Not Until Someday

- A Hope Springs Novel -

Valerie M. Bodden

Not Until Someday © 2020 by Valerie M. Bodden.

Cover design: Ideal Book Covers

Valerie M. Bodden
Visit me at www.valeriembodden.com

Hope Springs Series

Not Until Christmas
Not Until Forever
Not Until This Moment
Not Until You
Not Until Us
Not Until Christmas Morning
Not Until This Day
Not Until Someday
Not Until Now
Not Until Then
Not Until The End

River Falls Series

Pieces of Forever
Songs of Home
Memories of the Heart
Whispers of Truth

Contents

A Gift for You . . .

Members of my Reader's Club get a FREE book, available exclusively to my subscribers. When you sign up, you'll also be the first to know about new releases, book deals, and giveaways.

Visit www.valeriembodden.com/gift to join!

Need a refresher of who's who in the Hope Springs series?

If you love the whole gang in Hope Springs but need a refresher of who's who and how everyone is connected, check out the handy character map at https://www.valeriembodden.com/hscharacters.

Not as I will, but as you will.

—MATTHEW 26:39

Chapter 1

"*H*ey, aren't you Levi Donovan?"

Levi grabbed the bottled water out of the rest stop vending machine and turned toward the kid standing behind him.

"Sure am." His eyes tracked from the freckle-faced boy—maybe twelve years old, if Levi had to guess—to the attractive woman standing with her hand on the kid's shoulder. A hand that didn't sport a wedding ring. "I see you're a Titans fan." He gestured to the boy's cap. "You want me to autograph that?" He directed the question to the kid but kept his eyes on the mom.

The kid shrugged and passed his cap to Levi.

Levi patted the pocket of his leather riding jacket. Time was, he'd never left home without a pen for just such an occasion.

"You used to be pretty good," the kid said. "You ever going to play again?"

Pretty good? Levi resisted the urge to correct the kid. His rookie season, he'd set a new passing yards record. A record he'd then beaten three years in a row, until he'd been sidelined by an ACL injury.

"Nah. I'm retired now." At twenty-nine. Not that he'd had much of a choice. His comeback attempt had been less than stellar, with a broken thumb and a stress fracture in his foot.

Anyway, he'd been released, no teams had picked him up, and now here he was, getting a rush from signing some kid's cap in a rest stop.

Or not signing it. He gave his pocket another pat. "Sorry, Sport. I don't have a pen. Maybe your mom does?" He returned his gaze to the woman.

"I'm sure I do." She rummaged in her purse, retrieving a pen with a smile and passing it to Levi. He let his fingertips subtly brush hers as he took it, then signed his name across the cap with a flourish.

"Where you folks headed?" He passed the cap back to the kid.

"Disney World." The kid bounced on his toes. "Where are you going?"

"Nowhere as exciting as that." Actually, every time Levi thought about where he was going, he considered turning his Harley right back around.

"Thank you." The mom smiled at him. "This was sweet of you."

He tipped his chin and headed for the parking lot. "Have a good trip."

When he reached the Harley he'd purchased the moment he was no longer under a contract that prohibited riding, he tucked his water into the saddlebag and pulled on his helmet. He had hundreds of miles of open road ahead of him before he arrived in Hope Springs.

And he was going to enjoy them.

Because goodness knew he wasn't planning to enjoy his time there.

Grace dipped her head to pull in a deep breath of the mixed bouquet—asters, roses, tulips, some sort of lilies, and tiny white flowers she couldn't identify but that gave the whole arrangement a heavenly scent.

This was it. The perfect bouquet.

She meandered toward the flower shop's counter, smiling at the high school student working the register.

"These are pretty." The girl wrapped the flowers in paper. "Who are they for?"

"Myself. A birthday indulgence."

"You're buying yourself birthday flowers? That's so sad." The girl gave her a pitying look, eyeing her as if she were an old maid, and Grace bit her tongue against the urge to say she was only twenty-nine. She supposed that would seem like an old maid to a sixteen-year-old.

"Don't feel bad for me." Grace was careful not to let her smile slip. "I happen to love buying myself flowers. I always get the ones I want that way."

Actually, the last few years, a guy *had* bought her birthday flowers—but not the way the employee meant it. It had been her grandfather. This was her first birthday without him, and she'd found herself missing him so much that she'd decided to come out and buy herself a bouquet.

She took her credit card back, tucked it into her purse, and scooped up the flowers, keeping her chin up as she made her way to the door.

In the car, she nestled the flowers into the passenger seat, then leaned back against the headrest and blew out a long breath. It wasn't that she minded buying flowers for herself—or even that she minded being alone. It was just that she was so tired of everyone assuming that because she didn't have a boyfriend, her life was empty.

She wouldn't mind having someone someday—but only if it was the right someone. She'd learned the hard way that it was better to have no one than the wrong one.

It was why she kept a checklist in her head: loves and serves the Lord, good with kids, sensitive enough to show emotion, kind to others, and drives a sensible car.

If she could find a man who checked all those boxes, she'd be happy to settle down. But until then, she was perfectly content on her own.

She slid the key into the ignition, but before she could start the car, her phone rang. She dug it out of her purse, suppressing a groan as

Mama's picture flashed on the screen. Speaking of people who assumed she needed a man—not to mention, a passel of kids.

Maybe she should let it go to voicemail. But Mama would know Grace was ignoring her call. And she was probably only calling to wish Grace a happy birthday—maybe as a gift, she'd avoid mentioning Grace's lack of a boyfriend.

Here was hoping. "Hi, Mama."

"Happy birthday, Grace." Mama's Southern accent was soft but slightly more pronounced than Grace's. "How's your special day going?"

"Great." Grace made sure to fill her voice with cheer. "I just came from working on a fundraiser at church." She left out the part about buying flowers for herself. Mama would certainly take the flower shop cashier's view of things. "Now I'm headed home to make sure everything is ready to start the renovation on Grandfather's place next week."

A flutter of excitement went through her as she backed out of her parking space. She still couldn't believe Grandfather had left her the house that had been in the family for four generations. She'd spoken to him so many times about what a beautiful bed-and-breakfast it would make, but never had she imagined he would leave her the home—and the money to make her dream possible.

"I still don't understand why you feel the need to do this." Mama put on the voice she always assumed for guilt trips.

"I know you don't, Mama." Even though Grace had tried to explain it to her about a million times. "It's just something I need to do." She didn't add that it felt like a calling—like she'd at last found her purpose in life.

As far as Mama was concerned, she should only have one purpose. Babies.

"You're not getting any younger, you know."

"Yes, Mama, I know that." Mama had only reminded her every birthday for the past five years.

"By the time I was twenty-nine," Mama kept going, "I'd been married eight years and had five children."

"Four children, Mama. I'm number four."

"Whatever." Impatience shortened the word. "The point is, that's a lot more children than you currently have."

"Yes, Mama." That was a tension headache starting behind her eyes.

"Isn't it time to sell that old house and come home? Get married. Settle down. Give me some grandbabies."

"Mama, I told you, I don't—" Grace glanced down as the car's gas light dinged on.

"Before you tell me you're not interested in coming home, I've got some news that will change your mind," Mama chirped.

Grace shifted her phone to her other hand as she turned onto Hope Street and followed it past the fudge shop and the bakery and the antique store toward the edge of town.

"What are you talking about, Mama?"

"Remember Aaron Cooper? He just moved back to River Falls. He's our new youth pastor."

Grace could almost picture Mama waving pom-poms on the other end of the line.

"Of course I remember Aaron Cooper." His daddy and hers had served together at the Bible camp her daddy had run when Grace was younger. Aaron had practically been a part of her family, until the camp had closed when she was in middle school. Last she'd heard, his family had been in the mission field.

"Well, he's all grown up now. Very good-looking too. And single."

"That's nice, Mama."

"You know, I always thought he'd be a good match for you."

Grace snorted. "Mama, we were eleven when he moved away."

11

"I know, but if he had stayed, maybe everything with Hunter wouldn't have happened."

"But it did happen." She didn't exactly want to spend her birthday dwelling on the biggest mistake of her life.

She slowed and pulled into the gas station.

"Well, he's back now," Mama repeated. "And I still think you two would be perfect together."

"We haven't seen each other in nearly twenty years."

"Yes, but when I showed him your picture and told him you were single, he—"

"Mama!" Grace yanked the steering wheel toward a gas pump.

"What?" Mama's voice was all calm innocence. "He happens to be looking for a wife. It's perfect."

Grace shook her head violently enough that she'd be surprised if Mama didn't get dizzy through the phone. "Mama, it's not perfect." Heavens to Betsy, she couldn't believe they were having this conversation. "I don't even know Aaron Cooper anymore. And he's in River Falls, and I'm in Hope Springs."

"That's easy enough to fix."

"And I'm seeing someone." The words popped out of Grace's mouth before the thought had fully formed in her mind.

"You are?" Mama's voice rang with surprise. "Why didn't you say so?"

Grace rubbed at her temple. She couldn't very well say it was because she'd just thought of it.

"It's new, Mama." She opened her car door and stood waiting at the pump. There had to be a way to wrap up this conversation before she said anything even stupider.

"Well, who is he? What's his name? You're sure he's a good one? You know your judgment can be . . ."

A motorcycle roared up to the other side of Grace's gas pump.

Thank you, Lord.

"Sorry, Mama," she shouted to be heard over the motorcycle's engine. "I can't hear you. We'll talk more later." She hung up and tossed the phone into the car just as the motorcycle's engine cut off.

She lifted the gas pump, trying to figure out what she'd been thinking, telling Mama she was seeing someone when she hadn't been on a date in years.

She'd just have to pray that Mama would forget she'd said anything.

Sure. Mama was about as likely to forget as the right guy was to materialize right here at the gas station.

"Long day?"

The deep voice made her jump, and Grace spun around. "Excuse me?"

The motorcyclist on the other side of the pump had pulled his helmet off to reveal mussed dark hair and a charming smile, complete with dimple.

"Sorry, you looked like you were having one of those days. Can I get you a coffee? Cheer you up?"

"Ah, no. I'm fine, thanks." Grace gave him a tight smile. Though she usually enjoyed meeting new people, she was very much not in the mood for small talk right now.

"Do you have a piece of paper and a pen I could borrow?" the stranger asked.

"Uh. Sure." Ducking her head back into the car, Grace rummaged in her purse until she'd found the requested items, then passed them to the guy and busied herself washing the car windows.

When she was done, he was leaning against the gas pump, waiting. He passed her the pen, then the paper. "For you."

"What's this?" She glanced at the handwriting scrawled on the paper. A name and a phone number.

"My number. In case you decide you want that coffee after all. I'd love to take you out."

Grace stared at him. How could he know he'd love to take her out? Until two minutes ago, he'd never seen her before in his life.

"Thanks." She forced a smile as she passed the paper back to him. As certain as she was of what she wanted in a man, she was equally sure of what she *didn't* want. And a motorcycle-riding bad boy topped that list. She'd been down that road once before, and it had almost cost her everything.

"I'm actually seeing someone." Well, why not? If her imaginary boyfriend could get her out of a conversation with Mama, why not use him to make this guy back off too?

"Oh." He looked mildly surprised, as if no one had ever turned him down before. "Sorry. I should have realized." He gestured toward her car. "He must be a good one if he got you flowers."

"Yeah." Grace flipped the gas pump off though her tank wasn't full yet. "It was nice to meet you."

She jumped into her car and sped away before she had to tell any more lies about Mr. Invisible.

Chapter 2

*O*h well.

There'd be others.

Levi shrugged as he watched the woman drive off, then got on his bike and pulled away from the gas station.

It was her mocha eyes. That was what had made him ask her out in the first place. He'd always been a sucker for dark eyes.

That and the way she'd stood at the gas pump, looking so forlorn.

He'd been so sure she would be an easy yes that he hadn't even taken a moment to consider that she might turn him down.

It didn't matter. It wasn't like he'd been interested in anything more serious than a single date, maybe two.

Never more than that.

Levi leaned into a turn, the town feeling strangely familiar and yet new at the same time. He hadn't been home in over two years, and he suddenly couldn't remember if the awning over the antique store had always been blue and white or whether the sign at the marina had always been so big.

Too soon, he was slowing for the turn into his parents' driveway. As he parked and took off his helmet, the house too felt strangely new and old all at once. He would have sworn on his Super Bowl ring that the home he'd grown up in was yellow, but the siding was now taupe, with blue shutters. And the plum tree that he'd climbed as a kid was missing from the front yard. He double-checked the address.

Yep. This was the right place.

Modest. That was the word to describe this house.

Not bad. But nothing compared to what he could have bought his parents if they'd let him.

But every time he'd offered, he'd received the same answer—they were comfortable here.

So he'd stopped offering.

Hanging his helmet from the bike's handlebars, Levi grabbed his pack from the luggage rack, then made his way up the porch steps to the front door. It all felt a little surreal, as if maybe this was one of those dreams where everything was the same as in real life but different.

Until the front door sprang open and Mom was launching herself at him, pulling him into a ferocious hug. "I wasn't sure you'd come."

Levi squeezed her tight, her comforting citrus scent making him aware of how much he'd missed her. "I wasn't either."

He still wasn't sure why he was here. Only that Mom's message that Dad needed his help had touched something in him. After two years of refusing to speak to Levi, the fact that Dad would ask for his help felt like a big step.

When Mom finally let go, Levi took a step back, examining her. She had maybe one or two extra lines around her eyes now, but other than that, she looked as young and strong as ever.

"Hey, is that my brother?" The voice from behind Mom was deeper than Levi remembered but as cheerful as ever.

"Come see," Mom said over her shoulder, moving aside and gesturing for Levi to enter the house.

But he froze in the doorway, his chest tightening as his eyes fell on the cane in Luke's hand. Since the day his brother had been diagnosed with Becker muscular dystrophy eleven years ago, they'd all known

16

there might come a time when Luke would need help getting around—when he might even need a wheelchair. But Levi had assumed that day would be far in the future.

Luke was only twenty-five. He should be out running and throwing footballs. Not limping around with a cane.

"Hey, brother." Luke's grin swept from his mouth all the way to his eyes as he made his way to the door. "Long time no see."

"Yeah." Levi swallowed, painfully aware of his own smooth steps as he walked toward his brother and held out a hand, realizing too late that Luke held the cane in his right hand. Instead of taking his hand, Luke shifted his cane to the side and wrapped his other arm around Levi's back.

Levi gingerly put an arm around his brother.

"Dude, I'm not going to break." Luke tightened his grip on Levi until Levi lifted his other arm and pulled Luke in closer, still not one hundred percent sure he wouldn't hurt him.

When Luke finally let go, Levi looked around.

Though the outside of the house had changed, everything in here was identical to what he remembered. Pictures of Luke and Levi still decorated the walls. The big beige couch they'd piled on for family movie nights still took up one side of the living room. And Dad's old recliner was still tucked into the corner, his worn Bible perched on the table next to it.

"Where's Dad?" Might as well acknowledge the elephant in the room—or not in the room.

"At work." Mom gestured him toward the couch. "Come on, let's sit down."

"Maybe I should go over to the shop. Find out what he needs help with."

Mom and Luke exchanged a look.

"What?" Levi's head swiveled between them. Luke stared at the floor, and Mom busied herself rearranging throw pillows. "He didn't want me to come, did he?"

"It's not that." Mom gave up on the pillows.

"This is more of an intervention," Luke cut in. "Before he works himself to death."

"I'm sure there are plenty of people he could hire." Actually, this was good. It meant Levi didn't have to stay.

"Probably." But Mom's eyes filled, and Levi had to look away. He'd only seen his mom cry twice in his life—the day Luke was diagnosed, and the day Levi left for college—and he'd been shaken both times.

"But we wanted to see you." Luke had always been good at coming out and saying what he meant, whether or not it came across as sappy. "We've missed you."

Levi softened. "I've missed you guys too. But we all know Dad isn't going to be happy to see me here. I think it's best if I go now, before he gets home." He stood.

But the sound of the door from the garage to the kitchen pulled their attention toward the next room.

"Sandra, whose Harley is that blocking the garage?" Dad's voice boomed as loud as Levi remembered.

"Come and see." Mom pushed to her feet and moved toward the kitchen, throwing a pleading look at Levi over her shoulder.

He shook his head but dropped back onto the couch. It wasn't like he had much of a choice. He wasn't going to go sneaking out of here like some coward. He'd stay and face Dad.

Then he'd leave.

The murmur of Mom's low voice carried from the kitchen, followed by Dad's more explosive one.

"So how've you been?" Luke leaned forward, clearly trying to distract Levi.

"Bored." The word came out before Levi could think it through.

Funny. He hadn't been able to put his finger on the feeling before today. But that was it. He was bored.

He'd kept up with his training for the first year or so after he'd retired, until he'd realized there was no point. Mostly, he spent his days playing video games and his nights going out with friends.

It wasn't such a bad life, he supposed. But it lacked the thrill of getting onto the field, the satisfaction of a game well-played, the purpose of striving to be the best he could be.

"What about you?" Levi asked, but Dad burst into the room, followed by Mom.

"What are you doing here, Levi?" Dad's voice was flat. "You need money or something? Blow through your riches already?"

Seriously?

"No, Dad, I don't need money." He knew plenty of guys who blew through their salaries in record time, but he was smarter than that. He'd made enough on his investments that he'd probably never have to work another day in his life if he didn't want to.

"Well, I didn't know." Dad unbuttoned the Donovan Construction shirt he always wore over a white t-shirt. "All those pictures of you with all those women. Figured it must get expensive."

"Whatever, Dad." Judgment was the one thing Dad had always been good at. "I didn't come here so you could stand over me and judge me."

"What *did* you come for? To make a mockery of your family again?"

"A mockery?" Levi turned helplessly from Dad to Mom and Luke, who offered him a sympathetic look that was no help at all. "When did I ever—"

"That interview, Levi. Your whole lifestyle. Different woman every night."

"Hold on. I'm not with a different woman every night. And I didn't say anything against my family in that interview. All I said was—"

Mom stood, holding out a hand toward each of them. "Stop. Please."

Levi fell silent.

"I asked Levi to come." Mom's voice was firm as she turned to Dad. "You need help on your crews. You've had three guys quit in the last two weeks, and you're working yourself to death. And," she continued as Dad opened his mouth, "I need to see my son."

"She's right, Dad," Luke piped from his spot next to Levi. "We've got half a dozen jobs lined up for the next month alone. There's no way we're going to get them all done without help. And Levi knows what he's doing already. He doesn't need any training. He can step in and lead a crew."

That was true enough. From the time he could swing a hammer, Levi had been helping Dad on the various renovation projects he took on. During college, he'd spent summers managing the company's top crew. Before he'd been drafted into the NFL, he and Dad had talked about the possibility of partnering and expanding the company.

But none of that changed the fact that Dad no longer wanted anything to do with Levi.

The feeling was mutual.

"And you want to work for me?" Dad's cloudy blue eyes met Levi's.

The answer to that was an unequivocal no. But his gaze flicked to Mom, then to Luke. Both looked so hopeful.

He nodded once, painfully.

"Fine." Dad marched toward the kitchen. "Luke, get him up to speed on the Calvano project."

"Thank you." Mom squeezed his shoulder as she followed Dad out of the room.

Levi tried to muster a smile. It was only for the summer, he reminded himself. And if nothing else, at least he shouldn't be bored anymore.

Chapter 3

*G*race held the two paint samples against the dining room wall for the twentieth time.

She usually wasn't this indecisive, but she wanted everything in the house to be perfect by the time she had guests. She had to make a success of this, as much for Grandfather's sake as to prove to Mama that she wasn't wasting her time.

She stepped to the window, her eyes going from the vase of flowers she'd placed on the sill to the soft purple of the heather blanketing the hill that sloped down to the beach. That settled it. She'd go with a light lilac in here.

Grace watched the low waves chasing the seagulls along the shore. She may only have lived in Hope Springs for five years, but in that time it had become home. More than home, it was like this little town was a part of her, and the people here had become a second family.

Her phone dinged with a text, but Grace ignored it. Mama had been messaging all morning, asking for details about her mystery man, sending her all kinds of warnings about being careful what kind of man she dated, reminding her that Aaron Cooper was a pastor—exactly the right kind of man.

Grace knew she was going to have to fess up about her fib at some point, but for now she was still holding out hope that God might see fit to drop Mr. Right on her doorstep.

A loud knock from the front of the house made her jump.

"That was quick, Lord." She giggled to herself as she considered how ironic it would be if God had indeed brought Mr. Right to her doorstep. Then again, more miraculous things had happened. If Jesus could walk on water, surely he could deliver her the right man, right here and now.

Smoothing a hand over her unruly hair, she forced herself to wipe the silly smile off her face before opening the heavy wooden door.

"You?"

This was definitely not Mr. Right.

She'd known that the moment she'd laid eyes on him yesterday. From the motorcycle to the slick leather jacket to the arrogant way he'd asked her out, as if he couldn't fathom her saying no—everything about him had screamed that he was the kind of guy Mama had warned her to run far, far away from.

Just like Hunter.

She hadn't listened the first time.

But she'd learned her lesson.

"What are you doing here?" Was he stalking her or something? Grace gripped the front door, ready to slam it if he took so much as a step closer.

"I'm looking for Grace Calvano."

"That's me." How had he learned her name? This was getting creepier by the moment.

"You own this place?"

"Yes." Her knuckles tightened on the door.

"Wonderful." Was that sarcasm in his voice? "Can I come in?"

"No. I don't think so." She stepped back to swing the door closed. Hospitality was one thing. Stupidity was quite another. And she was pretty sure letting this guy in would be the height of stupidity.

He held out a hand to keep the door from latching, and Grace's heart just about stopped.

"What are you doing?"

"I need to take some measurements."

"Measurements?" She tried to nudge the door again, but his grip was firm.

"For your renovation." He spoke slowly, as if she were a child having a hard time grasping a new concept.

"I've already lined up the reno. With Donovan Construction."

"Right. And I'm Levi Donovan." He said it as if she should already know that.

What did he think? That she'd memorized the name on the piece of paper he'd tried to give her yesterday?

She peered over his shoulder, catching a glimpse of the Donovan Construction work truck in the driveway. "I thought I was working with Harold Donovan." She knew Harold and his family from church. This guy she'd never seen before yesterday.

"Well now you're working with me. I'm Harold's son. Are you going to let me in or what?"

She hesitated a moment longer. But she had to admit that his story seemed to check out. She let go of her grip on the door and stepped aside slowly.

"Thank you." He didn't sound particularly thankful.

"Where do you need to measure?" She brushed aside her annoyance as she led him toward the stairs. He may not be Mr. Right, but he was here to help her make her dreams of turning this place into a bed-and-breakfast a reality. The least she could do was be civil.

He smirked at her. "I can find my own way around, thanks."

Yeah, like she was going to let this stranger roam her house by himself. She spun toward the stairs. "Let me give you the tour."

He followed her, as she'd known he would. So much for Mr. I-Can-Find-My-Own-Way-Around.

She flipped on the light switch as she started up the staircase. Weak yellow light barely brightened the steps. "I need a bigger fixture here. Something to make it bright and cheerful."

"You're from the South, aren't you? I can hear it in the way you say 'I.'"

Grace stared at him. Was he paying attention to a word she was saying? "Yeah." She led the way to the first of six bedrooms.

"What brings you to Hope Springs?"

"I moved here to take care of my grandfather, if you must know. Anyway, up here I need the carpet ripped out of all the bedrooms." She bent to lift a corner of the carpet. "Grandfather never understood why his parents covered the hardwood floors."

"Your grandfather lives here too?" Levi peered over his shoulder, as if expecting Grandfather to appear out of the woodwork. "Maybe I should talk to him."

"Grandfather is happily in heaven right now, so I don't think he's going to have time to come by for a chat."

"Oh, I—" Levi pushed a hand through his hair, making a tuft stand up right in the middle of his head. "I'm sorry. I didn't mean—"

"It's fine." Grace slid easily past him. "I miss him, but I rejoice for him too."

Levi gave her an odd look but followed her as she led the way toward the bathrooms. "So where are you from then?"

"Tennessee." She flipped the light switch in the bathroom. "There are two bathrooms right now. Obviously, they need to be completely redone."

"Oh yeah? I played football in Tennessee."

Football. Add that to the strikes against him. Hunter had been a football player too.

Grace steered the conversation back to the topic at hand. "Actually, I'd really love to incorporate a bathroom into each of the guest rooms, if we can make it fit in the budget, which Luke seemed to think would be possible."

"Of course he did," Levi muttered. "He's not the one who has to put them in." He made a note in the tiny notebook he carried. "What else?"

Grace led him on a tour of the rest of the house, skipping over the small suite at the back of the first floor, which she used as her personal quarters, and pointing out the wall she wanted to take down between the living room and the dining room as well as the octagonal sitting room she wanted to transform into a library complete with floor-to-ceiling built-in bookshelves.

They ended the tour in the front parlor, which she hoped to turn into a comfy reception area for guests.

A thrill went up her spine at the word. Ever since she was a little girl, pretending to work at her own hotel, she'd dreamed of the day when she'd see to the needs of guests in her own establishment. And now it was really happening.

Levi finished scribbling something in his notebook, then looked up to study the large fireplace.

"It's beautiful, isn't it?" The stone-covered chimney was her favorite feature of the entire house.

Levi pursed his lips, and a low whistle slipped from between his teeth. "You can put one huge TV on that thing. Of course, you'll have to take the rock off. It's too uneven. But you could drywall it, or maybe cover it with tile or brick."

"A TV?" Grace shook her head until her hair flew into her face. "Absolutely not."

"You're not going to have a TV out here either?"

"Nope." She'd already told him there wouldn't be televisions in the guest rooms. Her bed-and-breakfast was a place for people to come to reconnect—with each other, with nature, and with God—not a place for them to rot their brains in front of a screen.

"You're going to seriously cut down on your business if you don't have a single TV on the property. No guy is going to go somewhere they can't catch the game."

"What game?"

He threw his arms up. "I don't know. Any game. Football. Don't you watch football?"

"Not really." With six brothers, she'd sat through enough football games to last a lifetime, though of course she enjoyed cheering them on.

Levi muttered something under his breath, making the pages of his notebook flap.

"Sorry, I didn't catch that."

"Nothing." Levi bounced his pencil against the notebook. "I need to get some measurements upstairs, so we can figure out the bathroom situation."

The grandfather clock in the corner of the room chimed five times. "Actually, I have plans tonight. Could we finish this another time?"

Levi waved her off. "Go do whatever you have to do. I can find my own way. I'll lock up on my way out."

"The plans are here."

Levi shrugged. "That works too." He strode toward the stairs, not bothering to wait for her approval.

Grace watched him climb the steps, thinking again of her earlier hope that God had delivered Mr. Right to her door.

Very funny, Lord. Apparently, she and God had gotten their signals crossed somewhere along the line.

She moved toward the kitchen, ignoring the sound of footsteps upstairs.

Like it or not, it looked like Levi Donovan was going to be spending a lot of time at her house.

Chapter 4

*W*hat was that delicious smell?

Levi retracted his tape measure and lifted his nose into the air, inhaling deeply.

Something garlicky, but he couldn't place what it was.

He worked out a knot in his back, then bent his head to write the measurements he'd just taken. He hadn't seen Grace in the past hour, and that was fine with him.

The way she'd looked at him when she'd opened the door to find him standing there—like he'd gone out of his way to track her down.

Don't flatter yourself.

Not that she wasn't pretty. She was.

But her no-makeup-messy-hair-t-shirt-athletic-shorts look wasn't really his thing.

Those eyes though.

Man alive. They'd almost pulled him in again today.

It wasn't the color so much as the warmth, he decided. That was what made them so enchanting.

And then there was her smell—sort of sweet and fruity, though he couldn't place it.

He shook himself out of it as he tucked his notebook into his pocket. She'd made it abundantly clear that she had no interest in him.

The sound of voices carried up the staircase as he traipsed down it. A lilting laugh, followed by a deeper voice.

Ah, the flower-buying boyfriend. He should have realized her plans were a date.

He wondered what the guy was like.

Probably scrawny and geeky—the kind of guy who needed to buy flowers to keep a girl.

At the bottom of the stairs, Levi froze.

It wasn't just one guy but a whole group of people.

Grace glanced toward him, and he thought for a second that she was going to ignore him.

But then she stepped forward. "Everyone—" She sounded less than enthusiastic. "This is—"

"Levi Donovan," a chorus of both male and female voices broke in.

Levi grinned, soaking up the surge that always went through him at being recognized. He shot a quick look at Grace to see if she'd noticed.

The surprise on her face was so worth it. "Y'all know him?"

"Not personally." A guy who looked close to Levi's own age stepped forward and held out a hand to Levi. "But he's a Hope Springs legend. Broke about every football record in the school. Played in the NFL. Nice to meet you, man. I'm Dan. This is my wife Jade and my daughter Hope." He gestured to a blond woman with a little girl on her lap and a very pregnant belly. "Heard you retired. Helping out your dad?" He gestured to the tape measure in Levi's hand.

"Just for the summer." Or less, if Levi could find someone to take over for him. Surely, one of the guys here would fit the bill.

"Anyway—" He turned to Grace. "I've got everything I need, so I'll be back bright and early Monday."

"You should stay for dinner." Dan looked to Grace. "Grace's baked ziti is the best. And we always have more than enough food. Right Grace?"

That was a forced smile if he'd ever seen one. But Grace's voice was cheerful as she said, "Of course you should stay. Let me introduce you to everyone else."

She kept that fake smile plastered on her face as she led him around the room. Levi tried to focus as she listed off names: Emma, Nate and Violet, Jared and Peyton, Ethan and Ariana and a little girl named Joy, Dan's sister Leah with her husband Austin and their teenage son Jackson, Sophie and Spencer and their twins Rylan and Aubrey. But mostly he concentrated on not being distracted by Grace's scent.

"Should we wait for Isabel and Tyler to eat?" Grace asked the woman she'd introduced as Sophie.

"Oh. I almost forgot. They decided to take a few extra days on their honeymoon. The kids were enjoying the beach so much."

"Why anyone would bring their kids on their honeymoon," Sophie's husband muttered, and she hit his shoulder playfully.

"You know they wanted the kids to have time to get used to their new family dynamic."

"Those kids couldn't be more family if they'd been raised together." Spencer stood, then helped his wife up, and they disappeared into the kitchen, the others trailing behind them.

"After you." Grace gestured Levi forward.

"We need the birthday girl," someone called from the kitchen. "Get in here, Grace."

"It's your birthday?" Nice. He'd crashed her birthday party.

"Yesterday."

"Ah, that explains the flowers. Where is your boyfriend anyway?" All the men she'd just introduced him to were married.

Pink tickled Grace's cheekbones. "Out of town."

"Oh. Well, happy birthday."

"Thanks." The mumbled word was barely out before Grace turned and practically sprinted to the kitchen.

The house was quiet at last.

Too quiet.

Grace settled onto the love seat in her small sitting room, a cup of hot cocoa curled in her hands despite the fact that it was the first day of June. Growing up, Mama had insisted cocoa was only for Christmastime, but Grandfather had been a year-round cocoa believer, and he'd easily converted Grace.

Sighing, Grace attempted to figure out what it was about tonight's birthday dinner that had fallen flat for her. She'd always loved meals like this, with all her friends, and she treasured them even more now as everyone's busy lives with marriage and kids had made them less frequent.

Her thoughts landed on Levi. The way he'd fit right in with everyone, as if he'd always been a part of the group. She supposed it helped that he'd grown up here—and that he was famous, apparently.

That was it. It was Levi being here that had ruined the night for her, though she couldn't put her finger on why.

Or she could, but she didn't want to admit it.

She was disappointed.

Disappointed that at the very moment she'd asked God to send Mr. Right, he'd sent Levi Donovan—who checked just about every box on the Mr. Wrong list—instead.

She supposed it served her right. She should know better than to tell God when and where to answer her prayers.

If only Dan hadn't invited him to stay for dinner, her evening might have been salvaged.

And the irony that when she'd first moved to Hope Springs she'd been convinced Dan would be her Mr. Right hadn't escaped her either. It had seemed to make so much sense at the time—why would God bring her right to a single, young pastor if she weren't intended to marry him? After all, she was a pastor's daughter, raised by Mama to be a pastor's wife. Now that she looked back on it, she could admit that she'd been more attracted to Dan's role as a pastor than to the man himself. Not that there was anything wrong with Dan—he was a wonderful man—but there was no spark between them, at least not beyond friendship. That, and Dan was still in love with his high school sweetheart—which Grace had helped them both see.

Anyway, that was five years ago, and Grace couldn't be happier for Dan and Jade, who'd quickly become her best friend.

It would just be nice to know that God had something like that planned for her.

It didn't have to be now.

She could be patient.

But someday. Someday she'd like to have a relationship like that. A family like that.

All she had to do was find another single, young pastor near Hope Springs. Which kind of limited her options.

Levi crossed her thoughts again.

No. Levi Donovan definitely wasn't an option.

She pulled out her phone. She'd felt at a disadvantage tonight, since everyone else seemed to know more about this guy who was working on her house than she did.

"Okay, Levi Donovan," she muttered to herself. "Let's see who you are."

Pictures of Levi in the light blue of the Titans popped onto her screen, interspersed with images of him dressed in suits and tuxes, a different woman at his side in each one.

Yep.

Levi Donovan was exactly the kind of guy she'd figured he was.

The kind of guy you ran away from as fast as you could.

As she scrolled, her eyes caught on the title of a video: "Levi Donovan Renounces Faith of His Family, Says God Is Irrelevant." It was dated two years ago.

Grace bit her lip. Did she really want to see this?

Her finger hovered over the video. After a second, she tapped it.

The Levi on her screen came to life, laughing at something the interviewer had said. His dimple was on full display, and he gave the camera a confident smile. The guy definitely had presence on the screen.

"But in all seriousness, Levi," a female voice said from off camera. "Fans have noticed that you used to give thanks to God after a win. You stopped doing that a few games before your big injury, and you haven't mentioned God since. Is there a reason for that?"

Levi's expression had sobered as the interviewer spoke, and he shifted in his seat. "I guess I hadn't noticed," he said at last.

"You were brought up in a fairly religious home?" the interviewer pushed.

"You could say that, yeah."

"Went to church every week?"

Levi nodded. "My dad didn't give us much of a choice." His voice became gruffer. "'As long as you live under my roof, you'll go to church.'"

"And now that you don't live under your father's roof, do you still go to church?"

"Nah." Levi shook his head. "Haven't in a while."

"Do you still believe in God?" The interviewer's voice was quiet, serious.

Levi's gaze slid to something offscreen, then back to the camera. "I don't know."

It was the most heartbreakingly honest answer Grace had ever heard, and she pressed her fingers to her mouth.

"What changed?" the interviewer asked.

Levi's sigh was deep enough that Grace could almost feel it through the screen. "I guess I started asking the hard questions."

"And you didn't like the answers?"

Levi's headshake was subtle. "More like I realized it didn't matter what the answers were. They wouldn't change anything. I guess I just realized that God is irrelevant."

Grace's finger tapped the screen to stop the video.

That confirmed that Levi definitely wasn't the man for her.

But it also meant she had her work cut out for her. Clearly God hadn't sent Levi here to be her Mr. Right. He'd sent Levi here so she could show him God was far from irrelevant.

He was the One thing Levi needed. Whether he knew it or not.

Chapter 5

Levi downed the last of his coffee as he turned into the driveway of the Calvano house Monday morning. The Victorian-style home was certainly grand, with its tall windows, wraparound porch, and octagonal tower. Thankfully, the exterior was in good shape, though a contrasting color on the door and shutters would add to the appeal.

Maybe he'd suggest it to Grace. Though he had a feeling she wouldn't listen—he got the distinct impression she didn't like him, bolstered by the look of relief on her face when he'd left the other night.

He hadn't expected to have a good time—honestly, he'd only stayed for the food—but Grace's friends turned out to be nice. Though they'd certainly shown an interest in his career, they also seemed to see him as more than a football player. He'd nearly forgotten what that was like, and it made for a nice change.

He parked the truck alongside the massive dumpster he'd ordered over the weekend and hopped out, jumping into the bed of the pickup to collect the tools he'd need for today's task: demo.

"What can I do to help?" Grace's voice came out of nowhere, and he lifted his head in surprise, smacking it on the ladder rack above him.

"Ouch. That looked like it hurt."

"It did. Thanks." He rubbed the tender spot on top of his head. "And as far as helping, the most helpful thing you can do is stay out of the way."

"I hope you're kidding." Grace reached up to tug the sledgehammer from his hands, then almost dropped it on her toes.

"Careful. And no, I'm not kidding." He'd learned early on that the last thing he needed was a homeowner hanging over his shoulder.

"I already told your father that I'm helping with this reno as much as possible. I want to put a part of myself into this house." Grace's look challenged him to defy her. "If you have a problem with that, maybe we need to call your dad and get this squared away."

Oh, she wanted to play hardball, did she? "If you're not careful with that sledgehammer, the only part of you you're going to be putting into this house is a broken foot. And if you want to help, fine. Be my guest. But don't complain to me when everything takes three times as long as it would without you." He vaulted down from the pickup bed and wrapped his tool belt around his waist, fumbling with the buckle.

"No offense, but you're sure you know what you're doing, right?"

A rough laugh burst out of him before he could stuff it down. This woman definitely said what was on her mind. "What part of that wasn't supposed to be offensive?"

She didn't smile. "Look, I'm sure you're a great football player and everything, but I don't see how that qualifies you to renovate my house."

"Believe it or not, I'm not just a dumb jock."

Her question had been fair enough. But the way she'd asked it made her disdain for his career plenty obvious.

"I managed my dad's top crew in college. And I have a degree in construction management. I know what I can do and what I can't do—and whatever I can't do, I know how to supervise the people who can do. That good enough for you?"

"That will do." Grace took a step toward the house, lugging the sledgehammer with her. "Where do we start?"

It was going to be a long morning.

"Where do we start?" Grace asked again as she followed Levi into the house, careful to keep the sledgehammer above the ground though it pulled at her muscles to hold it up.

"We'll take down this wall first." Levi strode through the living room to the far wall that blocked off the dining room. He set down the toolbox and drill case he'd been carrying and held out a hand, gesturing to the sledgehammer. "I'll need that."

She moved it out of his reach. "I think you mean I'll need it."

He smirked. "Sure. Take the first hit. You know how to use that?"

She shrugged. You swung and hit. Couldn't be that hard.

She hoisted the sledgehammer behind her head, not letting him see how it strained her triceps.

"Whoa. Whoa. Whoa. Not like that." Levi snatched it out of her hands, handling it as if it weighed no more than a regular hammer.

He held it parallel with the ground, one hand near the head, the other at the back of the handle, and pantomimed driving the sledgehammer forward to hit the wall head-on.

Then he held it out to her.

All right then. She'd do it that way.

Drawing the sledgehammer back, she paused for a moment, then rammed it forward with all her strength.

The shock of the blow traveled up her arms and into her shoulders as a small hole opened in the drywall.

She let out a cheer of triumph and glanced at Levi.

He was grinning too, though he wiped it away the moment he noticed her watching him.

Her smile grew.

See? She could do this.

"All right. My turn." Levi held out his hand again.

"Uh uh. That was too fun."

Levi crossed his arms in front of his chest, making his biceps bulge under his t-shirt. Grace looked away, concentrating on the wall as she lined up her next blow.

"And what am I going to do?" he asked. "Stand here and watch you?"

She couldn't quite tell if he was amused or annoyed, and she didn't really care. She took another hit at the wall, opening another small hole a few feet from the first.

Levi leaned against the wall, arms still crossed. "Maybe I'll take a nap. You're going to be at this all day at this rate."

"And I suppose you think you could do it faster?" Dumb question. With those arms, he'd probably have the wall down in two strikes.

But that wasn't the point.

Grace wanted to have a part in bringing out all the potential she saw in this place.

"I know I can." Levi pulled a regular hammer from his tool belt. "Ready?" He raised an eyebrow. "Set. Go."

He slammed his hammer into the wall before Grace realized it was supposed to be a race. In only two blows, he held a large chunk of drywall in his hands.

Well. Grace didn't have six brothers for nothing. She was as competitive as the rest of them.

She heaved the sledgehammer at the wall, this time creating a good-sized dent.

For the next ten minutes, the smack of their hammers against the drywall was the only sound in the room.

Finally, as she pulled the last piece of drywall off, Levi turned to her with a half-grin. "You're not too bad at that. What do you think?"

"Thanks." Grace was still panting slightly. "And I think I totally smoked you."

Levi laughed. "That's wishful thinking. But I meant what do you think about the room? With the wall down?"

Grace stood back to look. Light flooded from the back of the house to the front, and she could now see straight out to the lake from the front door. "I love it."

"Good. Because if you didn't, you'd be on your own." Levi winked, but Grace was pretty sure he was serious.

"What's next?"

"Normally, I'd do the kitchen right away, but since you're still going to be living here, we'll leave that for now. Let's go demo some bathrooms."

Grace gave a satisfied nod and followed him toward the stairs. At least it didn't look like she'd have to fight him on helping out with the reno anymore.

Maybe she'd even earned a little bit of his respect.

Not that she needed it.

Four hours later, Grace brushed her hair out of her eyes and examined the demolished bathroom. "I don't know about you, but I'm ready for some lunch. Would you like something?"

"Nah. I'm good."

"Come on. I have some leftover ziti." She hadn't failed to notice the three helpings he'd had the other night.

He set down the pry bar he'd been using to pull up the flooring. "I guess I can take a break for some ziti."

"Good." She led the way down the stairs and through the newly opened dining room.

"Looks like we got some dust on your flowers." Levi pointed to the vase on the dining room windowsill. "Sorry about that."

Grace brushed the drywall dust off the petals. "It's fine."

"So did your boyfriend make it back from his trip okay?"

Grace froze, concentrating on the flower petal in her hand. "Why are you so interested in my boyfriend?"

Levi watched her. "There is no boyfriend, is there?" He didn't sound mocking or accusatory. Just curious.

"What?"

"You made him up, right? To let me down easy."

"I didn't—"

"It's okay. I'm a big boy. I can handle it."

Grace dropped the act. There was no point in keeping up the ruse. "There is no boyfriend. I bought the flowers for myself." The pitying look of the cashier crossed her mind again—as if she were the most pathetic woman in the world.

"My grandfather used to buy me flowers for my birthday every year." Yeah, because that made her sound like less of a loser. "I bought them the other day because I was missing him."

"Good idea."

She turned in surprise. Levi wasn't looking at her with pity.

"And for the record," he added, "next time you don't want to go out with me, you can tell me. I can take it."

Grace laughed, even as those two words repeated in her head.

Next time?

There was so not going to be a next time he asked her out.

Right?

Chapter 6

$\mathcal{L}$evi finished sweeping the last of the debris into the garbage bag Grace held.

A week into this reno and he had to admit he was impressed. She'd worked alongside him every day, not exactly cutting the demo time in half but still contributing. And she hadn't complained once. Not even when she smashed her finger with the hammer.

"I need to run to the hardware store to grab a few things." He brushed his hands on his dusty jeans. "See you Monday?"

"Actually, I need to pick up some stuff for a fundraiser at church, so maybe I'll ride with you." Grace shoved a stray curl off her face. "If you don't mind."

Levi shrugged. "Why not?" Other than the fact that she'd made up a boyfriend to avoid going out with him, he had to admit she was pretty okay.

She was down-to-earth, funny, and easy to talk to. Plus, the fact that she had no interest in dating him took off all the pressure. He didn't have to be Levi Donovan, star quarterback, or Levi Donovan, ladies' man, or Levi Donovan, celebrity.

He could just be Levi Donovan, guy-who-was-renovating-her-house.

It was refreshing, actually.

Though he wouldn't have minded knowing why exactly she'd been so desperate to avoid a date with him. But so far he hadn't worked up the courage to ask. Some things a person was better off not knowing.

"Let me go change really quick." Grace rubbed at the streak of dirt on her shirt.

"You look fine." Levi snapped his tape measure onto his jeans pocket. "Everyone at the hardware store is a mess."

"Thanks." Grace made a face at him but followed him to the front door. "I think that's the nicest compliment I've gotten today."

Levi held the door for her. "Just call me Prince Charming."

They continued to banter as Levi steered the Donovan Construction truck toward the hardware store.

It was strange how comfortable Levi felt with her already. It reminded him of how things had been with Rayna.

Maybe it was a good thing Grace had said no when he'd asked her out. Because he had a feeling if he went out with her once, he'd want to go out with her again. And again.

And he'd promised himself the day Rayna had walked out that he'd never get involved in a serious relationship again.

He pulled into the parking lot of the hardware store and jumped out of the truck, waiting in front of it for Grace. Instinct told him to open her door for her. But that was what he did on a date—and this was anything but a date.

"So what do you need?" Grace came up beside him, and he was careful not to walk too close to her as they made their way inside.

Levi took out his phone and scrolled to his list. "A lot. Why don't you go find what you need, and I'll meet you outside when I'm done?"

"That sounds good." Grace disappeared down an aisle, and Levi let out a long breath.

Man alive, what was going on with him?

He'd been perfectly comfortable with Grace ten minutes ago—and nothing had changed between them since then.

41

It must have been the unexpected thoughts of Rayna in the car. That always threw him.

He scrolled through his list again.

What he needed was to focus on finding his supplies.

"Excuse me." A woman with blond highlights and a skirt that didn't leave much to the imagination stopped in front of Levi. "Do you know where I can find a staple gun?"

Levi looked at the display in front of him. "Right here."

The woman giggled and dropped a hand onto Levi's forearm. "I swear, I can be so dense sometimes." She lowered her eyelids, peering at him through her lashes. "You're Levi Donovan, right?"

The familiar surge went through him.

"In the flesh." He offered her his most inviting smile.

"Oh my goodness. I knew it. I'm Madeline Avery. I was a year younger than you in high school, but I was always too shy to say hi."

"You seem to have gotten over your shyness." He winked at her.

"That I have." She curled a piece of hair around her finger. Always a good sign. "In fact, I never would have done this when I was younger, but can I have your autograph?" She dug into her purse, pulling out a piece of paper and a pen and passing them to him. "And maybe your number?"

Grace checked blue paint off her list. Now she needed to find an inflatable swimming pool that was at least a few feet deep for the ink pool game they'd planned for the fundraiser.

She pushed her cart toward the pool displays she'd seen at the front of the store. The boxes were stacked pretty high, but if nothing else, she could always find Levi and ask him to help her reach one.

Much as she hated to admit it, working with him was growing on her. He was hardworking and dedicated—qualities that came from his athletic training, no doubt—but every once in a while he could be a goofball too, and he'd gotten her laughing for minutes at a time.

Not that she wanted to date him or anything. He was still the totally wrong kind of guy for that. But she was grateful that they'd managed to work together without any lingering awkwardness over the fact that he'd asked her out—and that she'd pretended to have a boyfriend to avoid it.

She turned her cart out of the aisle and toward the front of the store, then froze, glancing down at her stained clothes.

Really, Levi? Everyone goes to the hardware store a mess?

Tell that to the woman he was talking to, whose hair was perfect, face fully made up, clothes out of a designer store.

As Grace watched, Levi passed the woman a piece of paper and a pen.

"I'll call you." The woman winked and tucked the paper into her shirt, then sashayed toward the door.

"Wait," Levi called after her. "You forgot this." He held out what looked like a staple gun.

"Oh." The woman's laugh was flirtatious. "Confession: that was just a pretext."

Levi's laugh joined the woman's, and Grace rolled her eyes.

She waited until the woman had disappeared through the exit doors, then approached Levi.

"Looks like that's one thing you can cross off your list."

"What?"

But she stalked past him to the pool display. If he wanted to pick up women at the hardware store, that was his choice. It didn't matter one iota to her.

Fortunately, the pool she needed was on the lowest shelf.

She turned to tell Levi she'd be waiting for him at the truck. But he was nowhere in sight.

All the better.

She'd pay for her purchases and wait for him outside. And while she waited, she'd use the time to concentrate on not thinking about him.

"Thank you." Levi took the last bag from the cashier and tossed it into the cart, then hustled for the exit.

It hadn't taken Madeline long to call—and they'd arranged to meet for drinks and dinner in an hour. Which should give him just enough time to drop Grace off and run home to shower.

Outside, he nearly sprinted for the truck. But it was empty. He tossed his purchases into the back, then scanned the area for Grace. There was a grocery store next door. Maybe she'd run in there?

He tapped the tailgate impatiently, turning the other direction to see where else she might have gone. His eyes caught on a petite form with dark hair across the street. She was facing away from him, watching a group of kids toss a football around, but even from here he could tell it was Grace. He jogged through the parking lot and across the street.

"Sorry to keep you waiting. Ready to go?" The shouts of the kids on the field carried to them, and Levi couldn't help looking over. This very field was where he'd fallen in love with football.

Seemed like a lifetime ago.

"In a couple minutes." Grace didn't take her eyes off the boys on the field.

"I thought you didn't like football." Levi pulled out his phone to check the time. He now had forty-five minutes before he had to pick Madeline up.

"That's Leah and Austin's son over there." She pointed to a tall kid. "Jackson. He's pretty good, right?"

Levi watched for a moment as the kid faked a handoff, then threw a long spiral toward a receiver. The ball went long.

"Needs better control," he muttered. "It's not always about power. Now can we go?"

"What's the rush?" Grace turned to him, a teasing note in her voice. "Do you have a—" The teasing melted away as understanding dawned on her face. "You have a date," she said flatly.

"Actually, yeah, I do . . ." No reason to deny it.

She'd had her chance. And she'd turned him down.

"Hey, Mr. Donovan," a kid shouted from the field. "Want to come throw a few with us?"

Grace tilted her head, giving him a questioning look. She clearly thought he'd say no.

He checked his phone again.

He didn't want to give her the satisfaction of being right. And yet, he really didn't have time to play football with a bunch of kids.

"Not today," he called. "Maybe next time." He mostly succeeded in ignoring the disappointment on the kid's face.

The look on Grace's face, however—that was harder to ignore.

But he ignored it anyway.

Chapter 7

*L*evi pulled his pillow over his head as a sharp knock sounded on his bedroom door.

"It's Sunday." His father's voice was loud through the closed door.

"I know. That's why I'm sleeping in," he called back.

"Get up and get ready for church." The command was clear, and Levi pushed the pillow off his head.

Last week, he'd managed to be out of the house well before his family got up for church to avoid exactly this scenario. But this weekend, he'd decided to take his chances. He'd thought he'd be safe since Dad hadn't brought up church once since Levi had been home.

Apparently, Dad had been biding his time.

Levi grumbled out of the same bed he'd slept in as a teenager. It had been too small for him then and was like a baby bed for him now.

He yanked the bedroom door open, shoving a hand through his hair. "I'm not going to church."

"Yes, you are." Dad buttoned the collar of his dress shirt and wrapped a tie around his neck. "Put some clothes on. We leave in twenty minutes."

"You're not hearing me, Dad. I'm not going."

"As long as you're living under my roof, you'll go to church with your family."

Oh, that was nice.

"The only reason I'm living under your roof is because *you* needed help. You don't want me here, I can leave. You want me here, it's on *my* terms. And those terms are no church."

Dad pointed a finger at Levi's chest. "Someday, you're going to wake up and realize there's only one God. And it's not you."

The door next to Levi's room opened, and Luke poked his head out. "Lay off, Dad. You raised him to know the Lord, but you can't force him to believe."

Dad looked from Luke to Levi. "I swear, Levi, I don't know where we went wrong with you. We raised you the same as we raised your brother. So why did you turn out so different?"

"I don't know, Dad. Sorry to be such a *disappointment*." Wouldn't most fathers be proud their sons had made it to the NFL? But not his dad.

Dad jerked the knot of his tie tight. "Don't give me that hurt puppy dog look. If you want me to be proud of you, then be someone I can be proud of."

"If throwing four thousand yards my rookie season didn't make you proud . . ."

But Dad lifted a hand. "I'm proud of what you've accomplished." Dad didn't sound terribly proud. "But I want to be proud of *who* you are too. Understand?"

Levi stepped backward, rubbing at his chest as if he'd just taken a helmet to the solar plexus. Dad wasn't proud of *who Levi was*?

"Yeah. I got it." Levi backed into his room as Dad marched away.

"He didn't mean it the way it sounded." Luke took Dad's spot in the hallway.

"Not many other ways to mean it."

"That interview you did really hurt him. He's having a hard time getting over it."

Levi scrubbed his scratchy cheeks. "For the last time, that interview had nothing to do with my family. I didn't say a single word against any of you."

"Maybe not directly." Luke moved his cane to take a step closer. "But I think Dad takes you falling away as a personal affront. It was his job to raise you to know Jesus, and he feels like he failed."

"That's ridiculous." Levi crossed his arms, leaning on his door frame. "Like you said, he can't make me believe."

"But he would if he could. Because he loves you."

Levi snorted. "Funny way of showing it."

"Yeah, well, for the record, I'm still praying for you, that you'll see God's love for you. I'm not giving up on you. And neither is God."

"Whatever." Levi closed his door. "I'm going back to bed."

But there was no point. Dad's words kept colliding in his brain.

Be someone I can be proud of.

As if that wasn't what Levi had worked his whole life to be. As if that wasn't why he'd gotten up at five in the morning to work out from the time he was fourteen years old. As if that wasn't why he'd spent more time on the practice field than he'd spent in his own bed. As if that wasn't why he was here now.

He pushed out of bed the moment the sounds of his family faded.

Dad wanted to be proud of him?

Fine. Let him be proud of the way Levi got the bed-and-breakfast done in record time—and then left town for good.

Grace was still humming the last hymn as she walked out of church. As always, Dan's sermon had been challenging and uplifting and soul-filling all at once. It made her want to go out into the world and proclaim Christ's love from the rooftop of the bed-and-breakfast.

Or maybe inside its walls.

To Levi, the next time she saw him.

Not that she ever hid her faith from him—he'd seen her pray before their shared lunches, and he knew she was working on a fundraiser for church. But so far, she hadn't found a way to begin an actual discussion about God.

Mostly because every time she thought she'd worked up the nerve to do it, she pictured the video she'd watched. The one where he'd called God irrelevant. How was she supposed to overcome that?

But she wasn't the one who had to overcome it, she reminded herself yet again. Her job was simply to faithfully share God's Word—and trust the Holy Spirit to work in Levi's heart.

Please guide me in that, Lord, she prayed as she waved goodbye to her friends and emerged from the new, larger lobby that had been added onto the church after the tornado two summers ago.

"Grace."

She turned at the sound of her name and smiled as she spotted Harold Donovan, standing with his wife Sandra, Luke, and Luke's girlfriend May.

"Hello, Donovan family. How are y'all today?"

"We're well, dear." Sandra was soft-spoken, but Grace got the impression she could be ferocious when needed—when it came to protecting her sons.

"Levi said you've been right in the thick of things with the reno." Luke grinned at her. She'd only met him a few months ago, when they'd started attending the same Bible study, but already he had become a good friend. "Said you're tougher than you look."

A flush crept up Grace's neck. She hadn't been sure that she wasn't slowing the whole reno down, so the unexpected compliment boosted her confidence.

But Harold frowned at her. "He's making you do his job? He shouldn't—"

"Oh no, no," Grace jumped in. "Levi didn't want me to help, but I insisted. I want to make this place as much my own as possible. Put my blood, sweat, and tears into it."

Harold eyed her. "If you want to help, that's fine. But don't let him slack on you."

Slack? Grace was pretty sure Levi didn't know the meaning of the word.

"He's not." She didn't know why she kept feeling the need to jump in and defend him. "He's been busier than a moth in a mitten. We're ahead of schedule on most everything."

Apparently satisfied, Harold nodded.

"So what are y'all up to today?" Grace turned to Luke and May, smiling at their interlocked hands.

"We're going to a movie, if you want to join us," May offered.

From what she knew of May, the younger woman was quiet but sweet. And she'd love to get to know the couple better. But she didn't exactly feel like being a third wheel today.

"That's kind, thanks. But I have some things to get done at home. Y'all should come by for a tour sometime." She said goodbye to the Donovans and strolled to her car.

Though no one had said anything, the tension of Levi's absence from church had hung over them. She didn't have to imagine their heartache over Levi's turn from the faith. In college, her brother Judah had renounced his faith—and he still hadn't come back.

On the drive home, Grace prayed for her brother and for Levi—that God would open their hearts and call them back to him.

As she pulled into the driveway, her eyes tracked to the building's facade. Levi had suggested painting the doors and shutters a bright teal blue to contrast the white siding. Although she'd at first dismissed the suggestion, she could picture it now. It would certainly make a statement. She'd have to discuss it with him more tomorrow.

Grace steered around the dumpster to park in the shaded area off to the side of the driveway. It wasn't until she stepped around the dumpster that she spotted the motorcycle tucked next to it.

She only knew one person who drove a motorcycle—but what was he doing here?

Clearly not working, since he hadn't brought the truck.

Her stomach did a strange little dip.

He wasn't here to ask her out again, was he? Because she'd already made her feelings about that clear.

But then she remembered that he'd just asked that woman at the hardware store out two days ago.

She had nothing to worry about.

Chapter 8

With a hard shove, Levi rolled up the last remnants of the carpet in the largest bedroom. He'd already managed to pull up the carpet in the other five rooms. Which put him at least two full days ahead of schedule.

He wrapped his arms around the carpet roll in a bear hug and lugged it toward the stairs. The house had become familiar enough now that he could trundle down the stairs even with the massive carpet obstructing his view.

"Hey! Whoa!"

It took him a moment to register that the voice was Grace's. And that he'd nearly plowed her down the stairs.

He put on the brakes just in time, leaning back as the carpet's momentum tried to propel him forward.

He maneuvered the carpet so he could see around it. Grace stood two steps below, blinking up at him. In place of her usual athletic shorts and t-shirt, she wore a white and coral colored dress that set off her dark hair and eyes.

"Hey. You look nice." Oops. That was not supposed to come out. "I mean, are you okay?"

"What are you doing here?" Direct and to the point as always.

"Figured I might as well get a jump on the week." He shifted the weight of the rug.

"It's Sunday. Your father said Donovan doesn't work on Sundays."

"Well, I'm not my father. You weren't home, so I used the extra key you gave me."

"I was at church." She studied him, as if testing what his reaction would be. "Your family was there."

"Yeah." Not a conversation he was interested in having. "Would you mind moving out of the way? This thing isn't exactly getting lighter."

"Oh, sorry." Grace bounced down the steps ahead of him. "I'm going to get changed and make some lunch."

Levi's ears perked at the word. He was starving.

"I thought I'd make some pancakes. You want some?"

He should say no. She really didn't have to go to that trouble. But pancakes were his absolute favorite. "That'd be great."

He wrangled the carpet out the front door and tossed it into the dumpster.

By the time he got back inside, Grace was already pulling out mixing bowls and baking ingredients. She'd changed out of her dress and into her usual athletic gear.

She looked like a different person. And yet . . . not so different.

She was still beautiful in an entirely natural and unaffected kind of way.

"What?" Grace paused with her hand in the flour.

Levi shook himself. Had he been staring? "Nothing. You want some help?"

Her look screamed skepticism.

"What? You don't think I know how to make pancakes?"

"Do you?" She raised a challenging eyebrow.

"As a matter of fact, I make the best pancakes this side of the Mississippi. You sit down. I'll prove it."

He washed his hands, then took the measuring cup from her and nudged her aside.

"Levi, you don't have to—"

"You're never going to believe me unless I show you, right?"

"Well . . ."

"Okay. Then I'll show you." He started measuring flour into the bowl. Then the baking soda and baking powder.

He hadn't made pancakes since Rayna left, but as he fell into the rhythm, there was something soothing about it.

Or maybe it was this place. He was starting to feel at peace whenever he came here.

Or it could be Grace.

He turned the thought over. Was it her company he enjoyed?

"So how was your date the other night?" Her question pulled him out of his musing—probably for the best.

"It was fine."

"What did you do?"

He shrugged. "Dinner, a drink, a walk along the lake." Completely casual and uncomplicated. No commitment.

Exactly the way he liked it.

"Are you going out with her again?"

He stopped whisking. Since when was she so interested in his love life? "I don't know. Maybe. Why, you jealous?"

Grace's eye roll was more exaggerated than necessary, although he could have sworn there was a hint of pink in her cheeks. "You wish. How are those pancakes coming?"

"Patience. You can't rush perfection."

She watched him in silence as he separated the eggs and added the milk and butter. He was so used to her constant chatter as they worked that it was slightly unnerving that she wasn't talking now. But for some reason, he couldn't gather the nerve to ask her what she was thinking.

Finally, he flipped the first golden pancake onto her plate and passed her the syrup. He waited impatiently as she bowed her head and closed her eyes. The expression on her face as she prayed was so earnest that he was almost tempted to ask her what she was praying for.

When she at last looked up, she gave him a smile that he couldn't read and picked up her fork.

The moment she popped the pancake into her mouth, he could tell he'd convinced her.

"Told you. Best pancakes this side of the Mississippi."

She pointed her fork at him. "I need this recipe. This is going to be my Saturday breakfast for guests for sure."

He piled a stack of pancakes onto his own plate and crossed to the other side of the island to sit next to her. "You're going to do the full breakfast and everything, huh?"

"Of course." Grace's eyes went dreamy. "I've been practicing new recipes. But I hadn't found the perfect pancake recipe. Until now."

"It's not the recipe." Levi shoved a forkful into his mouth. "It's the chef."

"In that case, you're hired."

Levi laughed. "Sorry. That would require me to stay in Hope Springs."

"Isn't that what you're planning to do?" Grace paused with her next bite halfway to her mouth. "Stay here and work with your dad?"

"That is a definite no." Levi got up and moved to the refrigerator to get out the pitcher of orange juice he knew she always had in there, then grabbed two glasses. "I only came to help out for the summer. The sooner I can get out of here, the better. My dad and I don't exactly see eye-to-eye on a lot of things."

"Like religion?"

Levi set his fork down, his last bite still on it. "Yeah, among other things."

"I saw the interview you did with Sports World." Grace's comment was hesitant, and Levi tensed.

"Already got the lecture on that from my dad this morning, thanks."

Grace had just come from church. She'd obviously see things the same way as Dad.

She didn't take her eyes off him, but he couldn't find the condemnation in them.

"I thought it was really honest," she said at last.

Levi didn't know how to react to that. "My dad thought it was a personal attack. Sees me as a big disappointment."

"I'm sure he doesn't—"

"He told me as much just this morning, so . . ." He picked up his plate, scraping the last uneaten bite into the garbage.

"I'm sure he didn't mean it." But Grace's words rang hollow.

"Whatever. I'm sure your parents have never said anything like that to you."

Grace's face whitened, and she took a long drink of her juice. "Once." She said it more to her plate than to him. "But they had a good reason."

"I doubt that." Levi leaned on the counter. "You don't strike me as the kind of person who disappoints people often."

Grace stepped past him to put her plate and glass in the sink. "Looks can be deceiving. I let them down big time. Anyway, they'd be proud if I moved home, married a man I haven't seen since I was eleven, and had a passel of babies."

"And you don't want to do that? Get married and have babies?" Levi definitely would have pegged her as the family type—the very opposite of his type.

"Someday, yes. When I meet the right man."

"And what will the right man be like? You have a list, right?"

She was definitely the list-making type.

She busied herself putting away the baking ingredients. "Maybe."

He barely heard her mumble, but he grinned. "I knew it. What's on this list?"

"Nothing. Don't you have work to do?"

"Nope." He tipped his head at her. "It's Sunday, remember? Think I'll take Gloria out for a spin."

Grace gave him a blank look. "Gloria?"

"My Harley." He hesitated. "Want to come?"

Grace's reaction was instantaneous. She backed away from him, holding out her hands and shaking her head as if afraid he was going to physically abduct her and force her onto the bike.

"Your loss." He strode toward the front door, telling himself it wasn't his loss too.

Chapter 9

"How about Grandpa's Place?" Grace asked.

All week they'd been throwing around potential names for the bed-and-breakfast. Coming up with a name that conveyed exactly the homey feeling she wanted to portray was turning out to be a lot harder than she'd expected.

Levi groaned. "That's the worst one yet. Sounds like a bar. Or a bait stand."

She threw the sandpaper she'd been using on the dining room windowsill at him, but it went wide by a good three feet.

"Nice throw." He smirked.

"I don't hear you suggesting anything better." She retrieved the sandpaper and started working again, the sound mixing with that of the hammers and nail guns from the crew framing out the new bathrooms upstairs.

"It'd be tough to come up with anything worse," Levi teased, filling a nail hole.

Grace nearly threw the sandpaper again, then realized she'd only end up chasing it across the room again.

Levi lowered his putty knife and tapped his chin as if deep in thought, then pointed his finger into the air.

"How about Grace's Place?"

Grace wrinkled her nose. "It rhymes."

"I know. Think of the jingles. 'Grace's place. Where we have the space. So you can race. Don't forget—" Levi hesitated, looking skyward, obviously trying to come up with a rhyme. "Your mace," he finished.

A giggle escaped Grace. She had to admit that she quite liked it when Levi let his playful side escape.

But she tried to put on a stern look. "Didn't you learn that the customer is always right?"

Levi set down the putty and picked up a piece of sandpaper, joining her at the window. "Not when the customer is so obviously wrong."

Grace swatted at his arm before she could find the common sense to resist. Her hand met firm muscle, and she quickly pulled it back.

His cool, masculine scent—a mix of cedar and sandalwood—drifted to her, and she took a step sideways.

"Speaking of being wrong—" Levi spoke as he scrubbed the sandpaper against the window frame, taking off more paint in five seconds than she had in the past five minutes. "Are you still set on purple in here?"

"Nice." She almost swatted at him again but resisted this time. "You know I could fire you, right?"

"Dare you."

He had her there. She needed him if she had any prayer of getting this place done.

"To answer your question, no, I'm not still set on the *lilac*." She emphasized the word. Levi didn't seem to understand that there were hundreds of shades of every color. "You've made me second-guess. I hope you're happy."

"I aim to please. But you do have to make a decision by Monday so we can keep things moving."

Grace nodded, and they fell silent as they finished sanding the windows. She was about to suggest a break when there was a knock from the front door.

"I need a doorbell too." She brushed the dust off her hands and headed for the front of the house.

"Yes, ma'am," Levi called behind her. "Your wish is my command."

Ha. Yeah right. More like her wish was his to argue with. But she appreciated his honesty. She hadn't anticipated all the tiny decisions that went into a reno, from the shape of the drawer pulls in the bathrooms to whether she wanted dimmable lights in the guest rooms, not to mention the big decisions, like what to call the place.

"Grandpa's Place," she whispered to herself.

Yeah, now that she heard it out loud, she realized it wasn't going to work.

Too bad she had no idea what would.

She opened the front door, still pondering.

"Luke. May. I'm so glad y'all dropped by."

"Thanks for inviting us." May stepped forward to give Grace a quick hug, which she happily returned. Mama had raised her to be a hugger, and she didn't get enough opportunities for hugs these days.

"Come on in." She opened the door wider so Luke could get through with his cane. "Levi's in the dining room. We were just arguing about paint colors. Maybe y'all can help me decide."

She led the way to the dining room.

"Who was—" Levi froze as he turned, his eyes going straight to Luke's and May's joined hands.

"Hey, brother," Luke said.

Grace had never heard the man sound anything less than cheerful.

"Hey." Levi, on the other hand, was glowering.

Grace peered back and forth between the brothers.

From the way they both talked, she'd assumed they got along well. But that was not the impression she was getting right now—at least not from Levi.

"I want you to meet May. My girlfriend." If a man's chest could have burst with pride, Grace was pretty sure Luke's would have. "May, this is my brother. Levi."

May let go of Luke's hand and stepped forward, holding her hand out to Levi.

He stared at it, and for a moment Grace was sure he would refuse to shake it.

Finally, he reached out, pumped May's hand once, then turned back to the windowsill, working his sandpaper harder than before.

"So—" Grace sent Levi a daggers-to-the-eyeballs look, but he didn't so much as glance at her. "Y'all want a tour?"

"We'd love one." May's voice was warm and cheerful, though the hurt expression from Levi's snub hadn't yet disappeared. Luke, too, was looking at Levi as if he'd been betrayed.

Levi kept his focus on the window, but his voice reached them. "There are a lot of stairs."

Oh.

How could she have been so inconsiderate?

"I'm sorry. I wasn't thinking . . ." She turned to Luke.

"Nothing to apologize for. I'll be fine."

Her eyes shifted back to Levi, who dropped the sandpaper, shoulders stiff. "It's too much. I've seen the way you struggle on the little porch steps at home."

"He can do it." May's voice was quiet but certain, and Luke shot her a grateful look.

"Whatever." Levi threw his hands in the air. "But don't ask me for help when he falls."

Grace led them away. "So, this is going to be the library." She kept her voice low, walking into the octagonal room.

"I don't know what right he thinks—" Luke burst out as soon as they were out of earshot of Levi.

May laid a hand on his arm. "He's just worried about you." She leaned to kiss Luke's cheek and slipped her hand into his.

Luke drew in a short breath. "I guess. Sorry, Grace. Tell us more about this room."

When Grace had finished the tour of the first floor, she eyed the stairway.

Was Levi right? Was it too much for Luke?

But surely Luke was the best judge of that.

As if reading her mind, Luke stepped closer. "I'll be fine."

She nodded and started slowly up the stairs, glancing over her shoulder to watch as May helped him navigate the space.

Behind May, Levi appeared at the foot of the staircase. He didn't say a word, just watched as Luke made his way up one step at a time. The concentration on Levi's face said he was there out of more than curiosity. Despite what he'd said, Levi was there to make sure his brother didn't get hurt.

A shot of something unfamiliar went through Grace's chest.

For all his faults, it was just possible that Levi Donovan had a heart after all.

Chapter 10

*L*evi stepped out of the steaming bathroom, fastening the last button on his shirt. He'd needed that hot shower to pound away the tension in his shoulders before his date tonight.

Madeline had called after work to ask if he'd like to go to a movie, and he'd figured he might as well, even if he knew this would be their last date.

Two dates maximum. That was his rule.

From the hallway, he could hear the sound of Luke's forced cough, stimulated by the cough assist machine that helped keep his lungs clear. The sound had always bothered Levi, a constant reminder of his brother's illness.

In his own room, Levi tucked his wallet and keys into his pocket, then grabbed his cologne, trying to work up some enthusiasm for this date.

But instead of Madeline, he kept picturing Grace. The disapproving look she'd stuck him with when he didn't welcome May with open arms. The way she'd gone all quiet and distant after Luke and May had left.

She didn't understand. Not the way he did.

Having a girlfriend meant Luke was opening himself up to heartache. What happened when May got tired of Luke's illness? When she decided he wasn't what she wanted anymore?

Levi forced his thoughts off Grace. It didn't matter what she thought.

He stepped out of his room, checking the time. He'd spent longer in the shower than he'd meant to. He'd have to get a move on if he didn't want to be late.

As he reached Luke's room, the door opened, and Luke stepped out in front of him. Levi dodged to the side to scoot past his brother, but Luke widened his stance and planted his hands on either side of the hallway.

"What are you doing?" Levi took a step back. "Let me through."

"What was that all about today?" Luke didn't move a single muscle, aside from his jaw.

"What was what about? Look, come on, move. I have a date."

"Funny. I did too. And you were a jerk to her. You owe both of us an apology."

"I don't think so, man. Come on. Move." He feinted to the right, then moved to the left, but Luke didn't fall for it.

"You know I could easily make you move, right?" Not that he wanted to have to resort to force.

"Try it." Luke's lip curled.

"Seriously, Luke—"

"Oh, seriously?" Luke stepped forward and shoved Levi in the chest. "Seriously, you owe May an apology. She was in tears when we left."

Levi had made sure to be out of sight when they left, so he wouldn't know, but he sincerely doubted May had shed any tears over him.

"What's your problem with her?" Luke didn't shove him this time, but he didn't back off either. "Or is your problem with me? You're jealous I have a girl and you don't, is that it?"

"Don't be a moron. I'm going on a date right now, aren't I? So no, I'm not jealous that you have a girl. I can have any girl I want." Except maybe Grace. But he didn't want her anyway.

"Maybe." Luke pressed a finger to Levi's chest. "But you don't have love. And I do. And you can't stand that."

"Love?" Levi scoffed. "You think I want that? Love doesn't mean anything. Soon as things get hard, you think *love* is going to help? You think May's going to stick around when you're in the hospital? You think she's going to push you around when you're in a wheelchair?"

Levi never saw the punch coming.

One second, he was sneering at his brother, thinking how naive Luke was to believe love was real; the next, his hand was on his cheek, covering the throbbing spot on his jaw where Luke's fist had connected.

Levi straightened. If Luke had been anyone else, he'd already have a fist through his nose. Instead, Levi stood there, opening and closing his mouth a few times. Painful but not broken.

"Just because you didn't stick around—" Luke's voice shook. "Doesn't mean she won't." He took two halting steps into his room. "Some people actually know the meaning of love." His door slammed.

Levi stared at it for a moment, still rubbing his jaw. Then he spun on his heel and left for his date.

Luke thought he didn't know the meaning of love?

He did.

And he knew it always ended up with someone getting hurt.

Chapter 11

"Your jaw is looking better." Grace dipped her roller into the paint tray. When Levi had shown up last Monday with a black and blue jaw, she'd assumed he'd been in a bar fight or something. Even when he'd told her it was Luke, she'd had a hard time believing him. Until he'd given her the look that said he didn't want to talk about it.

And she hadn't brought it up. For two weeks.

But now that the bruise was nearly gone, she figured maybe it was time to talk.

"Yeah."

Then again, maybe not.

"I'm getting hungry. Want to get some lunch?"

"I'd rather finish up in here first." He gestured at the guest room walls they'd been painting a soft gray. "You go ahead though. I'll take care of it."

Grace crossed her arms in front of her, careful to adjust the roller so she wouldn't get paint on herself. "You think I'm slowing you down, don't you?"

Levi continued to roll paint onto the far wall, which he'd almost completed in the time it'd taken her to paint a quarter of hers. "You're not exactly setting any speed records."

"Just for that, I'm staying. And I bet I can finish this wall before you do that one." She pointed to the wall between them, which hadn't been touched yet.

"You want me to finish this wall and paint another whole wall before you finish the half a wall you have left?"

"It's three-quarters of a wall. And what's the matter? Afraid you can't do it?"

"Nope." Levi offered her the first true grin she'd seen from him in two weeks. "Just wanted to be certain of the terms of our bet. What are the stakes?"

"Lunch." Grace pressed a hand to her hungry stomach. "Loser buys lunch at the Hidden Cafe."

"You're on." Levi's roller took two long swipes down his wall. "Oh, and just so you know, I'm starved today. So I hope you have plenty of money for lunch."

"Little overconfident, aren't you? Don't forget you have another whole wall to do." But she filled her roller with paint and fell silent as she concentrated on rolling the wall as quickly as she could, trying to imitate Levi's long, smooth strokes.

After half an hour, her arm was burning. But she kept pushing, trying to ignore the fact that Levi was getting awfully close to done with his walls.

"Be right back." Levi set his roller down. "I need some water. You want anything?"

She shook her head. "I'm not stopping, you know."

"I wouldn't expect you to. I'm not worried." He sent her a smug smile. "I'll still beat you."

Grace put on a burst of speed as Levi's footsteps receded down the stairs. Ignoring the pain in her shoulders and neck, she sped toward the last section of the wall.

When she heard Levi's feet on the stairs ten minutes later, she was ready. She planted herself in the middle of the room, a smirk all set on her lips.

Levi stepped into the room, swigging from a water bottle. He lowered it as his eyes fell on her, and he looked from her to the wall.

"That's what you get for underestimating—" But something about his expression stopped her.

He didn't look surprised; he looked pleased with himself.

"You did that on purpose, didn't you?" Her hand went to her hip, tracking a line of paint onto her shorts.

"I don't know what you're talking about." Levi took another long drink.

"It didn't take you fifteen minutes to get water. You let me win."

Levi pointed at his chest. "Are you accusing me of throwing the game?" His look of feigned innocence clinched it.

"You're going to regret this." She waved her roller at him. "It just so happens that I'm starved today too."

So he'd thrown the paint race. Which was so not like him. He'd once made a bet with a kid on a plane ride that he could win a staring contest. And when he'd won, he'd happily taken the kid's airplane peanuts.

But for some reason he couldn't pinpoint, he really wanted to take Grace to lunch today.

Maybe it was because she'd somehow known that today's little race was exactly what he'd needed to get himself out of the funk he'd been in for the past two weeks. He and Luke had barely said a word to one another in that entire time, and much as he hated to admit it, it was wearing on him.

Part of the reason he'd agreed to come home for the summer was because he'd hoped he could make up for lost time with his brother. Instead, they were further apart than ever.

"Ready?" Grace emerged from her suite, looking fresh in a pair of denim shorts and a sleeveless shirt that accented her delicate shoulders.

"Yep. We'll have to take my Harley though."

"What?" Grace halted halfway through the kitchen. "Why?"

"It's what I drove this morning. My dad's Donovan truck is in the shop, so he needed mine."

"I can drive."

Levi shook his head. "I'm supposed to be taking you to lunch, if you remember."

"Then you can drive my car." Grace snatched her keys off the kitchen counter. "Please?"

He studied her. "There's nothing to be scared of, you know. The bike is quite safe. I even have an extra helmet."

"I'm not scared." Grace gave him a defiant look. "I just don't want to mess up my hair."

Levi snickered.

"What?"

"Nothing." He crossed the room to stand in front of her and lifted a strand of her hair. "You might want to get the paint out of your hair first."

Grace's eyes widened, and she snagged the strand from him. "One second."

"Yeah." But suddenly all he could think about was the feel of her hair in his fingers. And how he wanted to touch it again.

He jammed his hands into his pockets as she grabbed a paper towel and wet it, then rubbed it down her hair.

"There. Now am I presentable?"

Levi eyed her. She was more than presentable. She was beautiful. "You'll do."

"So you'll drive my car?" She held out her keys.

He considered pushing for her to ride the bike with him. But maybe it was best if they took a vehicle that didn't require them to sit so close together. Because this new awareness of her beauty was getting to him.

He took the keys and led her outside. He almost opened the car door for her but veered at the last second to go straight to the driver's side.

They spent the drive to the Hidden Cafe discussing what they'd already accomplished on the bed-and-breakfast and what they had left to do.

It was a big job, and with his crew shorthanded, it would likely be another few months before they finished.

The thought should have bothered him—but it didn't. Despite the tension at home with Dad and Luke, he was mostly enjoying his time in Hope Springs. It felt good to have a reason to get up and go to work every day. Maybe once he left Hope Springs, he'd have to look into getting a job—or starting his own company. Maybe he could specialize in bed-and-breakfast renovations.

Though he had a feeling he wouldn't enjoy them half as much if Grace wasn't there.

Uh uh. That was a dangerous thing to think. None of that.

Grace was a client and maybe a friend. Nothing more.

He pulled into a parking spot at the Hidden Cafe, then walked with her to the door, careful not to get too close to her. Even so, her sweet scent wafted toward him, teasing his senses. He held his breath as he opened the building's door. He didn't need that mystery fragrance to confuse him more than he already was.

Grace struck up a conversation with the hostess as she led them to a table, and Levi hung back a little, both to give himself some air and to watch Grace.

She was asking about the hostess's grandchildren, but the way she did it, it wasn't like other people. She really cared about the hostess's answer—really listened.

"A view of the lake is what you two lovebirds need." The older woman stopped at a table along the giant picture windows that overlooked the lake.

"Oh, we're not—" Grace started, but the woman pulled out a pad of paper.

"Can I start you with something to drink?"

Grace shot Levi a helpless look. He shrugged and sat down. He supposed it was harmless enough if this woman thought he and Grace were together.

They each requested a glass of water, and the woman swept toward the kitchen, promising to give them plenty of privacy.

"I wonder what she thinks we're going to do?" Levi peered around at the half dozen other customers in the restaurant.

"Levi!" But Grace giggled. "Mrs. Hurston is a hopeless romantic. Always trying to set people up."

"Ah, that explains it." Levi settled back in his seat, letting his gaze travel out the window. "The view is good."

"Yep." Grace was watching him thoughtfully. "Can I ask you a question?"

Levi blew out a long breath. He should have seen this coming. "Look, Grace, you're sweet and all, but—"

"What?" That was genuine confusion on her face.

"Nothing. Go ahead." Boy, Levi sure could use that water he'd ordered right about now.

"It's about Luke." Grace smoothed her hand across the table.

"Oh." That wasn't a topic he wanted to get into either. But he didn't see a way out of it. "What about him?"

"It's hard for you to see him like this, isn't it?"

A young waiter stopped at the table to drop off their waters, and Levi took a long drink as Grace placed her order for a cheeseburger and fries. He ordered the same.

When the waiter had left, Grace sat just looking at him. He took another long drink. At this rate, he was going to need more water before their food arrived.

"We don't have to talk about it if you don't want to," she said.

Levi played with the wrapper from his straw. "He wasn't using a cane the last time I saw him. That was a couple years ago, but I guess it feels like he's deteriorated really fast."

"When was he diagnosed?"

"My senior year of high school." Levi did the math in his head. "So eleven years ago."

He steepled his fingers under his chin. "He was never the fastest kid, but he wanted to play football."

"Like you." Grace lowered her hand to the table, letting it come to rest halfway between them. He studied her delicate fingers, covered with cuts and scratches from the work she'd been helping him with over the past few weeks.

"Yeah. Like me. By then, I was starting to hear talk of scouts, and I was training pretty hard. Anyway, I tried to train with him, but he couldn't keep up. I got so frustrated. I told him he should quit because there was no way he'd make the team." Regret burned hot and sharp in his chest. "He started training harder than ever. But the harder he trained, the more it seemed like he struggled. He started falling down when he'd go out running. Got skinned up pretty badly one time. Twisted an ankle another time."

He could still picture the look on his parents' faces when they'd come home from that doctor appointment. They'd anticipated a sprained ankle. Not a diagnosis that would change their lives.

"The doctors figured out it was Becker muscular dystrophy pretty quickly." He didn't add that the disease was genetic. That the chance his mother's sons would get it was fifty percent. That if his brother hadn't gotten it, he likely would have.

"That must have been hard." Grace's eyes on him were too intense, too sympathetic. He shifted to watch the white caps of the waves roll toward shore.

"Yeah." But not for the reason she thought. Levi had been a dumb kid then, with no awareness of how serious Luke's condition was. All he noticed was that because of Luke, his parents missed nearly all of his final season of high school football, including the game when six college scouts had come to see him play.

"And the bruise on your jaw?" Grace tapped her own face in the exact spot where his bruise from Luke's punch had mostly faded.

He shrugged. "He was upset because he thought I was rude to May."

"And did you apologize?"

He should have known she'd take Luke's side. "I was only trying to protect him."

"By being rude to his girlfriend?" She didn't say it ironically or like an accusation. More like she really didn't understand.

"By warning him that she won't stick around when things get hard. When he's not who she expects him to be."

"How can you know that? May is a sweet girl."

"Yeah. Well." Levi slid his empty water glass to the edge of the table. "Let's just say I know." Rayna had made sure of that. The moment he wasn't the NFL star she'd been after, she'd found herself a new star: his replacement on the field—and off.

"What—" But the waiter stopped at their table with a tray of food and piled it in front of them.

Grace bowed her head, and by the time she'd finished praying, he had half his burger gone.

Her eyes widened. "I guess you weren't kidding about being starved."

"Told you." He took another big bite.

Thankfully, she got the hint that he was done talking and bit into her own burger. For the rest of the meal, they resumed their argument about whether she should have at least one TV in the bed-and-breakfast.

When they were back in the car, Grace turned to him. "Can I ask you one more question?"

73

He shifted into drive without answering, which she apparently took as an invitation.

"Is that why you said you weren't sure if you believed in God anymore in that interview? Because of everything that happened to Luke?"

Levi turned onto Hope Street, keeping his eyes on the road and off of her. "Partly, yeah."

He waited for her to tell him that everything happened for a reason. That God had a plan in everything. That all he had to do was believe hard enough and everything would be fine.

But she was silent so long that he finally glanced over at her.

She turned to meet his gaze. "Thanks for telling me. All of it."

He nodded. He wasn't sure why he had. He'd never really talked to anyone about Luke. Not his teammates. Not his coaches. Not even his dates.

But talking to Grace had been surprisingly easy. And comforting.

He let himself relax into the seat just a little.

So long as he didn't get used to it.

Chapter 12

"Could you pass me the drill?"

Today's job was starting to build the shelves for the library, and Grace felt mostly useless, aside from holding up boards and passing Levi tools and screws.

She should really go finalize her plans for furniture. But she couldn't quite bring herself to leave the room.

She had been working a little too hard to convince herself it was because she wanted to be able to honestly say she'd had a hand in every part of the renovation.

But she couldn't deny that there was also something new in the air between her and Levi today. Maybe it was because of how they'd talked about Luke at lunch yesterday. Or maybe it was something in their coffee. Either way, he seemed friendlier and more open than usual, and she didn't want to jeopardize that.

She passed him the drill, and he gave her that same smile he'd been giving her all day. It was different than his usual smile—mostly in that it caused the slightest flutter in her belly.

Which she was studiously ignoring.

So he had a cute smile. That didn't mean she was attracted to him. More importantly, it didn't mean he was anywhere near the right kind of guy for her.

Which was why she wasn't in any danger from spending time with him now, flutters or no flutters.

From across the room, Grace's phone rang, and she wound around their pile of boards to dig through the various supplies that had accumulated on the floor.

"Where is it?" she muttered, picking up Levi's sweatshirt.

There.

She concentrated on not noticing the enticing sandalwood scent of the shirt as she answered the phone.

"Hey, Leah. What's up? Need me to pick up something for tomorrow?" It was hard to believe the fundraiser they'd spent months planning was finally here.

"Nope. Just calling to let you know I'm an aunt again. Jade had a baby boy this morning. Matthias Paul. He and Jade are healthy and happy. And Dan's over the moon, of course."

"That's wonderful. Tell them I say congratulations. I'll stop by the hospital to visit on my way to set up for the Messtival."

"If you can recruit anyone else to help tonight, that'd be awesome," Leah said. "We're obviously going to be short one pastor and his wife."

"I'll see what I can do." Grace sized up Levi as she hung up.

He finished screwing in a shelf and took a step back from it. "Good news?"

"Dan and Jade had their baby this morning. A boy."

"That's great." He picked up another board.

"Yeah."

Levi set the board back down, leaning it against the wall. "But . . ."

"How did you know there was a but?"

"I could see it in your face."

Oh. Did he know her that well? Warmth filled her, but she pushed it aside. Likely, anyone would have seen it.

She'd never had a good poker face.

"The Messtival is tomorrow, and without Dan and Jade, we're down two key team members. I'm not quite sure how we're going to pull it off."

Levi gave her a blank look. "Messtival?"

She rolled her eyes. So much for thinking he really knew her. "The fundraiser I've been talking about for the past month."

"Oh. That." He nodded, as if he had a clue.

"Whatever. You have no idea what I'm talking about."

"The fundraiser to raise money for the youth mission trip. The one where every activity is messy."

Grace felt her mouth open a crack. It seemed he did listen when she talked. There went that shot of warmth again.

She ignored it again.

"Anyway, we have a ton of stuff to set up tonight. And it's going to take a lot longer without them." She checked the time. "Actually, I might head over there now to get started." She hesitated, then decided to go for it. What did she have to lose? "You could come too, if you wanted. We could use the help."

"Sorry." Levi picked up the board again. "I'd love to help, but I have a date tonight."

"Oh." That was *not* disappointment Grace felt. Or, well, it was. But not over Levi having a date. It was only disappointment that she hadn't been able to recruit another helper. "Things with Madeline must be going well."

"I'm not going out with Madeline."

"Oh, that's too bad. What happened?"

Levi fit the board into place. "Nothing."

"But you're going out with someone else?"

"Yeah. Gina." He said it flippantly, as if it were completely normal to be going out with a different woman already. Then again, from what she'd seen when she Googled him, she supposed it *was* normal for him.

"All right, then. See you Monday." As she stepped out the door, she breathed a sigh of relief. At least now those little flutters she'd felt for Levi today would beat it.

He'd confirmed once again that he was the very opposite of her Mr. Right.

She thought of Jade and Dan, celebrating the birth of their new baby.

I do want that, Lord, she prayed as she got into her car. *And if you want to bring Mr. Right-for-Real into my life sooner rather than later, I won't complain. But if not, I'll keep waiting for someday.*

With one last glance in the mirror, Levi grabbed the keys to his Harley off his dresser and exited his room. He'd met Gina when he'd ridden his bike to the marina last weekend, and she'd been fascinated with it.

Unlike Grace, who looked freaked out at the mere mention of the bike, Gina had asked for a ride then and there. And he'd been happy to oblige. When he'd asked her out for tonight, she'd insisted he bring the bike.

Actually, Levi thought she might like the bike more than she liked him. But that was fine. He wasn't looking to fall in love. Just have a nice time and then go their own ways.

Voices carried down the hallway from the kitchen, and Levi hesitated.

Mom and Luke.

Maybe he should go out the front door. But his bike was in the garage—through the kitchen.

The moment he stepped into the room, Luke fell silent, shot him a glare, and got up from his seat at the table.

"I'm just passing through." Levi gestured for Luke to keep his seat.

But his brother retreated into the hallway.

"Suit yourself," Levi muttered.

"I don't understand what's going on with you two." Mom's brow creased. "But can't you make up?"

"Ask him that."

"I have." Mom's sigh ran deep. "He says he's waiting for you to apologize."

Levi snorted. "That's nice. He punches me in the jaw, and he wants me to apologize?"

"Can't you?" Mom turned pleading eyes on him. "I can't stand to see you two like this. You used to be so close. Until . . ."

"I didn't abandon him, Mom." A headache sprouted in Levi's temple as he struggled to believe his own words.

"I never thought you did." Mom offered a more than convincing look of shock. "I only wish your father and I had handled everything better. We were just so overwhelmed at first, and you were doing so well with everything, that I think we lost sight of the fact that you still needed us too. I hope you don't resent your brother for that." Mom blinked, but not before Levi spotted the glisten in her eyes.

"You did what you had to do, Mom. And I don't resent him. If anything, he resents me."

"Are you kidding me?" Mom sniffed and straightened her back. "He idolizes you."

"Right. That's why he punched me." Levi massaged his jaw, though it didn't hurt anymore. "I have to get going. Don't wait up for me. I'll see you tomorrow." He dropped a quick kiss on Mom's cheek.

"Another date with Madeline?" Mom sounded hopeful.

"No, actually. Gina."

The frown Mom directed at him could have rivaled some of Dad's best.

"What?" Not that he supposed he wanted to hear it.

"I know Rayna hurt you, but do you think this is the best way to deal with it? Going out with a different woman every week?"

"This has nothing to do with Rayna." Levi moved to the door.

VALERIE M. BODDEN

"Just because she left you doesn't mean every woman will." Mom stared him down. For such a small woman, she could still intimidate him.

"I know." They wouldn't leave him because he wouldn't give them a chance.

"You can't go through life alone, Levi, just because one woman hurt you. That'd be like never throwing another pass because of one sack. Don't you want to get married, have a family?"

"Not really, Mom." He opened the door to the garage. "I don't think I'm the family type. I gotta go. Love you."

"Someday you're going to change your mind about that," Mom called behind him.

But he closed the door and jumped on his Harley.

Mom might think he'd want a family someday.

But he knew better.

Chapter 13

Seven.

Levi was awake at seven o'clock on a Saturday morning.

And he had nothing to do with his day.

It didn't pay to go back to bed, since he'd gotten plenty of sleep, given that he'd been home from last night's date by ten o'clock. It wasn't that it'd been a bad date or that Gina hadn't been fun.

But somehow, the evening had been rather . . . blah.

After riding his Harley up and down the shoreline, they'd had a nice dinner, Gina asking the whole meal about what it was like to be in the NFL. Usually, he ate that up—dates who wanted to talk about his rise to stardom.

But for some reason, he couldn't stop thinking about the conversation he and Grace had had over lunch the day before.

It had been so . . . real.

Like Grace saw past the football player and had discovered the real person he was now. It was unnerving in some ways—but it also felt nice to really be seen. Understood.

And then there'd been his mom's words ringing in his head the entire date. *Don't you want to get married, have a family?*

He had wanted that once with Rayna.

He'd wanted it so much that he'd had the ring in his pocket the night she broke up with him.

Much as that had hurt, he would forever be grateful that something had held him back from proposing that night.

He'd learned an important lesson that night too: The moment you stopped being who people expected you to be, they walked away.

Even though he was sure Mom's prediction that he'd change his mind about marriage someday was wrong, it hadn't helped his date. Every time he'd looked at Gina, all he could think was, *This definitely is not the woman I'd choose to spend the rest of my life with.*

Finally, he'd given in, pleaded a headache, and dropped her off at home. The best he could do when she told him to call her sometime was offer a slight grunt that he hoped she'd taken as a gentle let down.

Kind of like Grace telling him she had a boyfriend.

He rolled out of bed. As long as he was awake, maybe he'd go make some progress on the bed-and-breakfast. Grace had her Messtival thing today, so he'd have the place all to himself.

Except the thought of working there without Grace fell flat for him.

Well then, what if he went over to the Messtival?

It sounded like they could use the help—and he could only imagine the look of surprise on Grace's face when he showed up.

That was enough motivation for him. He got up and got ready.

They were never going to get this all done.

Grace reviewed her checklist.

Over half the items had yet to be completed, and the Messtival opened in under two hours.

"Has anyone seen the squid?" a teenager called from the grassy area in front of the church where they'd set up the ink pool.

"The what now?" The deep, laughing voice behind Grace pulled her head in that direction.

She was sure she recognized it, but that couldn't be. He would never . . .

But there he was, striding toward her in khaki cargo shorts and a navy polo shirt.

"Levi." His name came out sounding more delighted than surprised, and she worked to rein that in. The only reason she was happy was that she might be able to rope him into helping. "What are you doing here?"

"Thought I'd check out this Messtival you keep talking about." He stopped a couple feet in front of her, hands in his pockets. "What's this about a squid?"

"Oh, yes." She turned toward the teen at the ink pool, who was still awaiting her instructions. "Did someone already put it in the pool?" she called across the lawn.

"Maybe," the girl called back, shrugging.

Grace exhaled, checking her clipboard again. "This day is not going as planned."

"What can I do to help?"

She could feel Levi reading over her shoulder.

"Seriously? You want to help? Actually, never mind." She seized his wrist and pulled him toward the far end of the parking lot. "You already offered. I'm not going to give you a chance to back out."

She pointed to the pile of ropes, plastic sheeting, and buckets of goop the teens had mixed up using water, paint, and food thickener. "Can you turn this into a tug-of-war pit? The plastic sheet goes on the ground, the goop on top of it, then the ropes—"

"Yeah. I've seen tug-of-war before. I've got this." He nudged her toward the teen who'd been calling for her. "Go take care of your squid emergency." He grinned. "There's a sentence I bet no one's ever said before."

"Thank you." Grace didn't have time to argue or to ask if he was sure he knew what he was doing. She jogged to the ink pool.

Fortunately, by the time she got there, another teen had found the missing squid. Grace watched as they threw it into the dark blue goop they'd filled the two-foot-deep pool with. Barely bigger than a quarter, the squid sank and disappeared from sight.

She hoped at least a few people would find it. It'd be disappointing if no one won the game.

"Grace, we need you over here."

She took off for the next emergency, spending the next hour locating a missing pinata, filling water balloons with paint, and lining up eggs for the egg toss.

Every once in a while, she peeked up to check on Levi's progress.

He'd finished the tug-of-war, and last she'd seen, he'd been surrounded by a group of teen boys, including Jackson, and was helping them set up the paint dodgeball course. He'd had the biggest smile on his face as he'd listened to one of the boys.

Grace had been tempted to pull out her phone and snap a picture, but then she'd been called away to sort out an issue with the prizes for the shaving cream slip-n-slide obstacle course.

By the time she had that all figured out, cars had started to fill the parking lot. Grace checked the time. Ten o'clock on the dot.

Then she checked her list. Every last item was done.

"Thank you, Lord," she breathed. "Please bless everyone who comes with a fun day."

"Now what?"

She jumped as Levi popped up next to her.

"Now I say thank you for helping. I don't think we'd have gotten it done without you."

"You're welcome." He stepped closer, watching families pour toward the ticket booth. "And now that you've thanked me, what's next?"

"Next?" Did he mean between them, or . . .

"Do you need help overseeing the games or anything?"

"Oh." She turned her back to him so she could survey the various activities—and so he wouldn't see the blush she could feel rising to her cheeks. "Nope. The teens should have that all covered."

"Good. Then let's go."

"Go? Levi, I can't go. I have to stay in case—"

But he grabbed her hand, tugging her toward the line that had formed at the ink pool. "I need to see what this squid thing is all about. Let's go play."

"Oh no, I really can't. I have to walk around and make sure there aren't any problems. Make sure everyone's having fun."

"Sure." Levi didn't let go of her. "But first *you* need to have some fun. You did all this hard work. Now you have to enjoy it."

"I *am* enjoying it." But she let him pull her into the line. She had to admit that for all the years she'd helped with this event, she'd never once played any of the games. And based on the shrieks coming from all around them, it was fun.

They ended up in line for the ink pool behind Tyler and Isabel, who were patiently answering the questions Isabel's daughter Gabby was tossing at them, while Tyler's twin boys threw a squishy ball back and forth. All five of them were covered with paint and goop already.

"Hey. I've barely seen y'all since you got back from your honeymoon." Grace pulled them each into a hug.

When she stepped back from Gabby's full-body launch, Isabel frowned. "We got you all covered in goop."

"No worries. Levi says I have to try the ink pool, so I guess I'm about to get messier."

"That's why they call it the Messtival." One of the twins grinned at her—Jeremiah she was pretty sure, though even after knowing them for five years, she still sometimes had a hard time telling them apart.

"And you must be Levi." Isabel stepped around Grace to hold out a hand to him.

"Oh, sorry. Levi, this is Isabel and her husband Tyler. And their kids—Gabby, Jonah, and Jeremiah. Y'all, this is Levi Donovan."

"Nice to meet you." Tyler held out a hand too. "Your name's pretty well known in these parts." He turned to his boys. "Levi used to play in the NFL. Isn't that cool?"

Instead of the overconfident smile he usually wore when someone recognized him, Levi looked a little bit . . . humble as Jonah and Jeremiah exclaimed over how awesome that was.

"We need a new coach for the boys' team," Tyler said to Levi. "If you're going to be around in fall."

"Oh. Uh—"

"Levi's only home for the summer," Grace jumped in. No point in letting the twins get their hopes up when Levi wouldn't be around by fall.

Levi gave her a strange look but nodded. "Sorry."

"All right, Weston family, you're up," the teen running the booth called.

Isabel smiled. "I love being called that." She turned and climbed into the goop-filled kiddie pool with the rest of her family.

"So what's the object of this game?" Levi's voice came from right behind her, and she jumped, moving forward a few steps to fill in the space vacated by the Westons.

"Basically, you get in the pool and try to be the first one to find the squid. You have three minutes."

"And if you find it?"

"You get to choose a prize, of course." She gestured to the display of prizes various shops around town had donated.

"Sounds easy enough. Prepare to be smoked by me. Again."

She shook her head. "If you recall, I won our last race."

He smirked. "Only because I let—" He broke off, eyes widening.

She poked an accusatory finger at his chest. "I knew you let me win."

"Busted." He chuckled, and she realized her finger was still pressed against him.

She pulled her hand back. "You should know I hate when people let me win. My brother Zeb did that once, and I punched him in the gut."

A loud, clear laugh burst from Levi. "You did not."

"Honest to goodness. I did. So you'd better not let me win this time."

Levi schooled his face into a mock serious expression and raised one hand, as if he were taking an oath. "I solemnly swear."

"Good." They watched as Isabel, Tyler, and the kids finished out their turn in the pool, giggling and shrieking but coming up empty-handed.

As they climbed out, the teen gestured for Levi and Grace to get into the pool.

The goop came up to Grace's knees as she stepped in. It was warmer than she'd expected it to be—and slimier. She slid her feet across the bottom of the pool to make room for Levi. He made a face as he got in.

"Kind of squeamish for a football player, aren't you?" She lifted a handful of the goop and lobbed it at him. It hit him square in the chest. "Kind of slow too."

"You think so, huh?" He picked up a much bigger handful of goop, chucking it at her.

But she managed to dodge out of the way before it could land on her cheek.

She reached for another scoop of the goop, as did Levi, but just then the teen called, "Ready. Go!"

They both dropped the goop from their hands and started feeling around under the opaque surface. Grace dropped to her knees, letting the goop cover her thighs.

She was going to win this one fair and square.

"What do you say? Winner gets to dunk the other person?" Levi's tongue poked out of the corner of his mouth as he slid his arms through the goop.

Grace spun to search the section behind her. "Hope you brought your nose plugs."

"I don't think I'll be needing them." Levi lifted his arm triumphantly from the goop and held it over his head. "Because I win."

"What?" Grace stood, examining his hand, which was dripping with goop but which also undoubtedly held the squid.

"You already had that when you made the bet, didn't you?"

He shot her a sneaky, boyish grin. "You told me not to let you win."

"I didn't tell you to cheat!"

"I wasn't cheating." Levi took a step closer to her. "I was being clever." He reached for her.

"You wouldn't!" Grace tried to back away from him. But the pool was too slippery. Before she could react, her feet had shot out from under her, and she was on her back, head submerged in the goop.

A flash of real panic shot through her. Was it possible to drown in two feet of goop? Was she going to be the first person to ever find out?

Something solid wrapped around her arms, and before she could figure out what it was, she was being hoisted into the air. Fresh air rushed into her nostrils, and she sputtered, trying to lift a hand to get the goop out of her eyes.

But her arms were still in that grip.

"For the record—" The pressure on Grace's arms eased, and something soft rubbed against her face, wiping the goop from her eyes. She opened them to find Levi lowering his goop-covered shirt. "I wasn't really going to dunk you."

He took her hand and led her to the side of the pool.

"So you say." But she squeezed his hand. "Thanks for saving me."

"Anytime you fall into goop, you know who to call." He supported her elbow as she stepped out of the pool, then followed her out.

They toweled off, then made their way to the prize booth, where Levi tried to make her choose the prize, even though he'd technically been the one to win it. When she refused, he picked a giant plush flamingo.

"That's not tacky at all." She wrinkled her nose as the teen handed it to him. "You should give that to your next date. She'll love it."

"I'm glad you feel that way." Levi grinned at her. "Because I got it for you."

"Um, no." Why was her heart hammering like that? It wasn't like Levi had meant that the way it'd sounded. He just wanted to offload the tacky stuffed toy on her.

Levi raised an eyebrow. "No to the flamingo, or no to the date?"

Or he did mean it the way it'd sounded.

She wiped a hand over a stray blob of goop that had fallen from her hair to her shoulder. "Both."

Right?

Yes. She definitely meant both. She didn't want some pink monstrosity of a bird in her house. And she definitely didn't want to date Levi.

"Fair enough." Levi tucked the bird under his arm. "Up for some tug-of-war? I hear it was set up by an expert."

"Is that so?" She followed him toward the rope, trying to figure out what the sudden tug-of-war in her heart was all about.

Chapter 14

"Where've you been hiding?" Levi looked up as Grace came into the bedroom where he'd been laying hardwood flooring. His crew had finished installing all the upstairs bathrooms, so things were moving along well.

"Why? Did you miss me?" Grace teased. She'd been doing that more this past week. Acting less guarded with him. More open.

He supposed that was what happened when you swam in goop together.

Levi made a face at her. So what if he had?

He was getting used to working side-by-side with her. "No. Just wondered how long you were going to slack off while I did all the work."

"For your information—" Grace passed him a steaming cup of coffee and a donut from the bakery. "I was getting fitted for my bridesmaid's dress for my brother's wedding. Trust me, I would have rather been here."

"Hey, if you're going to make a run to the bakery every morning, feel free to slack as much as you want." Levi shifted his weight to sit on the half-finished floor, and Grace plopped down across from him.

"So your brother's getting married? The one you punched in the gut for letting you win?"

"No. Zeb's already married. It's my oldest brother, Simeon, who's getting married this time."

"How many siblings do you have?" He wasn't sure why he was asking. Only that his donut was almost gone, and he didn't want her to disappear on him again.

"Six. All brothers."

He whistled. "That explains it."

"Explains what?" She tore off a piece of donut and popped it into her mouth, but her eyes challenged him.

"Your competitiveness. Your toughness. Your propensity to speak your mind."

"My—" But she laughed. "You make me sound like a rather unlikable person."

"Nope." He took a sip of his coffee, studying her over the rim. "Those are all likable qualities."

"If you say so." She brushed the powdered sugar from her hands. "So what are we doing today?"

Levi watched her. She didn't like receiving compliments, that much he'd learned. Then again, he supposed it had been a rather backhanded compliment.

Maybe he should be more direct. Come out and tell her she was stunning even in her faded purple t-shirt and running shorts.

Nope.

That would definitely not be a good idea.

He drained the rest of his coffee, then pushed to his feet. "Today you get to learn how to lay a hardwood floor."

Fortunately, she was a quick learner, and by late afternoon they had the floor finished.

Grace straightened her legs with a groan once the last board was in place. "No one told me you were going to work me this hard, Levi Donovan."

"You said you wanted to put a piece of yourself into this place. I'm just trying to help."

"Thanks for that." But the smile she gave him said she was sincere in spite of the sarcastic tone. "Be honest. This is harder than the NFL, isn't it?"

He laughed. "Ask me that after you've been tackled by a three-hundred-pound defensive end."

"Do you miss it?" Her question was quiet, no trace of teasing or sarcasm left.

He thought for a moment. "Sometimes, yeah. I miss the fields and the lights and the sound of the crowds. The smell of the turf. I especially loved the stadiums with natural grass. Always reminded me of the first time I played, in middle school."

"Have you thought at all about what Tyler said? About coaching here?"

He shook his head. "Like you said, I won't be here by fall."

"Right." She turned away, picking up the tools they'd left scattered on the floor. "It's Friday. If you want to quit early, it's fine."

"Why would I want to quit early?"

She lifted one shoulder.

"I don't have a date every Friday night, if that's what you were thinking."

"I wasn't thinking anything." But he could have sworn that was relief in her eyes. "You've just been working really hard here, and we got the room done, so I figured you deserved a break."

"How about this? We'll call it a day. But we go to the hardware store to get some more nails for the nail gun."

"You need me to come along for that?"

"No. I don't *need* you to." Though he did *want* her to. Which should probably concern him. "Just figured you might like to come. I could show you what I had in mind for the kitchen cabinets. But we can always do it another time."

"No. I'll come along." Grace's smile landed on him, making his insides do a weird sort of half-jump. He ordered them to settle down.

It was a ride to the hardware store for business. Nothing to get all excited about.

"Let me go change," Grace added. "Last time you told me everyone goes to the hardware store a mess, I discovered what a liar you are."

"Oh come on, you were the prettiest one in there." The words came out of their own volition.

Grace blinked at him, then turned and fled for the door. "I'll be ready in two minutes. Meet you in the car."

Great.

Hopefully those two minutes would give Levi enough time to relocate his common sense.

Because if he kept saying things like that, he had a feeling both he and Grace were going to regret it.

Chapter 15

"What do you think of these?" Grace pointed to a set of Shaker-style cabinet doors, glancing at Levi out of the corner of her eye. They'd been at the hardware store for an hour already, but he didn't show any signs of being in a hurry to leave.

"I like those. Maybe in white."

She turned to full-out stare at him.

"What?" His stubbly jaw line lifted in a smile.

"I think that might be the first time we've agreed on anything about this project."

"That's not true." Levi's eyes took on a playful glint, and he tugged on a strand of her hair that had escaped from her ponytail. "We also agreed that you were wrong about the dining room paint color and the showerheads and the whole TV situation."

Grace shoved him. "We did not agree about that last one." Though she had to admit she was glad she'd gone with his suggestions for the dining room and the showerheads. He had surprisingly good taste.

"I'll convince you yet." His wink was completely friendly, and yet it made Grace's heart quiver just a little.

"Excuse me?" A woman approached them, her gaze clearly on Levi alone. She looked a year or two younger than Grace but supremely more confident. "Do you happen to know where the faucets are?"

Grace ducked her head so neither of them would see her eye roll. Did women really think asking where to find things in the hardware store was a good way to pick up a man? Then again, judging by Levi's reaction last time, it apparently was.

"Over there." Levi pointed toward the far side of the store. "So I was thinking maybe we skip door pulls with these cabinets. Keep the lines clean and simple."

It took Grace a moment to realize he was talking to her. "What? Oh. Yeah. I mean, I agree."

The woman looked at Levi again, then at Grace, then walked off in the direction Levi had pointed. Grace swallowed a smile as she turned back to the cabinets.

She did *not* feel gratified that Levi had ignored another woman for her sake. Besides, it wasn't like he'd done it for her sake at all. The woman probably just wasn't his type.

And even if he had done it for her sake, he needn't have bothered. She had absolutely no interest in who Levi Donovan did or did not ignore.

"So I'll order these then?" Levi opened and closed the cabinet again.

"Yeah. That'd be great. What about the countertops?"

"You up for picking that out yet today? Otherwise we can come back next week."

"I'm game if you are. This is fun." The vision she'd had for the bed-and-breakfast was really coming together.

"All right." He grinned at her. "Don't want to stop your fun." If he thought she was lame for finding spending her Friday evening at the hardware store fun, he didn't let on.

For the next hour, he patiently led her through the options. After they'd agreed on a gray-black quartz, Levi led the way to the checkout, stopping at a small freezer and digging out two wrapped ice cream bars.

He paid for them, then passed one to her. "I ate two of these a day every day growing up. You have to try one."

She relented, unwrapping her bar as he held the exit door open for her.

Outside, Grace examined the streaks of orange and peach ribboning across the sky. "How long were we in there?" Somehow, the sun was nearly on the horizon. "Sorry to take up your whole night."

"The night is young yet." Levi pointed to her ice cream bar. "Now stop stalling and try that."

He watched as she took a bite. "How good is that?"

In truth, it tasted the same as every other ice cream bar Grace had ever eaten. But somehow, Levi's enthusiasm gave it a little extra something.

She smiled and took another bite. "Delicious."

"Good." Levi looked happy with himself as they walked to the truck, where he stashed the bags in the back. He lifted a hand to shield his eyes and peer toward the football field across the street, where a group of high school boys was playing.

"Is that tall one Jackson?"

Grace squinted. "Hard to tell from here. But I think so."

"He seems like a good kid."

"He is. Came from a rough background. Mom overdosed when he was little, and he was in and out of foster care for years before Leah adopted him. He's become a very thoughtful young man."

Levi watched the boys another minute. "You in a hurry?"

"No." She answered slowly, slightly apprehensively. What if he was about to ask her to dinner? "Why?"

"Come on." He took her hand and dragged her toward the road, not letting go even when she fell into step beside him.

She gently pulled her hand back, though he didn't seem to notice. Good.

That meant the handholding hadn't meant anything to him. Nor had it to her.

"Hey, guys," Levi called as they reached the field. "Got room for one more?"

Would wonders never cease? She turned to Levi, and he laughed.

"Don't look so surprised. I can actually be a pretty nice guy."

Yeah.

She'd been starting to notice that.

Levi jogged toward the boys, who had stopped playing to wait for him, their faces lit with the excitement of meeting a hero.

Grace settled onto the grass, telling herself it didn't make a hill of beans of difference to her if Levi was a nice guy. He might be kind and he might show the occasional emotion and he might even prove to be good with kids. But that didn't change the fact that he was the wrong man for her. If his overactive dating life wasn't enough to prove that, his attitude toward God was.

Not only was he not a pastor, but he had admitted to not being sure if he believed anymore. And while she was committed to sharing Christ's love with him in any way she could, dating him was out of the question.

Not that he was asking.

Still, as she watched him play, Grace couldn't help but appreciate the way he offered the boys encouragement and gentle correction without crushing their confidence. Tyler had been right—Levi would make a good coach.

If he were staying in Hope Springs.

Which he wasn't. And that was one more reason he could never be Mr. Right.

Levi and the boys played ball until the sun had fully set and dark started to creep over the field.

"All right, guys. I have to call it a night. I've kept my friend waiting too long already." Levi waved to the boys and jogged toward Grace.

Friend. She had to admit she liked the idea of being friends with Levi.

As long as that was what it remained.

They trooped across the street and into the truck.

"That was nice of you. Playing with those kids. Imagine the stories they'll be able to tell their kids someday."

Levi shrugged, looking uncharacteristically modest. "I had fun."

"I could tell."

"Yeah?" Levi sent her a questioning look. "How?"

"I don't know." Actually, she did know, but she didn't want to tell him that she'd watched him closely. That she knew the difference between his fake smile and his real smile. That when he was enjoying himself, his dimple just barely showed. "You just seemed to have a natural way with those kids."

They fell silent, though Levi still sported that happy look.

She was glad. He wore it much better than his usual surly expression.

He pulled into the driveway of the bed-and-breakfast and stopped the truck near the front porch, then cut the engine.

A ripple went through Grace's tummy. "You don't need to walk me to the door or anything."

"I know." But Levi pushed his door open. "I'm going to carry in the stuff we bought."

Oh yeah. A wave of foolishness washed over her. Why would she have thought Levi wanted to walk her to the door?

All these signs of interest she thought she was seeing in him were a figment of her imagination.

Levi lifted the bags out of the back of the truck as she scurried up the steps to unlock the front door. She waited in the entryway as Levi set the packages on the floor.

"I'll sort through everything on Monday." He straightened, meeting her eyes. "Thanks for coming with me. It was fun."

She nodded, and he shifted, then gave a self-conscious laugh and grabbed the door. "See you Monday then."

"Yep."

She watched as he bounded down the porch steps toward the truck.

"Levi?" Heavens to Betsy, what had made her call out like that?

"Yeah?" He took a step in her direction.

"A bunch of us are having dinner at Sophie and Spencer's tomorrow night. I'm sure they'd love it if you came too."

Levi ran a hand through his hair, looking uncertain. "Maybe I will. Thanks."

"Goodnight." Grace ducked into the house, closing the door behind her before she could say something else stupid.

Chapter 16

*L*evi raised a hand to knock on the door of the ranch-style house, glancing around him at the acres of cherry orchards surrounding the property.

He had gone back and forth a hundred times today about whether or not to come to the dinner at Sophie and Spencer's, which was unlike him—he was usually a decisive man. But when it came to Grace, he'd felt more and more like he was playing on a new field for the first time. Except she was a lot harder to figure out than football.

On the one hand, she was so not his type. Not to mention that she'd made it abundantly clear he was the furthest thing from her type.

But on the other hand, he couldn't deny that he enjoyed spending time with her. Or that, on occasion, she seemed to like being with him too.

The door opened to reveal Grace, her usual casual attire replaced by a simple yellow sundress. "I figured it had to be you. No one else knocks." She closed the door behind him. "I'm glad you came."

"Me too." He planted his hands in his pockets before he could brush away the piece of hair that had fallen across her forehead. "Where is everyone?"

"Out back." She pointed toward a patio door at the other end of the house.

He stepped that direction, but a hand on his arm stopped him.

Grace was biting her lip and studying the floor. "There's something I should probably tell you."

He eyed her. "Something I'm not going to like?"

"I don't know. Maybe." She drew up her shoulders as if preparing to do battle with him. "I invited Luke and May too."

"You— Why?" It was bad enough that Luke still wouldn't talk to him at home. He didn't need his brother to ruin his time here too.

"They're my friends." She gave him a defiant look. "And I think if you get to know May you'll like her. She's kind and sweet and—"

"That's not the point." Levi ran a hand through his hair. Why couldn't anyone else see it? "Luke has BMD."

Grace's eyes sparked. "Is that all you see when you look at your brother? His disability?" She crossed her arms in front of her. "Has it ever occurred to you that your brother is sweet and charming and kind and . . ."

Yeah. He got it. All the things he wasn't.

"That may be. But it doesn't change the fact that he's likely going to end up an invalid someday. Does May know what that's going to be like? Is she going to stick by his side through that? In my experience, people don't hang around when things don't turn out the way they expected. I don't want my brother to have to go through that."

"May's not like that." Grace seemed so earnest. "Just give her a chance. Please."

Levi shook his head. "Why does it matter so much to you?"

Grace chewed her lip again. "I don't like to see families torn apart," she said at last. "And I know how much it bothers you that you and Luke aren't speaking right now."

She couldn't know that. Because it didn't bother him one bit.

"I'm speaking to him. And he can speak to me anytime he wants."

The sound of voices approaching the front door drew their attention to the window.

Great.

"Please, Levi," Grace pleaded. "Just be nice. Give her a chance."

He sighed. He didn't see how he had much of a choice. His desire to stay and spend the evening with Grace—and her friends, of course—just slightly outweighed his desire to avoid his brother.

"Thank you," Grace said before he could respond. She scooted past him to open the door, and he took the opportunity to escape to the backyard. Just because he'd said he'd stay didn't mean he had to hang out and talk to Luke and May.

Grace's friends greeted him as he stepped outside onto the deck. To his surprise, he remembered most everyone's names from the last time they'd met.

Most of the group was gathered around Dan and Jade and their new baby, but Austin broke away to shake Levi's hand.

"Thanks for playing ball with Jackson and his friends last night. He hasn't stopped talking about it all day. When he wasn't in the yard lobbing passes at the tree."

"It was my pleasure," Levi said honestly. "Kid's got a good arm."

"You ever think about coaching? I know our high school program could use someone of your caliber."

What was it with everyone asking him about coaching? "Yeah. Maybe."

Wait.

Where had that answer come from? He didn't have any intention of coaching. Or of sticking around Hope Springs.

But before he could correct himself, Grace was emerging from the house with Luke and May. Her eyes zeroed in on him, and even from this distance he could read the disapproval in them. He didn't doubt she'd bring Luke and May straight to him, just to spite him.

But after letting her glare burn through him for a few more seconds, she led Luke and May toward the others gathered around Dan and Jade.

"Everyone." Grace's voice cut over the chatter. "I think most of y'all know these guys from church, but in case you don't, this is Luke Donovan. Levi's brother. And May. Luke's girlfriend." Grace directed a pointed look at Levi as a chorus of hellos and welcomes filled the evening.

"Luke Donovan. You were a baseball star at the high school, weren't you?" Ethan asked.

Luke ducked his head, but that didn't keep Levi from noticing his pleased expression.

"Levi is the star," Luke said. "But yeah, I played baseball."

"You were good," Ethan insisted. "I heard you almost made the All-State team your senior year."

He had? Levi stared at his brother. He'd known Luke liked baseball, but he'd assumed his brother's disease meant that he'd spent his seasons riding the bench.

"It was no big deal," Luke mumbled. "Not like it was the Super Bowl or anything." His eyes cut to Levi.

But what was he supposed to say to that?

"You still play?" someone asked.

"Once in a while. Getting a little tougher now, but I get in a game when I can."

"How about right now?" Grace asked. "The backyard is plenty big enough. We could get in a quick game before dinner."

"That's not a good—" Levi stepped forward. What was Grace thinking? Couldn't she see that Luke couldn't even *walk*? How was he supposed to play baseball?

"That sounds fun, actually." Luke glanced at May, who offered an encouraging nod.

Everyone except Jade, who was holding her baby, filed into the yard.

"Levi?" Grace called, the expectation in her voice clear.

"I'm good, thanks." He searched out a place to sit.

But Grace marched toward him. "You said you'd try," she hissed. "It's a game of baseball. You don't even have to talk."

"Fine." It was totally unfair that this woman could get him to do things he had no intention of doing. "But put us on different teams."

Grace rolled her eyes, but as they joined the others, she made sure both she and Levi were on the opposite team to Luke and May, who had taken up positions in the outfield.

Spencer batted first, hitting a line drive that got him onto first. Then Sophie was up, managing a pop fly that got her husband to third. Levi let himself relax. It didn't look like anyone here was going to knock one toward Luke.

Grace was up next, with a respectable hit down center field, but Tyler was quick on his feet and threw her out. She gave a good-natured shrug as she returned to the lineup.

"You're up, Levi," Spencer called from third base. "How about a homer?"

Levi grimaced. Baseball had never been his sport. But he'd never yet backed down from a challenge. He kept his eyes on the ball as Jared wound up, then released his pitch. It was low and to the outside, but Levi swung.

The bat connected with the ball, sending it up and over the heads of the infielders, directly toward Luke's position.

Instinct told Levi to run out there, put himself between Luke and the ball. But logic told him he'd never make it in time. He could only stand and watch, ignoring his teammates' shouts to run.

The ball reached the top of its arc and rocketed toward Luke, who let his cane fall to the ground and shifted two steps to the right, his eyes never leaving the sky.

He raised his gloved hand into the air, and the ball dropped into it with a perfect thud.

His team erupted into cheers, and Levi had to grin, even as a pang went through him. He should have been around more when Luke was in high school. His schedule with college ball and then the NFL had kept him too busy.

But that was mostly an excuse. In all honesty, he hadn't wanted to come back. Hadn't wanted to see Luke deteriorate. But maybe he'd missed out on the best years they could have spent together.

Levi forced his attention back to the game. Emma was up to bat next but struck out. As the teams switched positions, Levi moved to congratulate Luke on his catch.

But May ran to Luke's side and pressed a kiss to his cheek. "Nice catch."

Levi veered away, marching toward first base.

Why did it bother him so much, he wondered, Luke and May's relationship?

Grace had asked if the only thing he saw when he looked at Luke was his disability.

If he was honest, the answer was probably yes. But only because he *had* to see Luke that way. It was the only way to protect him.

Levi was so caught up in his thoughts that he missed an easy catch, allowing Tyler to get on first.

"You're up next, Luke," someone called.

"All right." Luke stood to make his way slowly to home plate. "I'm going to need a designated runner though. Legs aren't quite what they used to be."

"I'll run for you." May popped up next to him.

From across the field, Grace shot Levi a look that screamed "told you so."

Luke was almost at home plate when he went down.

It took Levi a moment to register that his brother was on the ground. But the moment he did, he sprinted for Luke's crumpled form.

He'd known baseball was a bad idea. But would anyone listen to him?

When he reached Luke, May was already crouching at his side, holding his cane out to him.

"What happened?" Levi scanned his brother for signs of injury.

The others began to reach them as well.

"Is he all right?" someone asked from the back of the group.

May stood, looking from Luke to the others. "Nothing to worry about. He just likes to practice his stunt double moves sometimes. He's expecting a call from James Bond any day."

Luke gave her a pained smile, but Levi glowered over May. "This is a joke to you?"

"No, of course not. I was only—"

"Get out of the way." Crouching behind Luke, Levi wrapped his hands under his brother's armpits.

"Oh, he can—" May started.

But Levi cut her off with a look, then hoisted Luke to his feet, waiting until he'd taken the cane and was steady on his feet to let go.

Luke gave him a long look, then shuffled away without a word.

"You're welcome," Levi muttered.

Grace appeared at his side. "That was kind of scary. You okay?"

Levi gave a terse nod, though it was a lie.

How could he be okay when his baby brother so clearly wasn't?

Chapter 17

" $\mathcal{I}$ think I'm going to take off." Levi leaned toward Grace, who'd been sitting next to him as they ate, lifting his empty plate off his lap. He'd managed to clear it, despite the fact that everything tasted like cardboard. Not that it wasn't perfectly good food—based on the last time he'd eaten with this group, he was sure it was all delicious. But his heart wasn't in food right now.

No matter what he did or how many times Grace tried to strike up a conversation, he couldn't get the image of Luke splayed on the ground out of his head. Or the way May had laughed at Luke. Or the way everyone was acting as if nothing had happened.

"Don't go." Grace set a hand on his arm, and the warmth of her fingers went through him.

But he pushed to his feet. "I'm not much fun right now."

Grace stood too. "It's going to be fine, you know. He's going to be fine." She looked so sincere and so concerned all at once that he had a sudden urge to step into her arms for a good old-fashioned hug. How long had it been since anyone had given him one of those?

"Yeah." He massaged a knot at the back of his neck. "I'll see you Monday, okay?"

She set those worried eyes on him again but nodded.

Levi brought his plate into the house, then made his way toward the front door, pausing at a family picture of Sophie and Spencer with their twins. Instead of looking at the camera, they were all looking at

Rylan, who appeared to be reaching for something in the grass. Levi peered closer.

A frog.

They looked like a happy family. A normal family. The kind of family he'd had until Luke had been diagnosed and they'd fallen apart.

"Levi?"

Though the voice was quiet, he jumped. He hadn't heard anyone else come into the house. He glanced over his shoulder.

"I was just leaving." He kept his tone short. He didn't have any desire to talk to May.

"I know." She looked tentative, as if one word from him might send her scurrying out the door. Definitely not the type of woman who was strong enough to stand up to the kinds of challenges Luke would face.

"I just wanted to say, I know it's hard for you to see Luke like this. But he's okay."

Levi ground his teeth. She had no idea what it was like for him.

This was the baby brother he'd grown up with. Played and climbed trees with. Run with. Thrown a ball with.

And now look at him. Luke very much was *not* okay.

He took a step toward her. "Is that why you laughed at him? Mocked him right in front of everyone else? Because he's okay?"

"What?" May's eyes widened, and she stepped back. "I didn't laugh—"

"You think he hasn't gone through enough in his life? The mocking, the bullying. You think he needs you to point out that he's no James Bond?"

"I wasn't trying to—"

But Levi didn't want to stand here and listen to her excuses. "Like I said, I have to go." He strode toward the front door.

"Levi, wait."

He yanked the door open, staring into the fading light for a moment, then faced her. "What do you want with Luke anyway? We

108

both know you're going to stick around until he gets too sick and then you'll get tired of him and be off, chasing after someone who's whole and complete and healthy. So why don't you save everyone involved some heartache and be on your way now?"

He lurched out the door and pulled it shut behind him, breathing heavily.

That had been completely unfair, and he knew it.

Because though he did worry that May would eventually desert his brother, those words had been directed not at her but at Rayna.

He huffed out a breath and jogged to his Harley. He'd have to apologize at some point, he supposed. But right now, all he wanted to do was put as much distance as possible between himself and other people.

"You okay?" Grace set the load of dishes she'd collected from outside on the counter, then moved toward the kitchen stool where May was sitting. The younger woman looked all trembly and shaken.

May sent her a weak smile that barely lifted her lips. "Can I ask you something?"

"Of course." Grace pulled out a stool and sat next to her. "What's up?"

"Do you think family is the most important thing?"

Grace frowned. "Most important for what?"

"I don't know. To keep together? Have a good relationship?"

"I do." Grace bit her lip. "Though we can't always please them." She thought of Mama, probably sitting at home right now scheming ways to get her to come home and marry Aaron.

"Do you have siblings?" May asked.

Grace laughed. "Yeah. Six brothers. Why?"

"I'm an only child, so I've always wished I could have had a brother or sister. Are you and your brothers close?"

The question brought the familiar ache to her soul. "Mostly. I'm in my brother Simeon's wedding in three weeks. But my brother Judah is estranged from the family. None of us have even seen him in six years."

"That's so sad." May set a hand on hers.

"It's hard. I don't think any of us realized how much we needed each other until he was gone." Grace patted May's hand. "But I pray for him every day. And I trust that God will bring him back to us—and back to the Lord—one day."

"I'll pray that too." May slid her chair back. "Thanks for the talk. I feel much better."

"Good." Grace waved her toward the backyard. "Now you'd better get out there. I'm sure there's one young man who's getting impatient to see you again."

"Yeah." A look of sadness flickered in May's eyes, but then she was gone out the door.

Grace moved into the kitchen and started putting food away. By the time everyone left, Sophie and Spencer would be exhausted and want to get the twins to bed.

She was almost done when Jade slipped into the room, a sleeping baby Matthias cradled in her arms.

Grace smiled at her, whispering, "You two look so happy."

"Which two?" Jade rubbed her baby's cheek. "Me and Dan? Or me and Matthias?"

"Both. All of you. I'm so happy for you."

"Thanks." Jade shifted Matthias to her shoulder, and he wiggled, scrunching his legs up under him. "I have to say, you've been looking pretty happy yourself."

"Me?" Grace grabbed a dishrag to wipe down the counter. "I'm excited with the progress on the bed-and-breakfast. I still can't believe it's really happening sometimes."

She felt Jade's eyes on her, and she scrubbed harder at a drip from the strawberry pie Peyton had brought.

When she couldn't scrub anymore, she looked up. "What?"

"Nothing." But Jade's knowing smile belied the word.

"Seriously, what?" Grace set the rag down and dried her hands.

"All right." Jade's smile grew. "I was just wondering if you're sure the renovation is the only thing making you so happy."

"I have a lot of things to be happy about. God's love. Singing in choir. How successful the Messtival was. Did you know we raised—"

"Levi Donovan," Jade cut in.

"What?"

"Levi Donovan is one of the things making you happy."

"Uh, no." But she could feel every drop of blood in her body rushing to her cheeks. "Levi makes me a lot of things—annoyed, irritated, frustrated—but not happy."

Jade only laughed.

"What?"

"Methinks the lady doth protest too much."

"Seriously, I don't—" But she made herself stop. No use solidifying Jade's opinion by protesting more. "He's become a friend. But I have zero interest in him in any other way. He's the complete opposite of my type."

"If you say so." Jade patted baby Matthias on the back as he started to fuss. "Just remember, Dan and I were the complete opposite of each other's type too." She made quiet shushing sounds to Matthias and glided out of the room.

Grace didn't need to be reminded of how different Dan and Jade had been. But now that she knew them, she couldn't imagine either of them with anyone else.

But that was Dan and Jade.

She and Levi were an entirely different story.

Levi had spent the night zoning in and out in front of a baseball game on television. But he had no idea what was happening or who was winning. He couldn't stop stewing over Luke's fall, Grace's compassion, May's hurt—and for good measure, he kept remembering the look of indifference on Rayna's face when she'd walked out on him.

He clicked the TV off and sat staring at the blank screen.

He had no idea how much time had passed when he heard the front door open. Luke's shuffling steps paused in the doorway.

"What are you doing?" Luke's voice was strained as he looked from Levi to the TV.

Levi shoved himself off the couch and moved toward his brother. "Waiting for you. About May . . ." He could at least apologize to Luke now, and maybe Luke could pass his apology on to May.

"You don't have to lecture me about her anymore." Luke pressed his fingers to his eyelids. "You were right." As Luke dropped his hand, Levi looked closer. His brother's eyes were red-rimmed and bloodshot.

"Right about what?" A sick feeling flooded Levi's stomach.

"That she wouldn't stick around." Luke's voice was hoarse. "She just broke up with me. Said she couldn't see us working out long term."

A brief flare of guilt rose in Levi's chest, but he squashed it down. If May couldn't handle a few honest questions about her relationship with Luke, then Levi had obviously been right in his assessment of her. She wouldn't stick around for the tough parts. And with Luke's condition, there were bound to be a lot tougher moments than this.

"Look, man." Levi clapped a hand to Luke's shoulder. "I know you don't want to hear this right now, but I really do think you're better off this way."

Luke rubbed at his eyes. "How can I be better off when I'm missing a part of myself?"

"Trust me." Levi patted Luke's shoulder again. "We'll be bachelor brothers. The Donovan boys. We can go out whenever we want, come in whenever we want, watch sports whenever we want." He thought of Grace's silly no-TVs- in-the-bed-and-breakfast rule.

"I'm going to bed." Luke shuffled toward the hallway, head down, shoulders slumped.

"Luke, wait," Levi called.

Luke turned.

"It'll be great." Levi had to work to sound enthusiastic.

But it *would* be great. Wouldn't it?

He'd been a bachelor for the past two years, and he'd never felt freer.

Sure, it was lonely sometimes.

As it had the habit of doing at the most inconvenient times, an image of Grace popped into his head. He was never lonely when he was with her.

But loneliness was a small price to pay to guarantee he'd never be hurt again.

Chapter 18

"This is all my fault." Grace sipped at her too-hot coffee, pulling it away from her mouth as it burned her tongue. She had to take off in a minute for her final dress fitting, but she couldn't leave until she'd drilled Levi on what he knew about Luke and May's breakup. When she'd noticed them sitting separately at church yesterday, she'd been concerned. But when she'd tried to ask each of them what had happened, both had politely said they didn't want to talk about it.

"Careful." Levi blew across his own mug. "And it's not your fault. It's May's. She's the one who decided to walk away from him."

"She was acting strange the other night. Asking all kinds of weird questions about family and stuff. I should have pressed harder to find out what it was all about. Maybe I could have changed her mind. They seemed so in love."

Levi shrugged. "Things aren't always what they seem."

Grace stared at him. How could he be so callous? "I suppose you're happy about this?"

"No." Was that hurt in his eyes? "Believe it or not, I don't want my brother to be unhappy. But I do think he's better off this way. Better that she leave him now than in another couple of months or years."

Grace picked up her keys. "Why were you so sure she'd leave?" Not that he'd been wrong.

"Experience," Levi said simply.

"Right. Because you get rejected by women so often."

"You rejected me," he pointed out.

She nearly choked on her coffee. "That's different. You're not—"

"Your type. I know." Levi set his coffee down. "So what is your type then, if you don't like the strong, handsome, athletic type?"

Grace rolled her eyes. "I'll be back in a little while."

"I see how it is," Levi's tone turned teasing. "Weaseling out of work again."

"Trust me, I'd rather stay here and work. But unless you want to go get fitted for a dress for me . . ."

Levi struck a ridiculous pose that Grace guessed was supposed to be modeling a dress. "I could pull it off."

"And you'd have to face my mama too."

"I bet I could take her."

Grace snorted. "You obviously haven't met my mama."

But forty-five minutes later, as she modeled her dress over a video call for Mama to see, she wished she'd taken Levi up on the offer to try on the dress—and deal with Mama—for her.

"There's plenty of time, Mama," she said into the phone. "This should be the last of the alterations, and the wedding isn't for three weeks yet."

"You sound like Abigail. 'Stop worrying, Mrs. Calvano. Everything is under control, Mrs. Calvano. I don't want a big fuss, Mrs. Calvano.'" Mama huffed. "As if any bride doesn't want a big fuss."

Grace lifted her arms so Harper could tack a pin into the seam of the empire waistline. "How's Simeon doing? Is he nervous?"

Grace already knew the answer to that question, since she'd been texting with her brother yesterday. Simeon had always been the most laid-back of her brothers, so she hadn't been surprised that he was taking it all in stride. His biggest worry was dealing with Mama. Grace had reassured him that in three weeks it'd be all over and Mama would stop meddling in his wedding—and start meddling in his marriage instead.

"You know your brother." She could picture Mama's embroidery needle flying through the pattern as she talked. "Won't say a word about how he's feeling. But he's nervous. Can't hide that from his mama."

Grace bit her tongue so that she wouldn't tell Mama the thing he was most nervous about was that his mother would drive his bride away before the wedding day.

"I wish you'd consider coming home earlier for the wedding. We have plenty of room for you. And we never get to see you anymore."

Grace let Harper spin her one hundred eighty degrees and switched her phone to her other hand.

"I know, Mama. But I have too much going on here. The renovation on the bed-and-breakfast is really coming along, and I can't afford to lose any momentum on it."

"I thought we raised you to appreciate your family." The comment was a perfectly crafted guilt trip, and Grace knew it.

But that didn't make it any less effective.

She dropped her arm, nearly getting stuck by a pin before quickly raising it again.

"Sorry," Harper whispered.

Grace shook her head. "I'll see what I can do, Mama. Maybe I can come a couple days early."

"Oh good," Mama's voice sparkled with triumph. "That will give you and Aaron more time to spend together. He's been asking after you. I'll make reservations for y'all. How about The Shed?"

Grace almost fell off the small platform she was standing on. Harper reached up to steady her.

"I'm not going to go on a date with Aaron, Mama."

"Why ever not?" Mama's voice was all innocence. "He's a wonderful man, loves the Lord, looking for a wife. I know God brought him here for you."

Why ever not? Grace raised her free hand to her forehead. She could not have this conversation with Mama one more time.

"Because I'm bringing someone," she blurted.

Silence crackled from the other end of the line, and Grace congratulated herself. It'd been a long time since she'd shocked Mama into speechlessness.

It only lasted a moment. "Is it that fellow you started seeing?"

Grace angled the phone away from her face. What fellow was Mama talking about?

And then she remembered the conversation she'd had with Mama on her birthday. The one where she'd made up a boyfriend to get Mama to stop talking about Aaron.

Well, it had worked then. She supposed it could work now.

"Yes, Mama. That's who I'm bringing."

"Are you sure that's a good idea, Grace? You haven't told me anything about him. And if you're too ashamed to tell your mama about him, he can't be good for you."

"I'm not ashamed to tell you about him, Mama." It was pretty hard to be ashamed of someone who didn't exist. "But I have to run for now. I'll see you soon."

She hung up before Mama could start demanding actual details, then stood there, staring at her phone.

Now all she had to do was find a man who was willing to come to her brother's wedding with her—and pretend to be her date.

No problem.

Chapter 19

"Got a minute?" Levi wiped a bead of sweat off his forehead and peered into the dining room, where Grace was seated at a makeshift table, her laptop open in front of her.

She smiled. "Yes, please. I'm going crazy trying to pick out table settings."

He waited for her to shut down her computer and stand up.

"Close your eyes."

"Why?" But she closed them. "This isn't some sort of prank, is it?"

"Nope." He wrapped an arm around her back to steer her. "A surprise."

"Oh, I like surprises." She let him pull her in closer, and he took the opportunity to draw in a breath of that sweet scent he could never place.

"I know." He felt like there were a lot of things he knew about her now. And it'd grown harder every day to convince himself that knowing her better didn't make him like her more.

Not that it mattered if it did. Like he'd told Luke, he was a bachelor, and he liked it that way.

Of course, that had been two weeks ago. Since then, his belief in his own statement had been sorely tested by his days with Grace.

He led her out the front door and down the porch steps, adding his other hand to her elbow to keep her from falling.

"Where are we going?" She giggled as he led her down the driveway.

Finally he stopped. He wanted her to get the full effect.

"Ready?" He leaned closer.

"Yes." Her voice brimmed with the excitement of a kid on Christmas morning.

"Open your eyes."

"Wow. Levi." She took in a deep breath. "I don't know how to say this, but . . . you were right."

Pleasure shot through his chest. "Saying it just like that works. So you like it?"

She took a few steps closer to the building. "I love it. That teal really pops on the shutters and the door. I guess I should trust you more often."

"That's what I'm saying." He pulled out his phone to check the time. "Oh man. I have to get going." He'd been so busy trying to get this done for Grace that he'd completely lost track of the time.

"Got a date?" Grace teased.

He hesitated. But there was no reason he shouldn't tell her. "Yeah."

"Oh." Her expression didn't change, but she started walking toward the house.

"How about you? What are you doing tonight?" He jogged to catch up with her.

"Me? I think I'll stay home and have a good cry."

"What?" He grabbed her elbow and pulled her to a stop. "What's wrong?" She wasn't really going to cry over him, was she? He'd cancel the date if it meant that much to her. Honestly, the only reason he'd made it was to fight off this growing desire he had to spend all his time with Grace.

"Nothing's wrong." Grace's face was completely serene, and he relaxed a little. "I just thought I'd watch *Marley and Me*. That movie wrecks me every time."

"I've never understood that." Levi scratched his head. "Why would a person choose to watch a movie they know is going to make them sad?"

Grace looked thoughtful. "Sometimes you just need a good cry."

"If you say so." He fished the truck keys out of his pocket. "Have fun, I guess."

"I will. You too." Grace ran up the porch steps and disappeared into the house without looking back.

Levi sat in his truck, uncertainty creeping over him. Was this what his life was always going to be like? Going on one or two dates with a woman, then moving on to the next? Never getting close to anyone because he didn't want to end up feeling like a fool again?

So far, it'd been easy. He hadn't met a woman he really wanted to get close to.

Until Grace.

He pulled his phone out of his pocket and dialed the number the woman from the grocery store had given him. When she didn't answer, he frowned. He'd much rather not do this over voicemail. But now that he'd made the decision, he couldn't imagine spending his night any other way.

He left a brief message, apologizing but being careful not to imply that he'd like to reschedule.

Then he hopped out of the truck and took the porch steps two at a time. Faced with the new teal door, he hesitated. On a normal workday, he'd use his key and walk right in.

But this wasn't a normal workday. He'd already said goodbye to Grace. If he walked in now, he might frighten her.

He lifted his hand to knock on the door frame, careful not to hit the wet paint on the door. As he waited for Grace to answer, he pulled out his phone and jotted a reminder to have her choose a doorbell.

He was still typing when Grace opened the door.

"Levi. Did you forget something?"

He put his phone away, meeting her slightly surprised expression. "Yeah. I mean no. I mean, I was wondering if you wanted some company while you cry your eyes out." The idea of anything making Grace sad fired a strange protective instinct in him. Maybe that was why he found himself standing here, watching her expression go from surprised to perplexed.

"I thought you had a date."

"Fell through. So what do you say? Can I tag along and watch—what was it again?"

"*Marley and Me.*"

"Yeah. Can I watch it with you? I've never seen it."

"There's probably going to be some ugly crying."

He doubted anything she did could be ugly. "I don't mind."

"All right then. I'll make some popcorn." She moved to let him in, and an inexplicable sense of peace came over him. Like this was where he was meant to be right now.

Ten minutes later, with popcorn bowls in hand, they entered the sitting room at the back of the house that made up part of her private quarters. He'd only been in this area once before, since she wasn't planning to remodel it.

The room was small, with mismatched furniture, but it looked out on the backyard and an incredible view of the lake below.

"Best view in the house." Levi moved to the window, not sure whether to sit on the love seat where Grace had settled or the room's lone chair, which was at a weird angle to the TV.

Outside, the sun had dropped behind the trees on the far shore, leaving deep shadows on the lake.

"It's starting." Grace kicked her feet up on the oversized ottoman and gestured for him to take a seat next to her.

He practically tiptoed across the room and eased himself onto the love seat, careful not to encroach on Grace's cushion by even a centimeter.

She sent him a quick smile, apparently completely unaware of how her sweet perfume toyed with his senses.

He stuffed a handful of popcorn into his mouth. At least if he was chewing, he should be able to resist the impulse to lean closer.

Chapter 20

$\mathcal{G}$ race fought to get the quaking in her lip under control.

This part of the movie always did her in. But much as she'd warned Levi about the ugly crying, she really didn't want to do it in front of him. She felt him look at her, and she blinked hard.

But then his hand landed on hers, and there was nothing she could do to prevent it any longer. The sob hiccupped out of her.

Instead of recoiling, Levi slid closer, and his fingers curled around hers.

"You weren't kidding about this movie." His voice was raspy, and out of her peripheral vision, she caught his other hand rubbing his eyes. It was there and gone in less than a second.

But it was enough to confirm what she'd begun to suspect: under his football-tough exterior, Levi Donovan was a softy.

She sniffed loudly. "It gets worse."

Levi's exclamation of disbelief tugged a laugh out of her even as the tears rained faster.

"We can turn it off," she said.

He shook his head, tightening his grip on her hand. "I can handle it if you can."

She nodded, resisting the urge to burrow her face into his shoulder, mostly so she wouldn't have to see what was coming next, but partly because she wondered what it would feel like to have his arms around her.

She was suddenly way too aware of how close he was sitting. She extracted her hand from his, leaning forward to pick up her water bottle. After she'd guzzled a long drink, she set it down, then settled back into the love seat, pressing her body against the armrest, as far from Levi as she could physically get on the too-small piece of furniture.

She'd forgotten herself for a moment. It was the emotion of the movie, that was all. And maybe the fact that Levi had asked to watch it with her.

She reminded herself that it wasn't like he'd gone out of his way to spend time with her. She was only a backup plan because his date had fallen through.

She directed her gaze to the screen, forcing herself to give all her attention to the movie. Every once in a while, Levi's head swiveled toward her. But she refused to let herself look back.

An hour later, she was wrung out but satisfied. She sighed as she wiped at her eyes. "What'd you think?"

Levi stared at her. If she wasn't mistaken, his eyes were a little red. "I think I'm glad I didn't watch that with the guys."

She clicked the TV off, leaving them in the near dark, the only light coming from a small floor lamp on the other side of the room. "I've never let anyone watch that movie with me before. I'm too much of a mess afterward." She scrubbed at her still-wet cheeks.

"You don't look like a mess." Levi's eyes met hers, and there was something in them she'd never seen before.

His hand lifted toward her cheek, and she was next to certain he was going to tuck her hair behind her ear.

She froze for half a second before her good sense kicked in, propelling her to her feet. She scooped up the popcorn bowls, trying to ignore the feel of Levi's eyes on her.

Thankfully, her phone rang, breaking the growing silence. She shifted the bowls to one hand and pulled out her phone with the other.

But the name on her screen made her groan.

"Is that your reaction whenever I call?" Levi asked.

Grace laughed. That was better. More like the Levi who loved to antagonize her. Less like the one who'd held her hand.

"It's my mama." She tucked the phone back into her pocket.

"I can go if you want to talk to her."

Grace shook her head. She'd hear it from Mama tomorrow. But she didn't have the energy to deal with Mama's hundred questions about her fellow tonight.

A fellow she still hadn't found. And she had exactly five days left before she had to get on a plane—with or without her imaginary boyfriend.

"She's just calling about Simeon's wedding."

"That's next week, right?"

"Yeah. I leave Wednesday. You sure you've got everything under control while I'm gone?"

He gave her a look, and she lifted her hands. She may have already asked that—more than once. "Sorry."

"Your mom still planning on setting you up with that guy you haven't seen since you were kids?"

Oh, why had she ever told him about that? "I don't think so."

"Yeah?" Levi's face brightened. "She came to her senses?"

"Not exactly. I told her I was bringing someone." The words spilled out like grape juice on white carpeting.

"You did? Who?" Surprise mingled in Levi's voice with something she couldn't identify.

"I don't know," she wailed. "There *is* no one. I just wanted her to stop hounding me."

"So find someone."

Grace looked at the floor. She was pretty sure no one in the history of the world had ever been as humiliated as she was right now. "There is no one. I haven't been on a date in years. All of my guy friends are married. Where am I supposed to find a single man who happens to be free to travel to Tennessee with me on less than a week's notice?"

"I'll do it." He said it simply, as if he were offering to run to the hardware store for her.

"You'll do what?"

"I'll come to Tennessee with you."

Whoa, Levi. What are you doing?

Had he just offered to go to Tennessee with Grace? More importantly, *why* had he just offered to go to Tennessee with Grace?

"You'll come to Tennessee with me?" She sounded as shocked as he felt.

"Sure. I mean, if it will help you out."

Grace bit her lip. "I don't know. I should probably call and tell my mama the truth. I don't want to deceive my family."

"You won't be deceiving them. You said you were bringing someone. And I'm someone." Why was he working so hard to convince her?

But now that he'd offered, he couldn't deny that he really wanted to spend some time with her away from work.

"I implied I was *dating* this person I'm bringing."

Levi rubbed his chin. "That *does* make it more complicated. I suppose we could go on a date first, so technically you'd be bringing someone you were dating."

"I— Wait. Are you asking me on a date?"

A strange sort of nervousness went through him.

What if she said no?

Well, then she said no. It wouldn't be the first time. And it wasn't like he was asking her on a real date this time. "Just for appearance's sake."

"I don't know." Grace set down the popcorn bowls she'd been holding and plopped back onto the love seat.

"I'm a good actor." Levi stepped in front of her. "Watch. Happy." He smiled and threw his head back as if someone had just told a joke. "Angry." He shook a fist in the air. "In love." He batted his eyelashes.

A laugh poured out of her, silky and light as air. It filled him.

"Is that a yes?"

"Okay." She slapped her palms against her legs. "Yes."

"Great." The grin that took control of his mouth was no act. "What time should I pick you up tomorrow night?"

"Tomorrow night?"

"We fly out Wednesday, right? That doesn't give us much time."

"True. How about seven? What should we do?"

"Leave that to me."

She eyed him. "Let's keep it simple though. And not romantic."

"Of course." He headed for the door. "Goodnight, Grace."

Her lilting goodnight followed him out the door and stuck with him all the way home.

Chapter 21

*G*race rummaged through her closet—again. She'd already changed six times.

But it wasn't her fault.

First of all, she had no idea what a person was supposed to wear on a date that wasn't really a date.

And second of all, Levi had texted to say she probably didn't want to wear a dress. Which left her worried about what he could possibly have planned.

She pulled out a peasant blouse and wrinkled her nose at it. It had to be at least a decade old.

A knock at the front door made her jump. Nerves zipped from her spine out to her limbs.

Only because she wasn't ready.

She glanced in the mirror. Her white capris and soft gray top would have to do.

She slipped on a pair of flats, grabbed her purse, and moved toward the door. She could see Levi through the window, though his back was to her. Good. That gave her a second to push aside the unexpected surge of attraction.

Levi Donovan was a handsome man, she'd never deny that.

But that didn't mean she needed to go getting all gaga over him. And it certainly didn't mean he was the right kind of man for her. All it meant was that she needed to be more on her guard.

Because Hunter had been an attractive man too. That was part of the problem.

With a quick inhale, she opened the door.

When Levi turned toward her, the first thing she noticed was his smile—wide and open and maybe a little nervous—and then the flowers he held out to her. Purple tulips.

"Oh." She took them awkwardly. Why was this feeling more and more like a date by the moment? "You didn't have to. It's not like this is a real date."

Levi shrugged. "You don't want to deceive your parents, right? So I thought it should be as much like a real date as possible."

Grace swallowed. As long as he didn't think a real date included any kissing.

Because that was so not happening.

"I'll put these in some water." She escaped to the kitchen, rummaging to find the vase that had held the flowers she'd bought for her birthday.

She wouldn't have expected then that only a month and a half later, a man would be buying her flowers.

He didn't buy you flowers, she reminded herself. *He got them as part of the act.*

"Allow me." Levi took the vase from her and filled it with water, then held the stems of the flowers under the faucet as he cut the bottoms off.

"Wow. You're an expert. You must buy a lot of flowers."

Levi cut the last stem and lowered the flowers into the vase. "Not really. My mom taught me when I was young, and I guess it stuck with me. I think the last time I bought flowers was three years ago. For my mom."

"Oh." Grace searched for a response to that, working not to feel special that he hadn't bought his other dates flowers. "That's sweet."

"There." Levi set the vase in the middle of the kitchen counter. "Ready to go?"

"I don't know. Am I dressed appropriately for whatever we're doing? I didn't wear a dress, as instructed."

"You look perfect." Levi's eyes landed on hers, then zipped away. "I mean, that's perfect for what we're doing."

"Which is?" Grace followed Levi to the front door and stepped through when he held it open for her. Her eyes stopped on the van in the driveway.

"I hope you don't mind. I borrowed my mom's van." He sounded strangely self-conscious. "I've been thinking about buying a car, but I haven't gotten around to it yet."

"I don't mind." Actually, it was kind of cute that he was driving his mom's van. Made him seem more like a normal guy.

"Good." He opened the door for her. "I didn't think you'd like to take the bike. Some women don't like to get their hair messed up on a date."

She touched a hand to her head. She wasn't sure which bothered her more—the fact that he kept acting like this was an actual date or the fact that he knew what "some women" liked on dates. She thought of the number of dates he'd been on just since she'd known him. Likely, he knew what a lot more women than "some" liked.

"You're not afraid of heights are you?" Levi asked as he pulled out of the driveway.

"Depends. What are we doing?"

Levi shook his head. "Nice try."

"No, I'm not afraid of heights," she admitted. "One time my brothers dared me to climb the town water tower, and I started to, but my daddy caught us before I got halfway up." She'd gotten quite the lecture that night—about how she'd face temptation in life, sometimes from people she loved, and she had to learn to say no to it.

They'd given her the same lecture the night they'd caught her with Hunter. Only stricter. And with more disappointment woven through it.

"What about water?"

She reeled her thoughts back to the present. To the man sitting next to her, who was a little too much like Hunter for her comfort. "What about water, what?"

"You're not scared of it, are you?"

"I live on the lake." What could they possibly be doing that involved both heights and water? Not cliff jumping. They were headed the wrong direction for that.

And then she knew. "Oh. *That's* what we're doing."

"What?" Levi's eyes darted to her. "You don't know what we're doing."

"Do too." She couldn't help the teasing note.

"Do not."

She just smiled at him. Let him have a taste of his own medicine.

"Prove it." He shot her a challenging look, before driving right past the road to the marina.

"I think you missed your turn."

He chuckled as he made a quick U-turn. "You *do* know what we're doing. Have you ever been?"

She shook her head. "I've always wanted to try it though."

"Good." He seemed genuinely pleased to have chosen something she would enjoy. "I thought it'd be pretty to watch the sunset from up there."

Grace stuffed down the flutter that trickled up from her belly. How many times had she seen couples riding together in the parasails at sunset and thought how romantic it would be to do that with her own special someone?

Oh well.

Levi might not be her special someone, but it should still be fun.

Levi parked the car, and she reached for the door handle.

"Freeze." His voice startled her into pulling her hand back.

"If this is a date, then I need to open your door for you." He ducked out of the vehicle before she could remind him yet again that this wasn't a date.

When he opened the door, she took her chance. "Levi, this isn't a—"

He held up a finger. "I don't want to hear that for the rest of the night. You want to be able to honestly tell your parents we're dating, then this is a date."

"But—"

Levi ignored her. "Let's see. The guy said to meet him at . . ." He squinted toward the docks, where rows of sailboats, yachts, and motorboats rocked in the gentle waves. "There he is."

He planted his hand on her lower back to steer her toward the white-haired man waving to them from the docks.

With a reminder to herself that the touch was only to keep up appearances, she took off faster than necessary. When she dared a glance at Levi, his hands were in his pockets, and he looked completely at ease.

As was she.

Why wouldn't she be?

Chapter 22

The higher the parasail got, the less tethered Levi felt to the world below. Up here there was no wondering if his dad would ever be proud of him. No worrying about Luke. No trying to figure out what he was going to do with the rest of his life. Up here there were no expectations.

There was only Grace.

Far from being afraid of heights, she was leaning forward, exclaiming at every new sight, from the lighthouse on the edge of the cliff to the pelicans flying alongside them to the small group of islands in the distance.

Sometimes Levi forgot how beautiful this place where he'd grown up really was. He had a brief flash of what his life could be like if he stayed here, but he dismissed it as quickly—Hope Springs might be beautiful, but it didn't hold anything else for him.

Except this woman next to you.

He dismissed that thought even faster.

Or at least he tried to. But the more he worked at it, the more he realized—he liked her.

He could tell himself all he wanted that he'd only offered to do this to help her out. But the truth was, pretending to date her gave him a chance to spend time with her without the risk.

She'd already rejected him once, and he was quite sure that if he asked her out for real again, she'd say no.

But a fake date?

There was no risk in that. And maybe if they spent enough time together, she'd realize that he wasn't so wrong for her after all.

"This was such a great idea." Grace's cheeks were bright, her eyes brighter.

He'd taken women to world-renowned restaurants, ushered them down the red carpet at awards shows, even flown them on private planes to house parties hosted by celebrities—but not one of them had ever looked at him like this.

Like they really appreciated the thought he'd put into the evening.

Then again, he wasn't sure he'd ever put as much thought into a date as this one.

"Oh look." Grace pointed toward the horizon. "The color in those clouds. It's like . . ." She closed her eyes as if searching for the perfect description.

Levi forced his eyes off her animated face to look toward the clouds sitting low in the western sky. They seemed to glow from the inside out with a color somewhere between red and orange.

"Tangerine," he said.

She opened her eyes, staring at him in wonder. "That's the word I just thought of."

"My mom used to take Luke and me outside to lay on a blanket and find shapes in the clouds." He'd forgotten about that until he said it, and nostalgia tightened his chest. That had been before they knew about Luke's diagnosis. Before his family's whole existence had shifted.

"Look. That one's a dragon." He pointed toward a cloud off to his side.

She squinted and leaned to look around him. "I don't see any cloud that looks remotely like a dragon."

"Right there." He pointed again. "See, there's the eyes. And the snout. And the puff of smoke from his fire. He even has wings." She had to see it. It was the biggest cloud in the sky.

But she shook her head. "Not seeing it."

"Here." He reached an arm around her and pulled her closer, then used his hand to turn her head ever so slightly. With his other arm, he pointed so that her line of sight would have to travel right past his finger.

Grace repositioned, bringing her head closer. "Oh that? That's not a dragon. It's a castle."

"What?" There was no way they were looking at the same thing. "That cloud. With the two giant wings sticking up from the back."

"Those are towers," Grace said patiently. "And that over there isn't a dragon snout. It's a princess waving to her subjects."

A laugh burst out of him, shaking his whole body.

The movement seemed to remind them both that his arm was still around her. He pulled away at the same time that she sat up.

They fell silent, watching the play of light on the clouds as it deepened from orange and red to pink and purple and finally to a deep blue that teetered on the brink of black.

"That was amazing," Grace said as the boat's captain began to reel in the parasail's rope.

Levi watched the water grow closer, trying not to feel the world closing back in.

Grace tried to reorient herself.

Her feet were firmly planted on the dock, and yet she still felt like she was flying.

She'd always figured she'd enjoy parasailing, but that had been beyond enjoyable. It had been . . . exhilarating.

She let herself watch Levi as he climbed off the boat behind her. Would she have enjoyed the ride as much if he hadn't been along? If she'd gone by herself? Or with another man? Someone more suited to her?

Somehow, she couldn't imagine it.

"Ready for some dinner?" Levi turned to walk up the dock.

"Oh, you don't have to take me out for dinner. This was more than enough." Grace tried to fall into step beside him. But she really did feel like everything was still swaying, and she stumbled.

Levi's hand landed on her elbow, and he kept it there even after she was steady on her feet.

She supposed she should pull away, but she had no desire to end up in the water tonight.

"What kind of date would this be if I sent you home hungry? Plus, I'm starving. We have reservations at Alessandro's."

"Alessandro's? Levi, that's too much."

The only restaurant on the peninsula with a Michelin star, Alessandro's was expensive. And romantic. Not exactly suited to fake dates.

"Come on." Levi steered her toward the van.

Soft music played in the vehicle, and Grace let herself relax into the seat.

"Can I ask you something?" Levi interrupted her silent musing on how she'd ended up here, going on a fake date with a man who was so totally wrong for her—and enjoying herself.

"Sure. As long as it's not what I'm going to order. I've heard everything at Alessandro's is delicious."

"You've never been there either?"

"A night of firsts for me, I guess." Including first fake date. "What'd you want to ask?"

"Why don't you date?"

Grace sat up straighter, suddenly on alert. "Who says I don't date?"

"You did. Last night. You said you haven't been on a date in years."

Grace didn't say anything. It wasn't like there was any reason to deny it.

"So why not?" Levi glanced sideways at her. "It's obviously not for lack of opportunity."

She spluttered. He was going to talk to her about opportunity—when he'd had more than his share of *opportunities* to date? "What is that supposed to mean?"

Levi lifted his hands off the wheel. "Nothing. Just that you're a beautiful woman, so I assume you get asked out all the time."

"I— Oh." How was she supposed to respond to that?

"I don't get asked out all that often," she confessed. "And when I do get asked, I guess I just don't . . . None of them have been the right kind of man."

"Ah." Levi nodded, as if he had her all figured out. "None of them checked all the boxes on your list."

She shrugged. "Maybe." That was nothing to be ashamed of. She'd made that list for a reason, and as long as she stuck to it, she wouldn't find herself in a compromising situation again.

"Fair enough." Levi pulled into the driveway at Alessandro's, and Grace glanced down at her casual outfit.

"Uh, Levi?"

"Yeah?" He pulled into a parking spot and shut off the van.

"I think this may be a bad idea."

Chapter 23

*L*evi sat with his hand still on the car keys. "Look, Grace. I know I probably don't meet half the qualifications on your checklist. But it's just a fake date. Surely I'll do for that."

"What?" She turned puzzled eyes on him.

"You said this was a bad idea. And I'm just saying—"

"Not that—" She gestured to her lap. "This. I think we're a little underdressed for Alessandro's."

"Oh." He looked from her capris to his own khaki shorts. "Does it matter?"

"I'll feel self-conscious."

"Okay then." He started the van back up. "How about ice cream for dinner?"

"Really?" Grace's eyes lit up but then fell. "Wait. You don't mean those hardware store ice cream bars, do you?"

"Ouch. Don't hate on my ice cream bars. But no. I was thinking the Chocolate Chicken."

"It's like you read my mind." She rested her hand on the console between the seats—only inches from his.

He swallowed, wishing he could read her mind about more than just ice cream. Like what did she really think of him? How far short of her list did he fall? And would he ever be able to convince her otherwise?

She looked peaceful and content, sitting here with him—and he took that as something. Maybe there was hope yet.

Levi pulled the van up to one of the last empty parking spots in front of the Chocolate Chicken. As they waited in line, they debated favorite ice cream flavors. She was a die-hard chocolate fan, while he preferred butter pecan.

Just one more thing about them that was different. But Levi didn't mind—it made life more interesting that she didn't simply agree with him on everything, like so many of his dates in the past had.

She challenged him in a way that he hadn't been challenged in a long time.

"Eat these in the park?" he asked as they walked out of the crowded building.

"Read my mind again."

They turned their steps toward the public gardens on the hill above the marina, settling in the large gazebo that overlooked the water below.

"This is one of my favorite spots in Hope Springs." Grace's sigh spoke contentment as she licked at a drip of ice cream. "I couldn't even tell you how many hours I've spent in here, praying."

"We toilet papered it once when I was in middle school. Some buddies and I."

Grace eyed him, as if she weren't sure whether to believe him. "You did not."

"We did. Got caught too. Got a nice ride home in a police cruiser."

Grace snickered. "I wouldn't lead with that when you meet my parents."

"Thanks for the tip." Levi finished off his ice cream. "What are your parents like?"

"Protective."

"Ah." In Levi's experience, protective meant intrusive. Maybe that was why Grace was so hesitant to date.

"Ah, what?"

"Nothing." Levi held up his hands. He had no desire to get into a fight with her about her parents.

"It's not like it sounds." Grace looked thoughtful as she stared over the water. "They just want what's best for me."

"It means a lot to you—what they think—doesn't it?"

She looked at him in surprise.

"I know you better than you think, Grace. Though I'm not quite sure *why* their opinion means so much to you." Like he was one to talk, working here all summer just to prove something to his dad.

Grace took a big bite of her cone, and he turned to watch the light at the end of the breakwater as it swiveled over the waves in the dark. It was none of his business, her relationship with her family.

"My senior year of high school—" Grace's voice was strained. "There was this guy who I was— Well, I thought I was in love with him. My parents saw right away that he wasn't the right kind of guy for me. But I didn't listen. And—"

His eyes followed her as she moved to the trash can to throw away her napkin.

And? He wanted to ask. But he held his tongue. If she wanted to tell him, she would. And if not, he wouldn't press her.

"And it turned out they were right," she said finally.

"So you made a list." It was all starting to make sense. "So you wouldn't end up with that kind of guy again. So you'd end up with the kind of guy your parents would approve of."

"Pretty much." Grace ran a finger over her lips, as if checking to make sure she didn't have any ice cream on them.

"You missed a little bit. Right there." He pointed to the corner of her lip, the part that turned up just so when she smiled.

"Thanks." She scrubbed her fingers at it. "Better?"

"Perfect." He worked to pull his eyes off her mouth. "Now what?"

"Now it's my turn to ask you a question."

He spread his arms wide. "Shoot. I'm an open book."

"Why do you date so many women?"

Grace watched as Levi shifted from one foot to the other. Her question had clearly made him uncomfortable. But he had asked about her dating life—it was only fair that she got to ask about his.

"Because it's fun, I guess." He took a step, as if to leave the gazebo.

"Levi." She wasn't buying it.

He sighed, brushing a hand over his hair. "I'm not some playboy or something."

"Okay." Grace waited. That hadn't really answered her question, had it?

Levi's cheeks puffed out as he exhaled. "You're not going to let me off the hook here, are you?"

She shook her head.

"Believe it or not, I had a long-term girlfriend. Someone I thought I was in love with. Someone I thought was in love with me."

Grace tried to picture Levi in love, taking his girlfriend on dates, curling up with his girlfriend to watch a movie, tucking his girlfriend's hair behind her ear.

Oddly, it didn't feel like that much of a stretch.

"What happened?"

He gave an ironic laugh. "Turns out she wasn't so much in love with me as with the idea of me. She walked the day I was cut." He turned his gaze away from Grace. "The day I was planning to propose."

"Oh." Grace had a distinct urge to knock that woman over the head. Levi might not be the right man for Grace, but that didn't mean he deserved to be treated like that. "I'm sorry."

He shrugged. "Anyway, I guess it's just easier not to let anyone else get too close. You know?"

She gave a slow nod. She supposed she did know, in a way. In the end, his dating a lot of women and her dating no one came from the same place—fear.

"On that note—" Levi seemed to snap out of his reverie. "I suppose we should call it a night."

"Probably." Grace tried to ignore the swoop of disappointment. It was only because it was such a beautiful night that she didn't want to go home yet. "I have to sing at church tomorrow, so I should get a good night's sleep."

"You sing?" Levi swiveled to look at her as they walked toward the van. "Why have I not heard you? We have the radio on every day."

Grace rubbed her arms, nerves she'd managed to push aside all week suddenly taking over. "I don't really like to sing in front of people."

"But you're singing for church?"

Grace pressed a fist to her stomach. "A solo. Don't ask me how they talked me into that. Do you think it's too late to back out?"

Levi chuckled as he opened the van door for her. "Probably. But I'm sure you'll be great."

Grace couldn't help the groan that escaped as she fastened her seatbelt. Now that she'd started thinking about it, the nerves were multiplying exponentially, as if they'd decided to host a party in her stomach.

Levi jumped into the driver's side. "What are you singing?"

"Great Is Thy Faithfulness."

He frowned. "Sounds familiar, but I can't think of how it goes. Sing it for me?"

"Uh, no." Grace blew out a breath. If just thinking about it was nearly making her sick, how would she get through singing it at church tomorrow?

"Please." Levi folded his hands on the steering wheel, as if begging.

But she shook her head. "If you want to hear it, you'll have to come to church. Assuming I don't die the minute I get up in front of all those people."

"You're that scared?"

Petrified was more like it. "I have no idea how you managed to play football in front of millions of people every week."

"I tried to remember why people were there. To watch a good game of football."

She made a face. "That doesn't help me."

"Well, why are people at church?"

"To hear God's Word." That one was pretty obvious.

"Okay then. Is that what you're going to do? Share God's Word?"

She nodded.

"There you go." He tapped her arm as if he'd just solved her problem.

"I'm still nervous, you know."

"I know." Levi smiled at her. "I'd be worried if you weren't. But you're going to have to trust me. You'll be great."

Grace leaned back in her seat. Easy for him to say.

He wasn't the one who was going to have hundreds of eyeballs on him tomorrow.

By the time Levi pulled up to her door, Grace was so worked up that she almost forgot her plan for the end of the evening. Although she was close to one hundred percent certain Levi wouldn't attempt to kiss her, she wasn't taking any chances.

"Well, goodnight." She sprang out of the van before he could put it in park.

But before she'd rounded the vehicle, he'd cut the ignition and was getting out.

"I'm fine." She kept plenty of space between them as she strode toward the house. "You don't have to walk me to the door."

He ignored the comment, his long legs keeping pace with her as if she had the stride of a child.

When they reached the door, she pulled out her keys and turned them in the lock, then allowed herself to tilt her head ever so slightly, so she could just see his face.

The moonlight hit it, illuminating the way his smile ended in a dimple.

"Thanks. This was nice." Nice? The guy had taken her on the best date of her life, and all she had to say was that it was nice?

"I thought so too." Levi took a step closer, and she got ready to duck into the house.

They were *not* going to kiss.

But instead of lowering his head, he raised a hand, squeezed her arm gently, then turned and jogged down the steps.

"Goodnight, Grace," he called over his shoulder. "See you tomorrow."

"Goodnight, Levi." She was too busy noticing the tingle that lingered where his fingers had met her skin to ask what he meant about seeing her tomorrow. And by the time she thought to ask, he was already driving away.

Chapter 24

*L*evi held up two ties, debating. He didn't know when he'd decided that he'd go to church today. Only that Grace had looked so vulnerable when she'd confessed to being nervous about singing. And he'd thought that if he could be there for her, maybe somehow that would help. Which sounded crazy now. But he'd already told her he'd be there. And he had no desire to let her down.

Their date last night had been . . . He didn't know how to describe it.

Fun. Playful. But also honest. Open. Unguarded.

All those things he never allowed himself to be around other women.

He picked up the ties again, then tossed them both on his bed. No need to go overboard.

All activity in the kitchen stopped the moment he walked in. You'd think he was some kind of exotic zoo creature, the way every member of his family was staring at him. Even Luke, who'd been entirely oblivious to the world around him since he and May had broken up. Although the lovesick expression he'd worn for two weeks didn't change, his eyes did flick to Levi's dress clothes with a hint of interest.

Mom recovered first. "Breakfast? I made eggs."

"That'd be great, Mom. Thanks." Levi took the plate she passed him.

"We leave in five minutes." Dad's voice was gruff, but under it, Levi could hear the hope.

He wanted to tell him not to get his hopes up. This didn't mean he was going to become a choirboy or something. It simply meant that for this one day he was going to give church a chance.

Four minutes later—Levi checked the clock—Dad was ushering them all to the van. Levi shoveled in a last bite of eggs on the way to the door.

In the van, Mom and Dad struck up their own conversation, and Levi turned to glance at Luke. A fresh wave of nostalgia rippled through him. It wouldn't take much to imagine they'd traveled back in time twenty years. All Levi had to do was reach out and act like he was going to poke Luke, then Luke would complain to Mom and Dad that Levi was touching him, then Levi would point out that he wasn't, then Mom would tell them to stop, then, when they didn't, Dad would yell and threaten to pull over.

Levi turned away from Luke to gaze out his window.

Those days when their biggest problem was who was touching whom were long past.

Mom turned in her seat to look at him, as if she was afraid he might have jumped out while the car was moving. "You know that Pastor Zellner's son Dan is pastor now?"

He nodded. "Grace introduced us. Seems like a decent guy."

"Oh that's right, he's friends with Grace." The way Mom said it, Levi knew she hadn't forgotten that for one second. It was simply a way for her to "subtly" sneak in her next question. Which should be arriving in five, four, three, two—

"What did you and Grace end up doing last night?"

Levi held in his groan. His mom was only curious—his parents had never been stifling the way it sounded like Grace's had been.

"I took her parasailing."

Mom gasped. "What if she was scared of heights?"

"She loved it."

Mom shook her head. "Why anyone would attach themselves to that contraption and let themselves be suspended over the lake like that . . ." She shuddered and looked at Dad. "Don't *ever* ask me to do that."

"Wasn't going to," Dad replied.

Levi's gaze slipped to his father's profile as Mom faced forward again. His parents loved each other, he'd never doubted that. But it'd always seemed to him more like a workman type of love—more like a partnership than a romantic whirlwind. He had no idea when the last time his parents had been on a date was.

He wondered what that would be like—not worrying about wining and dining a woman. Just putting your head down and doing the work together—going through life together. Facing the hard times together.

An image of working side-by-side with Grace sprang into his head.

That kind of life might not be so bad.

As Dad pulled into the parking lot of Hope Church, Levi leaned forward. "It looks different."

"We had to rebuild after the tornado," Mom said. "I called and left you a message about it."

Now that she mentioned it, Levi did vaguely remember a message about a storm, but he hadn't paid too much attention to it, other than registering the fact that his family was safe.

"It looks bigger."

"Yeah. Hope Springs has been growing, and so has the church. We added some new meeting rooms and classrooms. Plus a much bigger lobby." Dad parked the car, and Levi tugged at his open collar. What was he doing here? He didn't belong among all these people who went to church every week. Who hadn't spent the last few years questioning whether God really mattered. Sometimes wondering if he even existed.

"Come on." Dad gestured for him to hurry. "Service will be starting in a minute." Same old Dad. Considered five minutes early to be late.

Inside the lobby, Levi was greeted by several of Grace's friends as he followed his family into the sanctuary. He smirked as Dad led them to the exact spot his family had always sat when Levi was growing up: right side of the church, third row from the front.

He took the seat on the aisle, sitting with his hands on his knees as the rest of his family bent their heads to pray. Levi stared straight ahead. It'd been so long since he'd prayed, he was pretty sure God wouldn't remember who he was. Besides, he wasn't convinced that the various prayers he'd sent up over the years—prayers for victory, prayers for his career, prayers for Luke—weren't just floating somewhere in space, unheard and unheeded by this so-called God who was supposed to love him.

Levi might not be an expert in love, but even he knew that if you claimed to love someone, you listened to them.

Music started from the far side of the sanctuary, and Levi turned to see a band warming up. Nate sat at the piano bench, smiling like there was nothing he'd rather be doing.

A moment later, a line of people wearing black pants and maroon shirts filed in behind the band.

The choir?

Levi had been expecting them to be wearing robes. He searched the faces a little too eagerly until his eyes picked out Grace. Though she was dressed the same as everyone else and was shorter than the women on either side of her, still she managed to stand out.

Maybe it was the joy that always radiated from her, highlighted by the shaft of sunlight that fell on her face from the large windows at the side of the church. Or maybe it was the fact that she kept pushing her hair behind her ear, then pulling it in front of her again, then pushing it back again. She was nervous.

And that made him nervous.

An overwhelming desire to run over there and give her a pep talk came over him. But that wouldn't exactly be a churchy thing to do.

Instead, he kept his eyes on her, willing her to look his way. All he wanted was a chance to smile at her, to let her know he was here for her.

She scanned the crowd, like she was looking for someone.

Him?

But her eyes were far from him when the smile broke across her face. Levi followed her gaze, a tiny hit of jealousy taking him down a notch. Had she been lying about there being no one she wanted to date? Maybe she'd been trying to work up the nerve to ask someone else when he'd stepped in and volunteered himself.

There.

His eyes landed on the row she was focused on. Jade's little girl, Hope, was waving at her like crazy.

Levi turned back to Grace, who grinned at Hope, sent her a small wave, and then resumed her search of the sanctuary.

"Good morning." Dan's welcome from the front of the church pulled Levi's attention off of Grace, only for a second. But it was long enough for her to pick up her choir binder. He guessed he'd never know if her eyes had been on their way to him next.

She was going to vomit.

Right here and now, in front of the whole church.

Why had she ever agreed to do this? Just because the choir director had been begging her for years to do it and just because everyone in the choir had urged her to do it and just because she hated to disappoint people, that didn't mean she should have accepted.

She'd had stage fright since she'd run off the stage in tears at her first piano recital in second grade.

Put her in a group, put her behind the scenes, and she was fine.

But put her in front of people, and she froze up like a pig on an ice pond.

And it didn't help that she'd been on edge all morning wondering if Levi would be here. That had to have been what he'd meant when he'd said "See you tomorrow," didn't it? The thought had made her half-giddy—Levi was going to hear God's Word—and half-petrified—Levi was going to hear her sing.

But it turned out it didn't matter. She'd searched nearly the entire sanctuary before Dan had started the service, and she hadn't seen a sign of him.

"Our opening hymn this morning will be sung by our choir, accompanied by the worship band," Dan was saying now.

Grace tried to swallow, though her mouth had turned into a cotton field. She couldn't worry about Levi now. She had to focus.

Which would be a whole lot easier to do if the words on the page weren't blurring in front of her.

This was it. She was going to pass out. Topple over and knock the rest of the choir down with her, like dominoes.

The director gave her the cue to come forward to the microphone they'd adjusted to her height before church. She stepped forward, her eyes scanning wildly over the packed seats in front of her.

There were so many people. Too many people.

She couldn't do—

Her eyes fell on him.

Levi.

He was watching her, and the moment her eyes locked on his, he sent her a confident smile.

You can do it, he mouthed.

What had he said last night? To remember what all these people were here for.

They were here to listen to God's Word. And she was here to share it in the form of song.

She sucked in what may have been the deepest breath of her life and closed her eyes.

Her stomach was still flopping around like a fish on a riverbank, but the words came out clear and true: "Great is thy faithfulness, O God my Father."

She risked opening her eyes, letting them travel to Levi. He wasn't smiling anymore—he looked serious. Thoughtful.

Please let your Word touch him, Lord. Show him your love. Grace sent up the prayer even as she continued to sing, and somehow she wasn't afraid anymore. She let her eyes scan the rest of the sanctuary.

Some people were watching her and smiling, some had their eyes closed and were swaying to the music. Little kids were coloring or munching on snacks, and Jade and Dan's daughter Hope was clapping along to the music.

A swell of joy rolled through her as she took a step back from the microphone to join the choir in the refrain. This was her church family. None of these people were perfect. They were all sinners. But they were all people Christ had died for. People God had shown his faithfulness.

Her voice was stronger on the second verse, and so strong on the third verse that she wondered if it was even her singing anymore. As she sang, the words hit her as if she were hearing them for the first time:

"Pardon for sin and a peace that endureth,
Thine own dear presence to cheer and to guide,
Strength for today and bright hope for tomorrow—
Blessings all mine, with ten thousand beside!"

As the last words faded, Grace switched off the microphone and ducked her head, stepping back to follow the choir to their designated seats on the left side of the church. They'd be singing another song later in the service—one she didn't have a solo in, thankfully. Because now that the song was done, she had no idea how she'd gotten through it. The nerves came back in fresh, rolling waves.

She'd managed not to get sick in front of the church, but she wasn't sure how much longer that would last.

As the people around her whispered that she'd done a good job, she mumbled an apology and rushed for the nearest exit.

Chapter 25

As a kid, Levi had been yelled at for fidgeting in church more times than he could count. But Grace's singing had stunned him into stillness.

It wasn't just her voice—though that was amazing. And it wasn't just the expression of joy on her face—also incredible. It was the depth she put into the words—like she really believed them. Like they were really true and she had experienced them.

Some small part of Levi wanted to know what that was like.

As Dan called for the congregation to stand, Levi realized he was still staring at the now-empty microphone. His gaze skipped to the rows where the choir members had settled, but he couldn't pick out Grace. A flash of movement behind them caught his eye as someone slipped out the sanctuary door into the lobby. He didn't know why, but he was sure it was Grace.

"I'll be right back," he leaned over to whisper to Mom.

She shot him a concerned look, but he offered a reassuring hand pat before striding down the aisle toward the back of the church. A couple of people smiled at him, but most didn't even seem to notice him.

When he reached the lobby, he stopped, scanning the area. Other than Jade, who was swaying with a crying Matthias in her arms, he didn't see a sign of anyone.

"Looking for Grace?" Jade shifted the baby to her shoulder, and he stopped crying for a moment to stare at Levi.

"Hey there." He made a funny face, and Matthias's wails started in again, more intense than ever.

"Sorry." He took a step back. "I didn't mean to scare him."

Jade shook her head, rubbing the baby's back. "He's tired. Decided to stay up and party all night. Grace went in the women's room."

Ah. Well, that made sense. And there was no point in him standing out here to wait for her. How clingy would that seem?

"Actually, she was looking kind of peaked. I was going to go check on her, but Matthias wasn't having it. If you want to hold him for a second, I'll go." She held Matthias out toward him, as if she were handing off a football.

Levi lifted his hands to his sides, a clear signal that he did *not* want to hold the child.

"It's all right. He doesn't bite." Jade bounced the baby a little. "And I know you won't drop him. You always hold onto the ball."

Yeah. The ball. Not a *kid*.

But Levi's hands came together, and Jade placed the baby into them.

The child was heavier than a football. Definitely squirmier. And louder.

But somehow holding him didn't feel weird.

"I'll be right back." Jade hurried toward the far side of the lobby, and Levi stood there, staring down at the baby.

The volume of the kid's cries lowered a little, and Levi bent his knees, then straightened, bouncing gently the way Jade had been doing.

After a couple of seconds, the cries lowered to a soft whimper.

"See, it's okay, buddy. I've got you."

The baby made a strange noise, one like Levi had never heard before. If he had to describe it, he'd say the baby had cooed, kind of like a pigeon.

"You like that?" He bounced some more, eliciting more coos.

"How did you get him to stop crying?"

Levi startled as Jade came up beside him, looking like she was about to hug him. Behind her, Grace was watching him, her lips curved up slightly.

He passed the baby back. "Honestly? I have no idea."

"Well, thank you. Now I can sit down again." Jade gathered the baby to her shoulder, then slipped through the doors back into the sanctuary.

"You're good at that," Grace whispered, stepping into the spot Jade had vacated. "What are you doing here?"

"Oh, I—" Did she mean "here" at church or "here" in the lobby? Either way, the answer was the same.

Looking for her.

"You sounded amazing. From now on, I'm going to have to insist that you sing along with the radio."

"Thanks." She ducked her head, letting her hair cover her face.

Over the speaker that piped the service into the lobby, he heard Dan begin another Bible reading.

"I should get back in there," Grace whispered.

"Yeah."

"I'm over on that side."

"Okay." Great time to lose the ability to string together a sentence of more than one word.

She offered him one more quick smile, then crossed in front of him to pass through the door to the sanctuary. He almost called out to her to wait. Almost asked her to lunch after the service. But he stopped himself. That felt a little too much like opening himself up to rejection.

Besides, he'd be spending the next week with her. He could go one afternoon without her.

In fact, he probably *should* go one afternoon without her.

Levi waited a few seconds after Grace had gone back into the sanctuary to reenter through the doors at the other side.

As he slipped into his seat, Dan stepped to the podium at the front of the church. Ah, time for the sermon. Never his favorite part of the service.

He sat back in his seat, kicking his legs out under the row in front of him, and started counting the number of tiles on the floor.

"Let me ask you something." Dan sounded like he was talking to an old friend instead of an entire church full of people. In spite of himself, Levi looked up from his counting. Dan stepped out from behind the podium, bringing himself closer to the congregation. "What are you doing here?"

Levi snorted to himself. Seemed to be a popular question today.

One he couldn't answer.

"I don't mean here, as in at church this morning," Dan continued. "Although I suppose plenty of people would ask us that. But why are you *here* here? On this earth. Right now, at this specific time, in this specific place."

Levi gave up counting the floor tiles and leaned forward in spite of himself. The truth was, he had no idea what the answer to that question was. Ever since he'd lost the ability to play football, it was like he'd lost his whole reason for being. He was floating around like some useless piece of space debris.

Or at least he had been, until he'd started working on Grace's renovation.

His eyes traveled the sanctuary, settling again on the spot where she sat with the rest of the choir members. The look of intense concentration on her face said she was one hundred percent interested in Dan's sermon.

Definitely not thinking about Levi.

"I guess what I'm really asking is—" Dan was still talking, and Levi picked up on the thread of the sermon. "What is your purpose?"

Purpose.

Something about that word struck a chord with Levi. Was that what he was looking for? Purpose? If Dan could tell him how to find that, maybe he was worth listening to.

"So many people are looking for purpose in so many places. In success. In money. In meditation. In being a good person. But there is only one purpose."

Levi glanced around the church. Was anyone buying this? Dan wanted them to believe that every single person in the world had the same purpose? There was no way. Obviously they weren't all going to be pro athletes or brain surgeons or even parents.

"I can hear you now," Dan said. "You're telling me to get on with it and tell you this purpose already." There were a few chuckles across the congregation. "I'll do you one better," Dan continued. "I'll let *God* tell you what your purpose is." He lifted a Bible off the podium behind him and opened it, letting his finger scan down the page.

"Listen to the purpose God calls you to. In John chapter eight, Jesus tells us: 'If you hold to my teaching, you are really my disciples. Then you will know the truth, and the truth will set you free.'" Dan closed the Bible, keeping his finger in the pages. "Do you see your purpose there?"

Levi almost shook his head. How on earth was that verse supposed to show him his purpose? What did it even have to do with anything?

"Your purpose," Dan announced, "is to hold to God's Word."

Levi sat back, disappointment pulling his shoulders down. He should have known he wouldn't find any useful advice here. Just a bunch of platitudes about how everything would be fine if he simply read the Bible and prayed. Well, he'd tried that, and it hadn't worked.

"But why?" Dan asked. "Why does Jesus tell us to hold onto—to remain in—his Word? To boost his own ego? To show us everything we're doing wrong? To make life easier for ourselves?"

He scanned the entire congregation before continuing. "No, no, and no." He counted off on his fingers. "He tells us why we need to remain in him—so we will know the Truth."

Right. Truth. Who even knew what the truth was anymore?

Dan paused. "That's a slippery word these days, isn't it? Truth? People will tell you it's relative. They'll say that just because something is true for you doesn't mean it's true for them."

Dan hung his head a moment before lifting his chin. "They're wrong. They're so, so wrong. There is only One Truth. And he doesn't want anyone to die without knowing him. Jesus is that Truth. He tells us that himself: 'I am the way and the truth and the life.'"

Dan paced toward Levi's side of the church. "Knowing that is the only thing that matters. Nothing else we do, nothing else we learn or achieve means anything without the Truth."

"When you don't know that Truth, when it eludes you and you're searching for your purpose in all the wrong places—searching in your job or in your money or even in your family—you're never going to know true peace. Something will always be missing."

Those words. They caught at Levi.

Something missing.

As much as he tried to deny it, even to himself, there had been plenty of days when he'd felt like something was missing.

"God's purpose for you is right here." Dan picked up his Bible, holding it over his head. "It's the purpose of knowing the Truth that you are saved in Christ. That Jesus went to the cross for you. That he suffered the punishment for your sins. That he rose from the dead to give you the promise of eternal life."

Dan's smile traveled across the room. "That purpose has nothing to do with who you are or what you've done. It's all about the One who is 'the way and the truth and the life.' And it's an *eternal* purpose."

Levi shifted, sure the sermon was over, but Dan spoke again. "Maybe you're thinking that's all well and good, but what you really need is a purpose for *right now*. For while you're here on earth. Before you die."

Yeah. That would be nice. But as far as he knew, the Bible didn't deal with the here and now, except to make rules.

"All right, then," Dan said. "That can be summed up in one word: glorify. Our purpose in this world is to hear God's Word, worship him, and share his glory with the whole world. I don't know about you, but that's bigger than any other purpose I could ever come up with. In fact, it feels too big sometimes, doesn't it?" His smile said he had an answer for that too. "God tells us how to do that too, and it's actually quite simple: 'Whatever you do, do it all for the glory of God.' Share his Word. Shine the light of his love to others. That's it. Plain and simple."

As Dan finished the sermon, Levi stood with the rest of the congregation. The word *purpose* was still echoing in his head.

Maybe purpose was what he needed.

But was that purpose really Jesus?

He'd been so sure for so many years that it wasn't.

But now—now he wasn't quite so certain.

Chapter 26

*G*race watched out of the corner of her eye as Levi grabbed a bottle of water out of the fridge while she boxed up dishes in preparation for the kitchen demo when they got back from Tennessee.

She'd asked him yesterday what he'd thought of church, and he'd said it was fine. Not a word more. And she hadn't yet figured out how to bring it up again.

"What?" Levi raised an eyebrow.

Great. He'd caught her staring at him.

"Nothing. We should prob—" A lilting chime dinged from above them, and she swiveled, searching for the source. "What was that?"

Levi grinned. "Your new doorbell. Like it?"

She actually did. Very much. But— "I thought I was going to pick one out?"

"I know." Levi capped his water bottle. "But I knew you'd like this one, so I thought I'd surprise you. Worked, didn't it?"

"Yes, but—"

"Come on. That's probably Tori at the door. Don't want to give her a bad impression by making her wait all day."

Grace pressed down a fresh onslaught of nerves. No big deal. It was only a chat between two women. Even if one of them did have a national travel blog.

Levi reached the door before she did and gave her a thumbs-up before opening it.

Grace's mouth dropped as the woman outside the door stepped into Levi's open arms for a bear hug. There was no way to describe the woman other than gorgeous.

Grace had dressed with care this morning, putting on a flowing skirt and a sleeveless blouse and even a subtle layer of makeup.

But next to the woman in Levi's arms, who wore a fitted black dress, perfect hair, and long legs, she looked like a ragamuffin.

Well, that was fine. It wasn't like anyone would see her.

She cleared her throat and stepped forward as Levi released the woman. "I'm Grace Calvano. You must be Tori." She held out a hand, and the woman shook it with a gracious smile.

"It's so nice to meet you." Tori glanced around the unfinished space. "Looks like a beautiful place you have here."

"Thank you. Please come this way. We're in the middle of the remodel, so I thought we could enjoy the view in the backyard."

She led the way to the back patio.

"This is quite a view." Tori sat in the lounge chair Grace indicated. She pulled out her phone and tapped the screen. "You don't mind if I video record our interview, do you? I like to include a couple of brief clips with each post."

"Oh. Uh—" Blind panic. That's what this feeling must be.

"It's fine," Levi cut in, smiling at Tori.

"And I assume you'll be joining us for the interview?" Her comment was directed to Levi.

"Sure. Why not?" Levi settled into the chair between Grace and Tori.

"Great." Tori pulled an expandable tripod out of her bag and attached her phone to it, setting it up so that it would have a clear shot of all three of them.

"So—" Tori leaned back in her chair, seeming to be completely at ease in front of the camera. "How did you manage to snag Levi Donovan to renovate your bed-and-breakfast?"

"Um." Grace licked her lips. She'd thought this interview was supposed to be about why she wanted to open the bed-and-breakfast, the kind of experience she wanted to create for guests, that sort of thing. But she supposed the renovation was part of it. "He kind of just showed up at my door one day, saying he worked for the construction company I'd hired."

Tori laughed. "Your lucky day, I guess."

Levi flashed a self-confident smile at the camera.

"I guess." Grace crossed her legs in front of her in a vain attempt to appear as confident as Tori and Levi. "Actually, I—"

"And Levi, what brought you to work for this construction company? I'm guessing you don't need the money."

"Nah." Levi shrugged, and Grace recognized the false humility in his smile. It wasn't nearly as attractive as the real humility he could show on occasion. "It's my dad's company. I came home to help out for the summer."

"That's sweet." Tori jotted something on her paper. "So what kind of work are you doing here?"

Levi settled back into his chair. "Let's see, I took out a wall between the living room and dining room, put bathrooms in all the guest rooms, refinished the floors throughout the house, painted, built a library . . . You name it, I pretty much did it to this place. Oh, and I just put in a new doorbell."

Grace gaped at him. *He* had taken out a wall? *He* had added bathrooms? *He* had refinished the floors and painted and built the library? What about her? She'd been part of every single one of those projects. She'd poured her blood, sweat, and tears into this place. Not to mention all the work his crew had done.

"Actually, we did a lot of that together. I really thought it was important that I—"

"Oh yeah." Levi's smile felt condescending. "Grace has been a great helper."

Helper? This was her home. Her bed-and-breakfast. If anyone was the helper here, it was him.

"So what next? After this is done?" Tori's question was directed to Levi. "Will you stay in construction? Stay in Hope Springs?"

"I'm not sure what I'll do." Levi leaned forward. "Right now I'm weighing my options"

Options? She'd give him options.

Right now, he had the option to leave voluntarily or risk her throwing him out. On camera.

"Is there any chance—"

"Would you like a tour?" Grace interrupted Tori's next question to Levi.

Tori looked surprised. "I was under the impression that the place wasn't ready for tours yet."

"It's not." Grace fumbled. "But—"

"The library is almost done," Levi cut in smoothly. "You'll love it." He sent Grace a look that said *you're welcome.*

She barely resisted kicking him in the shin.

In the library, Levi pointed out the shelves *he* had built, the floor *he* had finished, the window seat *he* had designed. Okay, Grace would give him that one. But she'd added the cushions and pillows to make it cozy.

"It's nice." Tori panned the space with her camera. "But where are all the books?"

"That's Grace's department." Levi waved at her.

Oh, was she really going to get a chance to talk at her own interview?

Tori turned the camera on her, and Grace's tongue latched to the roof of her mouth.

"What kinds of books will you have in here?" Tori prompted. "Will guests be able to check them out?"

Grace managed a mute nod.

"Let me ask you something." Levi stepped in front of the camera, blocking Grace's view of Tori.

At last, she managed to pull in a breath. "Yes, guests will be able to check out books," she blurted from behind Levi.

Tori stepped around Levi, who turned to peer at Grace too.

"That's good." Tori pointed her camera back to Levi.

"And if they're in the middle of a book when their stay is done—" Grace rushed on, causing Tori's camera to swing back to her. "They can bring it home."

"That's great." Tori's smile was patronizing as she turned away from Grace to talk to Levi again. "You wanted to ask something."

Levi leaned against an empty shelf, looking totally at ease, totally photogenic. "Do most places like this have TVs?"

Grace shook her head. Not this old argument again.

"Some do. Some don't," Tori answered.

Grace threw a triumphant look at Levi. So there. She wasn't crazy not to want a TV.

But Levi was still looking at Tori. "And which do people like better, the ones with or without TVs?"

"I suppose it depends on what people are looking for," Tori said. "But I'd say the ones with TVs are more common."

"Thank you." Levi turned to Grace. "I rest my case."

"I take it this is an ongoing argument?" Tori watched them with an amused smile.

Levi laughed. "You could say that. Grace wants people to come here to connect. I say you can connect over TV. Like while watching a sad movie together." Levi's eyes darted her way.

Grace froze. That was so not what had happened while they were watching the movie the other night. They hadn't made a connection.

"Let me show you the fireplace. It's original to the house." She left the room without checking that Tori and Levi were following her.

"It's the perfect place to put a TV too," she heard Levi mutter behind her.

She chose to ignore him. She didn't want to be seen yelling on video.

"I think that went well." Levi closed the door behind Tori. "Should drum up plenty of business for this place."

Grace spun away from the door and marched to the kitchen, the clattering of dishes soon carrying through the house.

She'd seemed off all afternoon, but he'd chalked it up to stage fright. She definitely hadn't been comfortable in front of the camera. He probably should have warned her about that.

Fortunately, he'd done a pretty good job of covering for her.

He winced at the sound of shattering glass and sprinted for the kitchen.

"You okay?" He found Grace standing barefoot in a minefield of glass.

"Stay put. I'll go get a broom."

"I got it." Grace picked her way through the shards.

"Seriously Grace. You're going to get cut. Stay there. I got it."

"Just like you do everything else around here too?" Grace pelted the question at him.

"What?"

She winced and pulled her foot back from the spot she'd been about to step.

"For crying out loud. You're so stubborn." In three quick strides he'd crossed to the closet that held the broom and pulled it out.

When he reached Grace, he started to sweep the glass, but the broom was yanked unceremoniously from his hands.

"What on—" He looked up to find Grace sweeping glass with a vengeance.

"I said I've got it." Her voice was hard, and she didn't look at him.

"Grace? What's going on? Are you upset that I didn't warn you Tori was going to film? Because I'm sorry. I should have known—" He fumbled as her incredulous stare landed on him.

"You really don't know why I'm upset? Are you that self-involved?"

Levi took an involuntary step backwards. "Self-involved?"

"I was under the impression that the interview was supposed to be about the bed-and-breakfast. Not the Levi Donovan show."

"What are you talking about?" He gripped the back of his neck. She was crazy. "All we talked about was the bed-and-breakfast."

"Yeah. And all the work the wonderful and famous Levi Donovan is doing on it. Oh, Levi—" She put on the false, high-pitched voice of a belle. "Whatever would I do without you?"

"What did you want me to do? Say I wasn't working on it?"

"You called me your little helper, Levi." Her voice was dangerously quiet.

Levi held up his hands. "I never said little."

"You might as well have."

"Look, I don't know what you're complaining about. If I hadn't called in a favor with Tori, you wouldn't have had the interview in the first place."

"Yeah. It looked like a real hardship for you to ask for that favor from Tori."

"What's that supposed to mean?"

Grace glared at him a moment, then looked away. "Nothing. Never mind."

Levi grasped for a way to turn this conversation around. "It will be good for business. People will want to come to the bed-and-breakfast Levi Donovan decorated. It's a selling point."

That was obviously not the right thing to say.

Grace drew in a long breath, then exhaled all at once. "I think you should leave now."

"Look—" Was it possible he *had* taken over the interview? He was so used to being the star that it hadn't occurred to him that he was hogging the limelight. "I'm sorry, okay? I wasn't trying to steal your show. All I wanted to do was help."

"Yeah. I know." But her tone said she didn't know. And she didn't forgive him.

"I have to finish packing." She rubbed at her temples. "I'll see you tomorrow, okay? Our flight leaves at nine, so if you want to be here at six, that should be plenty of time to get to the airport and get checked in."

"Will do." At least she still wanted him to go to Tennessee with her. "And I really am sorry. I didn't mean—"

"Okay." Her voice was tired, like she couldn't deal with him anymore today.

He watched her a moment longer. He'd screwed up, and he had no idea how to fix it.

With Rayna, jewelry had always worked. But he had a feeling that wouldn't cut it with Grace. Not to mention they weren't really in the type of relationship where it would be appropriate for him to buy her jewelry.

Not yet, anyway.

Not ever, probably, if he couldn't fix this.

"I'll see you tomorrow." He grabbed his keys. "Have a good night."

Chapter 27

"*H*ere."

Grace eyed the steaming cup of coffee Levi held out to her—a peace offering, she supposed.

She'd hardly gotten a wink of sleep last night, thinking about that interview. And though Levi had apologized again this morning when he'd pulled up to her house ten minutes early, the drive to the airport had been nearly silent.

"Try it. I got you hazelnut."

She made a face. He knew she drank her coffee unflavored and black. But the caffeine called to her, and she brought it to her lips, taking a cautious sip.

The warm liquid swirled on her tongue, a hint of bitter mixed with the slightest taste of sweetness.

Oh, that was good.

She lowered the cup, trying for an indifferent expression.

"So?"

She shrugged. "It's fine. Thanks."

"Come on, admit it. You love it. You just don't want to forgive me."

She grabbed the handle of her carry-on and dragged it behind her toward their gate. So what if he was right? She knew she had to forgive him—eventually. But she wasn't quite ready for that yet.

"The problem is—" Levi easily kept pace with her, though he had his carry-on duffel draped over his shoulder. "You can't stay mad at me. It's physically impossible."

She snorted. Watch her.

"All right. Just remember that you brought this on yourself."

"Brought what on—" But she cut off as Levi stopped dead in the middle of the path, forcing the people who had been following them to veer off to the sides.

He dropped his bag, then flung his arms wide and . . . sang.

"I'm sorry. So sorry . . ."

Or at least she thought that was supposed to be singing.

The words were scratchy and off-pitch and oh-so-loud. The man couldn't carry a tune in a bucket with a lid, bless him.

She lifted a hand to hide her eyes and ducked her head, slinking a step farther away from him. But a firm hand gripped hers and drew her closer. His other arm wrapped around her back, snugging her right up to him.

And still he was singing.

She took a quick, wild glance around her, searching for an escape route, but a crowd had started to gather around them.

"Levi, stop," she hissed.

But he shook his head, laughing, as the song continued to pour out of him.

Someone in the crowd whistled, and Levi waved with one hand, his other still firmly planted on her back. She ducked her head farther, burying it in his sweatshirt. This was mortifying. But also kind of . . . *No, it was not kind of sweet. It was mortifying. Period.*

At long last, the song ended. A smattering of applause broke out around them.

Fire licked up Grace's cheeks, and yet, they also felt a little bit strange. As if she was . . . Yes, she was smiling.

Why was she smiling?

"What'd you do?" a voice from the crowd called.

"I was an idiot." Levi's whole chest moved as he responded, and Grace suddenly realized her face was still pressed against him.

She took one very large step backward, keeping her head down so she wouldn't have to see the people gathered around them.

"Do you forgive him?" that same voice called.

Grace raised her eyes to Levi's. He was watching her with a goofy yet pleading look. He folded his hands in front of him, angelic style, and mouthed, "Please."

Grace gave one quick nod.

Forgiving him was better than standing here with all these people staring at her.

"Kiss her." That ever-so-helpful spectator again.

Grace balked.

Of course Levi wasn't going to kiss her.

And she wasn't going to kiss him.

But he looked at her, raising both eyebrows. She gave an emphatic shake of her head.

No way.

She was not kissing Levi Donovan in front of all these people.

She was not kissing Levi Donovan. Ever. Period. End of story.

Levi was still watching her, and for half a second, she was sure he was going to do it anyway. Her blood thundered in her ears, drowning out the voice that was repeating the request.

But then Levi stooped to pick up their bags. "She's shy."

He winked at her, then turned and started walking toward their gate again.

She scurried after him, unwilling to be left alone with the crowd. When she reached his side, he still sported an overly large grin.

"I can't believe you did that."

"I told you, you brought it on yourself. Oh, and just so you know, Tori and I never dated. That wasn't why I called in a favor. I helped her get an interview with Lawrence Brooks—who she ended up marrying."

"I— Oh." Why he thought she would care about his connection to Tori was beyond her. "That's . . . interesting."

"Is it?" He lifted a shoulder. "Come on, we don't want to miss our flight."

"So are we friends again?" Levi didn't dare lean closer to Grace, though he kept his voice low. She'd been acting weird since the moment they'd gotten on the plane. And he'd seen the look on her face when that guy in the airport had said he should kiss her—pure terror.

Did she really find him that repulsive? That undesirable?

"Yeah." Her sigh said she'd given the answer against her better judgment. "We're friends."

"Friends who pretend to be more?"

"I guess. Wouldn't be much point in dragging you along otherwise."

"Speaking of, we should probably practice."

Grace gave him a blank look. "Practice?"

"Acting like a couple. You know, holding hands. Talking. Hugging." He raised an eyebrow. He really shouldn't push it right now, but he had to see how she'd react. "Kissing."

Alarm lit her eyes. "We are not kissing. If you think—"

He laughed. "Relax. I was kidding. I know I'm not your type. Here." He held out his hand, palm up, fingers splayed.

Grace stared at it, and he nodded his chin at her hand.

Slowly, she lifted it and let her palm come to a rest against his.

He folded his fingers around hers. "There. That's not so bad, is it?"

She didn't reply.

"Now, what's our story?" He tightened his grip on her hand, feeling the scrapes and callouses from the weeks of hard work at his side.

Though nearly every woman's hand he'd ever held had been soft and smooth, he preferred Grace's without question.

"Our story?"

"You know, how did we meet? What do we enjoy doing together? That sort of thing."

A flitter of panic crossed Grace's face. "Maybe this was a mistake. I don't want to make up a whole lie to tell my family."

"Okay. We'll tell them the truth."

"But—"

"We met when I started working on the bed-and-breakfast. And we like to work together, eat ice cream, and parasail. See?" He turned to her. "None of that is a lie, right? Unless you don't like doing those things with me?"

"No. I do. But . . ."

"Good. Now how about pet names? Pookey, Snookums, Honey Bear? Which do you want to be?"

Grace laughed, and the anxiety slipped from her face. "Who have you ever heard call someone Pookey? Let's stick with Grace and Levi."

"Fair enough. Now for the important part."

Grace gave him a wary look.

"I need a primer on your family. I aim to make a good impression."

For the next hour, Grace told him all about her family, her hand planted firmly in his the whole while. By the time the plane landed, Levi knew that Grace was closest to her brother Zeb, who was only a year older than her and a cop. He knew that Simeon had met his bride on a mission trip, that Judah was a doctor and likely wouldn't be at the wedding, since he had cut himself off from the family, that Asher was a park ranger, Joseph was studying to be a vet, and Benjamin played football, had just graduated from high school, and wanted to become a chef.

He also got the impression that all six of them were fiercely protective of their sister.

As they filed off the plane, Grace slid her hand into his. He looked down at her with a smile, his heart making a short, quick trip to his throat until he reminded himself that she was just doing what they'd practiced.

"Last chance. You sure you want to do this?" She sounded adorably nervous.

But he wasn't sure if it was because she was afraid he'd say no—or afraid he'd say yes.

"I'm sure." He leaned over to take her bag from her. "Let's do this, Pookey."

She swatted at his arm, but the smile that lit her face made it so worth it.

Chapter 28

"Benjamin!" Grace shrieked as she threw herself into her baby brother's arms. He had to have grown at least three inches since she'd seen him at Christmas. The worst thing about being the only girl in a family of boys was that everyone was taller than her. Well, that and the perpetual mess in the bathroom.

"Hey, sis." Benjamin's long arms squeezed her tight, and he ducked his head, whispering, "You could have mentioned that the someone you were bringing was Levi Donovan."

She supposed she could have, but it hadn't occurred to her. Somehow, she usually forgot that Levi was a big football star everyone knew. To her, he was simply the guy renovating her house. And pretending to be her boyfriend.

She let go of her brother. "Sorry. Benjamin, this is Levi. Levi, my youngest brother Benjamin."

"Ah." Levi shook Benjamin's hand. "The football star."

Benjamin's cheeks colored, and Grace turned to look at Levi. He'd remembered what she'd told him on the plane?

"I'm not a star," Benjamin mumbled.

"You are too." Grace slugged him. "You don't take your team to state three years in a row without being a star."

"She's right, man." Levi slung an arm over Grace's shoulders.

She stiffened but didn't move away.

He's supposed to be your boyfriend, she reminded herself. *That's what boyfriends do.*

"Maybe we can get in a game while we're here. If your sister doesn't mind." He leaned over and brushed the lightest kiss onto Grace's hair.

Pulling away slightly, she shot him a look. Hadn't she said no kissing? And she'd meant it.

Even if his gesture had felt sweet and friendly more than passionate or romantic.

"Come on. I'd better get y'all home." Benjamin opened the passenger door of his ridiculously tiny Gremlin. "Mama's been in a tizzy all day long, waiting to meet Grace's special fellow. Wait till she finds out it's Levi Donovan. I can't believe you didn't tell us."

Actually, now that he said it, Grace couldn't believe it either. What *would* her family think when they learned she was dating Levi Donovan?

She moved to climb into the car's tiny backseat, but Levi pulled her back. "You take shotgun. Catch up with your brother."

She eyed Levi's long legs. "There's no way you're going to fit back there."

Without waiting for him to argue, she climbed in. Once she was settled, Levi crammed himself into the seat in front of her.

"You sure you're okay back there?" He craned his neck to check on her.

"Positive." If okay meant having some sort of spring sticking out of the seat into her back, then she was great.

"Sorry." Benjamin crammed the luggage onto the seat next to her, then climbed into the driver's seat. "She needs a little work, but I'm going to fix her up." He pulled into traffic. "Levi Donovan," he muttered. "Unbelievable. How did you two even meet?"

Levi launched into the story of how he was helping with the bed-and-breakfast. Every once in a while, he sought her confirmation, and she nodded absently. She was too busy worrying to jump in. What if Mama and Daddy didn't like Levi? Didn't approve of him?

She studied what she could see of his profile from back here. He was good-looking, that was for sure. But her parents wouldn't care a lick about that.

And he was a nice enough guy, charming when he wanted to be. Which seemed to be a lot more often lately.

She told herself it didn't matter what her parents thought of him. It wasn't like he was really her boyfriend. Just a convenient stand-in to keep them off her back while she was home. Even so, she really wanted them to like him.

To approve of her choice.

Even if he wasn't really her choice.

Ugh. Her head spun.

Levi and Benjamin's conversation moved from how Levi and Grace had met to football, then to Benjamin's plans for next year.

"Grace says you want to go to culinary school?"

Grace's eyes about dropped out of her head. It wasn't only football that he'd been paying attention to on the plane.

"Yeah. It's not exactly the NFL, but . . ."

"It's a good choice," Levi interrupted. "Women love a man who can cook. Just ask your sister. I made her pancakes, and that was the moment she knew she was in love with me."

Grace choked on her own spit, gasping for air around her coughs.

Levi turned to peer at her. "You okay, Honey Bear?"

The most Grace could do was curl a lip at him, and he laughed.

"If cooking is your passion," he said to Benjamin, "that's what you should do."

"Thanks, man. You're pretty cool."

Levi swiveled to look at Grace again. "You hear that? I'm pretty cool."

She smirked. "Don't let it go to your head."

But yeah, he actually was pretty cool. The way he was encouraging her brother, who as the baby of the family had always been a little less sure of himself, was more than pretty cool.

Not that he needed to know she thought that.

"I think we're off to a good start," Levi whispered to Grace as he held out a hand to help pry her out of the backseat of Benjamin's Gremlin. "Your family likes me."

"Benjamin's the easiest one," Grace whispered back. "Especially since he apparently idolizes you." But she was happy about that, he could tell. "Mama's going to be the tough nut."

"There y'all are." A woman who looked strikingly like Grace, only older, stepped onto the wide front porch of the spacious Revival-style home.

Grace shot him a deer-in-the-headlights look.

"Relax. It's going to be great. She'll like me, you'll see."

Grace gripped his forearm. "Whatever you do, don't mention your Harley."

"I don't see how it would come up. Why?"

But Grace's mother had descended the porch stairs and was beelining for them.

"Mama." Grace left his side and wrapped her mother in a hug.

When the two women pulled apart Levi held out a hand. "I'm Levi Donovan. It's so nice to meet you."

Mrs. Calvano gave him a long, appraising look before shaking his hand. "Heather Calvano."

"That's a lovely name."

"Hmm." Mrs. Calvano turned to Grace. "Abigail and Carly are bunking with you in your old room." Levi made a mental checklist—Abigail was the bride, Carly was Zeb's wife.

177

"I put Levi in with the boys." She turned to him. "I hope you don't mind sleeping on the floor. We don't have enough beds."

"Mama, can't Benjamin—"

"Of course I don't mind," Levi cut in. "I'm just grateful for the invitation to come. I don't know how I'd handle five days without my girl."

Mrs. Calvano scrutinized him, and Grace frowned. Okay, maybe that had been a tad over the top.

But her mother seemed like the kind of person it would take over the top to impress.

"Well, I hope you weren't planning on spending too much time with her while you're here." Mrs. Calvano shepherded them toward the house. "As a bridesmaid, Grace is going to be plenty busy with wedding activities."

"Oh. I'm sure I won't be *that* busy. Levi and I will still have time to spend together."

"Maybe." Mrs. Calvano gave a polite nod. "Come on. Everyone's out back."

As they followed Mrs. Calvano, Grace sent him her best told-you-so look.

Fine. He could admit he had his work cut out for him, getting her mother to like him. But he was up for the challenge.

Chapter 29

"What are you doing out here?" Grace closed the French doors that led to the back patio Mama and Daddy had put in last summer. The morning was warm and sticky, the sun just starting to burn off the dew sparkling in the grass all the way down to the river.

Levi was sprawled on a chaise lounge, and she padded closer, cup of coffee in hand. She'd planned to sneak out here for some quiet time in prayer before the rest of the family woke and chaos took over. She'd assumed Levi was still sleeping.

"Your brothers sound like they're sawing down a forest in there. I couldn't sleep." He eyed her coffee.

"Here." She passed the mug to him. "You look like you need this more than I do."

"Thank you. Have a seat." He moved his legs to make room for her at the foot of the chair. After taking a sip of the coffee, he held the mug out to her. She gave it a dubious look.

"What? I promise I don't have cooties."

No, maybe not. But sharing a cup of coffee felt a little too intimate.

She set the mug on the arm of the chair, and he shrugged, then took another sip.

"So this is where you grew up?"

She nodded, taking in the sweeping view of the backyard that ran right down to the banks of the Serenity River. "From sixth grade on, yes. Before that, my dad helped run a Bible camp nearby, so we lived in a cabin at the camp."

"That explains a lot."

"What does that mean?"

Levi took a slow drink of coffee, obviously enjoying making her wait for an explanation.

"Levi."

He laughed, holding up a protective hand. "Nothing. Just that you're a hard worker, not afraid to get dirty or break a nail. Not a girly girl."

"Oh." Was that supposed to be a compliment or an insult?

"That's a good thing, by the way." Levi's smile was too warm—or rather, it made her too warm.

"So what are we doing today?" He was apparently oblivious to the effect of his smile on her—as he should be.

"I'm not sure what Mama has planned."

Levi's smile transformed to a grimace. "Whatever it is, I'm sure it doesn't involve me. She was pretty clear that she didn't plan to give us much time together."

"She's just a little wound up about the wedding. Mama's the kind of person who wants everything to be perfect."

"Hmm. I wonder if I know anyone else like that," Levi teased.

She swatted at him, making him slosh coffee onto his arm.

"Hey." Levi wiped at the coffee with his other hand. "Here's a thought—you could try doing what you want to do today, instead of letting your mom tell you what to do."

"And what do I want to do today?"

"You'll think of something."

They both turned at the sound of someone stepping onto the patio.

"Speak of the—" Levi muttered, but Grace shot him a quelling look.

"What?" His expression was all innocence. "I was going to say 'mother.'"

Right.

"Good morning, Mama."

Mama's eyes traveled from her to Levi. "Did y'all sleep out here all night?" It was subtle, but Grace heard the suspicion—the unspoken accusation—in the question.

If Levi noticed, he didn't give any indication. "No, ma'am. Just stepped out this morning to watch the glorious sunrise. This is a beautiful view you have." He gave her mother an angelic smile that somehow didn't look the least forced or fake.

Grace could have hugged him. He was trying so hard to get Mama to like him. Daddy and the boys had been a shoo-in—they'd even asked him to golf with them tomorrow. But like she'd warned Levi, Mama would be a tougher nut. Maybe impossible.

Not that it mattered too much what Mama thought about Levi—as long as she was convinced enough that they were dating that she didn't try to meddle and set Grace up with Aaron.

Ignoring Levi, Mama turned to Grace. "I need to go over to the church this morning to finalize some things with Pastor Cooper. I thought you could come with me. Might be nice to catch up."

Grace stared at Mama. Why would she want to catch up with Daddy's old associate? And then it hit her—Pastor Cooper was Aaron's name now too.

Her mouth opened. Here she was, with her *boyfriend*, as far as Mama knew, and still Mama wanted to set her up with Aaron. Mama would never be satisfied with anyone Grace chose for herself. Grace had shown her lack of judgment once, and Mama was forever going to hold it over her head.

She turned to Levi, who watched her, a question in his eyes. Was she going to do what Mama told her to? Or was she going to make her own decision?

Her gaze snapped back to Mama. "Actually, Mama, I promised Levi I'd take him on a tour of River Falls today. Since I'll be doing bridesmaid stuff all day tomorrow and Saturday."

Mama waved off her protest. "That won't take long. Y'all can do it later."

"Sorry, Mama." Grace called on all her gumption. "We wanted to get an early start. Tell Pastor Cooper I say hi, though."

Mama's eyes grew three times bigger, and her mouth opened, but she spun and disappeared into the house without a word.

Grace blew out a long breath.

"So," Levi piped from beside her. "I guess we're touring River Falls today?" There was a chuckle in his voice but also maybe a bit of admiration.

Grace nodded, but inside a new worry was working its way up. Now she had to spend the entire day with Levi.

And she was looking forward to it way more than she should.

Chapter 30

"Pull over here."

Levi obeyed Grace's directions, pulling into a scenic overlook on the hilly road they'd been navigating in the Gremlin Benjamin had lent them for the day. He turned off the car, and Grace opened her door, bouncing out. She seemed to be full of a strange sort of energy today that had propelled them through downtown River Falls, to the banks of the river, and now up onto a high mountain overview.

And he wouldn't change it for the world. This time alone with her—time when they weren't working but simply being—was turning out to be pretty incredible.

Grace walked to the edge of the overlook, which sloped gently down the tree-covered mountainside to a valley below, where he could make out a few of the buildings Grace had taken him to earlier.

Grace pointed to an arc in the river that threaded between the buildings. "See how the town's right in the middle of that heart-shaped curve in the river?"

Levi squinted. "Looks more like a kidney bean to me."

Grace smacked his arm, and Levi grinned. He would never admit it to her, but he'd been saying things to provoke her all morning, just so she'd do that. He couldn't get enough of that contact with her. But even though they'd practiced holding hands so diligently on the plane,

Grace hadn't once taken his hand since the moment her mom had come out of the house to greet them yesterday.

Levi's stomach rumbled, and he glanced at the time. Two o'clock. No wonder he was starved. "As usual, you worked me right through lunch. Want to grab a bite?"

"Pie." Grace's eyes gleamed. "I'm craving some pie from Daisy's."

"Pie for lunch?" Levi bumped his shoulder against hers. "I had no idea you were so rebellious."

They stuffed themselves into the Gremlin, and Grace directed him back into town. He tried to imagine her growing up here, riding through these streets on her bicycle, meeting up with friends, maybe a boyfriend.

No. That he didn't want to imagine.

Anyway, it was difficult to picture Grace living anywhere aside from Hope Springs. She was so woven into the fabric of that community.

As they walked into the pie shop, he let himself wonder, not for the first time in the last few weeks, what it would be like if he did that too—wove himself into the community of Hope Springs. He wasn't sure yet that he was ready to take such a drastic step. But each time he thought about it, it became just a little more appealing. Maybe because each time he thought about it, his thoughts lingered just a little longer on Grace.

"Levi?"

"What? Sorry." Levi shook himself out of his nonsensical thoughts, focusing on the woman behind the counter, who was apparently waiting to get his pie order.

"I'll go with . . ." He scanned the rows and rows of pies in the display case. "A slice of cherry and a slice of apple."

Grace raised her eyebrows.

"What? If you want me to have pie for lunch, I need one for my meal and one for dessert."

Grace unzipped her purse and pulled out a credit card, but he already had his ready. "I got this."

But she shook her head and plucked his card out of his fingers, passing the cashier hers instead.

"Grace—"

Her look stopped him. "You flew all this way for me. The least I can do is buy you a piece of pie."

"Two pieces," he corrected.

"Okay, then." Her laughing eyes met his. "Two pieces."

They carried their pie to a small table near a window that overlooked the river outside.

Levi took a bite, closing his eyes as the pastry flaked on his tongue and the tart cherries popped against his taste buds.

"Good, right?"

When he opened his eyes, Grace's smile bumped right up against his heart.

"You have to taste it." He loaded his fork with a generous bite and lifted it toward her mouth.

She considered it, and for a second he was sure she was going to refuse it as she had the coffee earlier. But then she leaned forward and opened her mouth, and he gently steered the fork into it.

Her eyes closed too as she chewed. "I wonder if I can get Daisy to deliver these to Hope Springs. My guests would never want to leave then."

They dug into their pie slices in earnest, Levi easily outpacing her, finishing both his pieces before she'd gotten halfway through her one slice of French silk pie. Finally, she scooped the last bite onto her fork, then held it out to him.

His eyes met hers, and again he was drawn in by their mocha color, nearly an exact match to the chocolate of her pie.

"I couldn't. That's your last bite."

She bounced the pie lightly. "I had some of yours. It's only fair."

She moved her fork closer, almost sending the pie toppling off. Levi reached to steady her hand, wrapping his own around hers and bringing the fork to his mouth.

This time he didn't close his eyes, instead keeping them focused on her. She swallowed and ducked her head as she slid her hand out of his.

"Like it?" Her words sounded forced.

"I do."

She looked up, her eyes widening and her face growing pale.

"Sorry. I didn't mean to make you—"

But she was staring beyond him, toward the door. Levi swiveled in his seat to get a better view.

A guy in full motorcycle gear strode toward the register, pulling off a pair of aviators. He didn't glance in their direction.

Levi turned to Grace. But if anything, she'd gone even paler.

"What's wrong?"

"We have to go," she whispered, as if they were fugitives and the guy was FBI.

"Why? Who is that?"

Grace shook her head. "A mistake."

Levi peered at the counter again. The guy was talking with the cashier as she rang up his order. Didn't exactly seem like a threat.

"Okay." Levi pushed his chair back. "Let's go."

Grace stood too, just as the guy took his pie and started in their direction.

"Oh no." Grace's whisper was so quiet Levi wasn't sure that was what she'd said.

But he turned toward her, reached out his arms, and pulled her in close for a hug, tucking her face against his chest. She squirmed for a second but then reached her arms around his back. Levi let his head drop to rest on top of hers, that sweet smelling perfume doing crazy things to his imagination as he wondered what it would be like to hug her for real.

He waited for the guy to pass and take a seat at the far end of the shop.

"Okay." He spoke low and into Grace's hair. "Coast is clear. Stay in front of me."

He reluctantly let her go, steering her in front of him so that his larger form would shield her from the other guy's view, should he look over.

When they were safely outside, he pointed to the river. "Want to go for a walk? Or do you want to go back to your parents'?"

Grace looked over her shoulder at the pie shop, then toward the water.

"Walk," she finally said.

"You got it."

They'd been walking for ten minutes before Grace felt like she could breathe normally again. As far as she knew, Hunter had moved to Nashville after high school. She had been totally unprepared to see him today. But she'd acted a little bit like a lunatic, and she should probably apologize to Levi for that.

"You probably think I'm crazy."

He laughed. "Well, yes. But I've known that for a long time now."

"Funny." But his teasing took a weight off her. "Sorry I acted so weird back there. I really didn't want to run into Hunter."

"Yeah. I gathered that." Something squeezed her fingers, and she looked down. How long had they been holding hands? And why did it feel so natural?

They lapsed into silence again, though Grace threw furtive glances at Levi every few seconds.

Finally, he stopped and turned toward her. "Why do you keep looking at me like that?"

"Like what?" She looked away. "I'm not looking at you."

"Yes you are. You're wondering what I think of you. If you should explain what happened between you and Hunter or not. So I'll answer you." He tugged her back into a walk. "You don't have to tell me if you don't want to. The past is in the past. Sometimes it's best to keep it there."

Grace sighed. She didn't have to tell him. But for some reason, she wanted to.

"You remember I told you about not trusting my parents' judgment about a guy I was seeing?"

Levi nodded.

"Hunter was that guy." She pulled her hand out of his and wrapped her arms around herself. "He had been pressuring me for a long time to show him that I really loved him. So one night, he took me to this secluded little pond. I didn't realize my parents had followed us—I think one of my brothers tipped them off—and let's just say they caught us . . ." Heat and shame rushed to her cheeks, but she made herself finish the thought. "In a compromising position."

"Oh." Levi's expression didn't change.

"I promised them I'd never see him again. And I haven't."

"I don't think they meant you literally have to hide if he comes into a room."

"I know." Grace covered her face with her hands. "I don't know what came over me back there."

Though it hadn't been so bad having Levi hold her close. "Thanks for your quick thinking."

"At your service." He gave a slight bow, and they resumed walking.

Chapter 31

"*R*eady to go?" Grace's dad, whom Levi couldn't quite bring himself to call Abe, though he'd insisted on it three times already, closed his SUV's hatch.

"Yes, sir." Levi checked to make sure his credit card was in his pocket. A sure way to impress Grace's dad would be to pick up the tab today. "Let me run inside and say goodbye to Grace."

"Didn't you already say goodbye?" Asher called to his back.

Levi tossed a grin over his shoulder. Didn't hurt to throw in an extra goodbye for her family's benefit, just in case any of them doubted he and Grace were really in love.

Inside, Grace sat with her mother at the kitchen table, which had been transformed into a makeshift greenhouse for assembling the centerpieces.

"Those look nice."

Grace glanced up, a surprised smile lifting her lips. "What are you doing in here? Don't tell me they left without you. They did that to Judah once."

Grace's mother stiffened at the name. Grace hadn't gone into much detail about what had happened with her older brother, and Levi got the impression that the family avoided talking about it.

"No, they're waiting for me. I think." He turned to check out the window. The SUV was still there. "I didn't want to leave without saying goodbye."

Grace's eyes widened, but Levi's gaze shifted to Mrs. Calvano. She barely seemed to notice he was there. So much for impressing her with his attentiveness to her daughter.

He crossed the room and pressed a kiss onto the top of Grace's head, her sweet scent making him want to linger.

She froze, the flowers she'd been cutting floating in mid-air. He was probably going to hear about this later—he knew she'd said no kisses—but desperate times called for desperate measures.

"Those look a lot like the flowers I gave you for our first date. Remember?" He straightened, and Grace offered him a half-amused look.

"I remember." He could tell it was on the tip of her tongue to say *since it was only last week*, but she resisted. She turned to her mother. "They were beautiful, Mama. Purple tulips. You should have seen them."

"That's nice." Mrs. Calvano didn't look up from her arranging. "You'd best get going before you make the boys miss their tee time."

Well, he'd tried.

"See you later." It'd probably be pushing it to kiss Grace again, so he squeezed her shoulder.

Then he jogged out to the car and squished into the backseat with Asher and Joseph. Zeb sat in the front, and Benjamin had insisted on driving Simeon in his Gremlin.

The brothers spent most of the car ride ribbing each other in that way that showed how close they really were. A small pang went through Levi, as he wondered if he and Luke would have been closer if life had been different. If he hadn't been so busy with college and then the NFL. If Luke hadn't gotten sick.

By the time they got to the golf course, Levi's cheeks hurt from laughing so much. They piled out of the vehicle and grabbed their clubs, joining Simeon and Benjamin at the clubhouse.

A sweet scent caught Levi's attention as he was about to enter the building. He stopped abruptly.

Grace?

But there was no one around aside from her brothers. And he knew from spending the past half hour in the car with them that the sweet smell definitely wasn't them.

Next to him, a vine wound up a trellis, pink and orange flowers covering its green stem. He stepped closer to it, inhaling deeply.

This was it. This was what Grace smelled like.

"You good, man?" Zeb sounded amused to find Levi stopping to smell the flowers.

"Yeah." He stepped back and went through the door Zeb still held. "What kind of plant is that?"

"Honeysuckle, I think. Why?"

"No reason." He sped up to reach the counter, where Grace's dad was about to pay for the group.

"I've got this, sir." He pulled out his card and reached past Grace's dad to hand it to the concierge.

"That's not necessary." Grace's dad gave him a searching look, and Levi felt oddly exposed.

"Yeah, we all like you already," Joseph quipped.

"I know it's not. But I'd like to. If you don't mind. You've all been so good about welcoming me into the family."

"Thankfully, I'm not too proud to accept a gift." Grace's dad put his card away. "Thank you."

"My pleasure." Levi felt suddenly like he'd passed some sort of test.

As they moved onto the course, he settled into an easy camaraderie with the brothers. Even Grace's dad was personable and easy to get along with, which at first threw Levi for a bit of a loop. But after a while, he was joking about Pastor Calvano's slice along with the others.

At the ninth hole, as they paused for a water break, Zeb pulled Levi aside.

"Look man, I wanted to talk to you a minute." Zeb seemed to be the most serious of the brothers.

"Okay. What about?"

"Grace." Zeb folded his arms across his chest, which may have been broader than Levi's. "I like you. I can see that she likes you. You make her happy."

He did? That was good to hear. He could never tell.

"But your reputation isn't exactly as a one-woman man, if you know what I mean."

"I—"

Zeb raised a hand. "Hey, I believe people can change. I see it all the time. And I hope you really do care for her the way you seem to."

"I do." The words came out effortlessly. It wasn't his feelings for Grace he questioned. It was hers for him.

"Good. Because you may be Levi Donovan, but if you hurt her, you'll have to answer to us."

Levi swallowed. "I won't hurt her." Right? How could he hurt her if she had no real feelings for him?

Zeb slapped his shoulder. "That's good to hear."

Levi nodded, lifting his water bottle for a long swig.

"I look forward to when we can do this for your wedding," Zeb said as he walked to join the others.

Levi gasped with the water bottle still to his mouth, sucking liquid right down into his lungs.

He sputtered and coughed for a full minute before he finally had it under control.

"You okay?" Benjamin gave him a concerned look.

"I'm great." Levi picked up his clubs and followed the others. They didn't really expect him to marry Grace, did they?

When he didn't, would they make things worse for her than they'd been to begin with?

Maybe this whole thing had been a big mistake. Maybe he should have let Grace come back alone to reconnect with this Aaron guy.

The guy was a pastor, for crying out loud. He probably ticked every box on Grace's checklist.

Whereas Levi doubted he checked a single one.

Chapter 32

Levi searched the crowded backyard for the familiar tumble of dark hair.

He'd barely seen Grace since he'd left this morning. By the time they'd gotten back from golfing, she'd already left to prepare for the rehearsal. There hadn't been a moment to talk to her during the rehearsal either, since she was in the wedding party.

As he'd watched her walk down the aisle in her soft blue sundress, Zeb's comment from earlier had come back to him. After Rayna, he'd been sure he'd never consider marriage again. But maybe . . .

Levi shook himself. That was way too far in the future to think about.

Finally, he spotted her at a table for two. Nice. It would be good to have a chance to talk alone. Even if they were surrounded by people. But as he stepped closer, a guy with bleached blond hair and a smile that seemed to touch his ears slid into the seat across from her.

Levi picked up his pace, ready to tell the guy to scram—that was his girl—but Grace offered the stranger a welcoming smile and took the glass of punch he held out to her.

Levi stopped.

An elbow to the gut would have been more pleasant.

He debated. He could go over there and tell the stranger to bug off, remind Grace that she might want to put on a better show of being his girlfriend for her family. Or he could walk away.

"Hey man. Looking for somewhere to sit?" Benjamin came up next to him.

"Who's that guy sitting with Grace?"

Benjamin followed the direction of Levi's head bob. "Pastor Cooper? He's pretty cool. Got a lot of the kids involved in youth group. We're all over by that picnic table. Unless you're going to sit by Grace?"

Levi had never been one to walk away from a challenge. But he knew when to fold. Grace might think she didn't want to be set up with the man her mom wanted her to be with. But she was only fooling herself.

He wouldn't let her fool him too.

"Nah." He followed Benjamin. "I'm not going to sit by Grace."

Where was he?

Grace had been searching the guests gathered in her parents' backyard for half an hour, trying to find Levi.

It wasn't until she heard the shouts from the front yard that she realized her brothers must have gotten a game of football going. That had to be where Levi was.

She followed the sounds around the house but slowed as she spotted the group. Though dark had fallen a good hour ago, the front yard was well-lit, and she spotted Levi instantly. He was huddled with Asher and Benjamin and had an arm over each.

A tickle of joy went through her at the way he fit so easily into her family, followed by a wave of regret. Her brothers would be crushed when she and Levi "broke up."

Unless they didn't. Break up.

The thought had taken hold of her earlier today, when Levi had kissed her head again. The gesture had been so sweet and spontaneous, and she'd found herself wondering what it would be like if he did that all the time. For real.

Grace shook herself as she plopped onto the grass to watch the football game.

This was only pretend. Levi was only putting on an act for her family. Come Sunday evening, she'd have to return to reality. Better not to wander too far from it now.

Especially since, even on the off chance that Levi would be interested in making this real, it didn't change the fact that he wasn't the right man for her.

When the game finally broke up, Grace pushed to her feet. "Y'all looked like you were having fun out there."

"Yeah, your boyfriend's not too bad at football," Simeon joked.

"You guys gave me a run for my money." Levi exchanged fist bumps with them as they dissipated.

"Thanks for playing with them." Grace stepped to Levi's side.

He tossed the football from hand to hand. "They're fun guys."

"I'm sorry we haven't had a chance to see each other much today. Mama had the bridal party running all over the place."

Levi shrugged. "It was fine."

Grace set a hand on his arm, and he stopped tossing the ball. "Is something wrong?"

"Nope."

"How was golfing?"

"Good."

She crossed her arms. "If nothing's wrong, why are you being like this?"

"Being like what?"

Grace huffed. This man was maddening sometimes. "So short with me."

"Sorry. I figured you were tired of talking after your long conversation with Pastor Cooper."

"Pastor Cooper?" Was that what this was about? "We only talked for a few minutes. He had a youth group thing to get to."

"Well, maybe *y'all*"—his lips sneered around the word—"can sneak in a quick date tomorrow after the wedding."

"A date?" Wasn't that what Levi was here to prevent? "I don't want to go on a date with Aaron."

"Could have fooled me. You two looked pretty happy together. Just wish you hadn't dragged me all the way here to keep your mom off your back about him only to turn around and throw yourself at him."

Grace drew back her shoulders. "Throw myself at him?"

"Don't worry. I'm sure your mom will be happy. Just tell her we broke up. Say I realized I'd never live up to who you want me to be." Levi tossed the football over his shoulder and marched toward the house.

Chapter 33

*G*race flipped onto her back. Then to her side. Then to her back again.

If she didn't get some sleep, she was going to look like a wreck for Simeon's wedding tomorrow.

But how could she sleep, after the way Levi had treated her before?

The man had dated more women than she could count. And he had the nerve to call her out for talking to a man her mother happened to want to set her up with?

She wasn't going to deny that catching up with Aaron had been nice. But that was all it had been.

She'd found herself sitting there, thinking about Levi, even telling Aaron about him.

He'd said he was happy for her, hadn't said a word about missing her or wanting to marry her.

So either Mama's reports of his interest in her had been wildly exaggerated or Aaron respected the fact that she was with someone else.

Someone who had retreated to the boys' bedroom right after their fight.

Grace turned to her side again. What she couldn't figure out was why Levi cared so much.

They were doing this whole ruse for her benefit, not his. So what did it matter to him if she talked to another man? He'd acted as if he were . . . jealous.

Grace's eyes popped open, and she rolled to stare at the ceiling.

But he couldn't have been. Right?

She thought of those moments when his acting had been so good he'd almost convinced her his feelings were real. Like when he'd kissed her head. Or held her hand. Or sent her that smile that said . . . all kinds of things she hadn't let herself think it said. She'd told herself he was just a good actor, but what if . . .

Grace sat upright.

There was no way she was going to be able to sleep now.

She tiptoed out of the room so she wouldn't wake Abigail, then crept through the hallway, pausing for a moment to listen to the honking snores coming from the boys' room. No wonder Levi hadn't been able to sleep the other night.

She opened the French doors as quietly as possible and slipped outside.

The night had grown damp, with a slight chill, but it was alive with the calls of bullfrogs and katydids.

She padded to the chaise lounge she and Levi had shared the other morning.

A soft scream escaped her at the sight of a body on it.

The eyes flew open.

"Levi." She pressed a hand to her galloping heart. "What are you doing out here?"

"Couldn't sleep." He blinked at her. "Why aren't you in bed?"

"Couldn't sleep either." She rocked from foot to foot on the cool flagstones as they looked at each other.

Levi moved his feet and gestured to the end of the chair just as he had the other morning. Hesitantly, she sat.

"Stars are beautiful tonight." Levi's voice was low, suited for the dark and the late hour.

She tilted her head back to study the sky.

"That's Venus over there," Levi said.

She followed his arm toward a bright dot straight above them. "I didn't know you liked astronomy."

"I told you. Not just a dumb jock."

"I know." She dropped her chin to look at him. "About before. I'm sorry. I wasn't trying to make you uncomfortable by talking to Aaron. You were right, I did drag you all the way down here, and I should have been more considerate instead of leaving you to fend for yourself with my family."

"About that." Levi gave her a sheepish grin. "I think I may have overreacted a little. You can talk to whoever you want. And for the record, you didn't drag me here. I volunteered."

"You did, didn't you?" Grace almost asked him why, but she wasn't sure whether he'd say it was because he wanted to spend time with her or because he needed a diversion. And she wasn't sure which she wanted it to be.

Levi tipped his head back toward the stars, and Grace followed suit. They sat like that, silent but peaceful, until the chill air started to seep through Grace's skin.

She rubbed her hands on her arms. She wasn't ready to go inside yet.

"Here." Levi slid to the side of the chair and patted the spot next to him.

Grace contemplated it. There was definitely enough room for her. But was it a good idea?

Levi waited, not pressuring her.

Another shiver went through her, and she pictured her cozy bed inside. But for some reason it didn't hold as much appeal as sitting out here with Levi.

She scooted up the seat until she was planted next to him, but his shoulders were too broad for her to sit back.

"One second." Levi repositioned himself, and she felt his arm across her shoulders. "There, now sit back."

She did, tentatively, and he adjusted his position so that his hand rested lightly on her upper arm.

"There. That's better."

She nodded, his clean sandalwood scent sneaking past her defenses.

"You smell good," Levi murmured. "Like honeysuckle."

Grace twisted her neck to look over at him. "Not many guys could pick out the smell of honeysuckle."

"It's been driving me crazy for weeks, trying to place the smell. Then I walked past these flowers at the golf course, and Zeb said they were honeysuckle."

Grace giggled at the image. "You asked my brother about flowers? You could have asked me what the smell was if you wanted to know."

Did he say he'd been thinking about her scent for weeks?

She sat back, nestling into his arm, and closed her eyes, letting the sounds of the night wash over her. The crickets had quieted now, but the bullfrogs still thumped out their rhythm, and in the distance an owl hooted. Next to her, the steady in and out of Levi's breath lulled her.

"Can I ask you something?" Levi asked after a while.

"Mmm hmm." She was feeling pleasantly warm and sleepy in his arms, but she opened her eyes.

"Dan's sermon the other day. Do you really believe that?"

Grace held her breath. She'd been praying for an opportunity like this. "Which part? I mean, I believe all of it, but which part are you wondering about?"

"About there only being one purpose." Levi said the words slowly, as if he were putting a lot of thought into them. "About holding onto

God's Word and there only being one truth. About our role on earth being to glorify God." He chuckled low in his throat. "So basically, all of it."

"I do." Grace angled her head so that she was facing him, her ear pressed to his upper arm.

"So why do you bother with the bed-and-breakfast then? Or with anything that isn't reading God's Word or preaching about him? If that's supposedly our purpose."

"Those things are our purpose, yes." Grace searched for a way to explain it. "But that doesn't mean we can't carry them out in lots of ways, including running a bed-and-breakfast. Or playing football. It's more that as we do those things, we keep God first in our hearts. And we give him glory for everything he's given us, including our talents and skills."

"Hmm." Levi reached to tuck a strand of hair behind her ear, as if he'd done it a thousand times before. "You make it sound so easy."

"Easy?" Grace laughed. "It's definitely not easy. At least not all the time. But I find that the more time I spend in prayer and in God's Word, the more I want to spend time with him. It's like when you meet someone new and you want to know more and more about them."

Levi was watching her with a strange smile.

"What?"

He shook his head. "Nothing. I like how you describe that. I guess I always saw church as something I had to do because my parents made me and the Bible as just a bunch of rules. I haven't spent a lot of time reading the Bible or praying on my own."

"It's never too late to start. God's Word is . . ." She searched for an adequate description. "It's the greatest love story ever told." She bit her lip. "I suppose that sounds corny, but it's true. It's the story of a love so great God would do anything to make us his own. Even give up his Son. Reading it fills me. And it makes me want to live my life in a way that will please him. Not to follow the rules, but to show my love for him. Not that I always succeed."

Levi scoffed. "If I've ever met anyone who was in line for angel-of-the-year, it'd be you."

Grace shook her head. "First of all, people can't be angels. And second of all, you of all people should know I struggle with this."

"Why me of all people?"

"Because I had a hard time being civil to you when we first met. You managed to rile me up all the time so I couldn't control my tongue."

"Only when we first met?" Levi teased.

"Yes." She smacked his chest. "I'm much nicer now."

"Why is that?" His eyes met hers and held on.

Her mouth went completely dry. What was she supposed to say to that?

"I'm not sure," she mumbled.

Levi's eyes traveled to the dark yard.

"But I do know," she rushed to fill in, "that God loves you, Levi." She broke off. It felt suddenly like an intensely personal thing to say to someone.

"Yeah." Levi didn't sound certain, but he didn't sound hostile either. "Thanks."

She nodded, turning to face forward again.

Peace washed over her as she thanked God for giving her the opportunity to talk to Levi about him. She had no way of knowing if it had made an impact. But she trusted that the Holy Spirit could take this little seed she'd planted and grow it into something strong and beautiful.

Next to her, Levi's breaths deepened, and she let her head droop to his shoulder. Just a little longer . . . she'd let herself stay in his arms just a little longer, then go inside.

Chapter 34

*W*ow.

Levi had no words as he watched Grace glide down the aisle of the church.

He hadn't seen her since he'd woken on the chaise lounge at three in the morning to find her asleep on his shoulder. He'd sneaked a kiss to her forehead, then gently woken her so they could tiptoe back to their bedrooms for a few more hours of sleep.

When he'd woken, she'd already been whisked off to the salon with the rest of the wedding party.

As she reached the pew he sat in now, she slipped him a soft smile. A twinge in his chest told him what he already suspected—he had it bad for this woman.

And he had no idea what to do about it.

Usually, when he saw a woman he was interested in, he simply asked if she'd like to go out and she said yes and that was the end of the story.

But Grace had already rejected him once. And he had next to no confidence that if he asked her out again she wouldn't do the same, their talk last night notwithstanding.

That talk had been—it had probably been the deepest conversation he'd ever had with anyone in his life. Usually, he found talk of faith off-putting, but Grace's sincerity and passion for God had struck against something in him that he had been sure was hard and dried up.

She'd said learning about God was like getting to know someone new. Like wanting to know everything about that person.

There was no denying that was how he'd been feeling about her lately. So if he picked up a Bible and started reading it, would he feel that way about God too?

He wasn't sure if he was ready to find out.

He directed his focus to the front of the church, where Simeon and Abigail faced each other, tears streaming down their cheeks.

According to Grace, Simeon had been a confirmed bachelor with no intention of ever marrying before he'd met Abigail. And then he'd fallen hard and fast, proposing within three months.

Levi thought again of the ring he'd bought for Rayna. They'd been together for three years before he'd felt ready for that step. And even that hadn't been long enough to know who Rayna really was. What she really cared about.

I look forward to when we can do this for your wedding, Zeb had said yesterday.

But could Levi ever imagine himself standing up there, pledging his life to one woman?

His eyes went to Grace, who had tears on her cheeks as she watched her brother and his bride.

Maybe, if—

Nah. Levi Donovan was not the marrying type, and he knew it. Didn't he?

Grace dropped onto a soft chair in the ballroom lobby and eased her feet out of her shoes with a groan. She wasn't sure her toes would ever be the same again.

"Better?"

She jumped but smiled involuntarily at the sound of Levi's voice behind her. She hadn't had a chance to talk to him all day, and she had missed him.

"Much. I'm not sure how I survived this long."

"Well, you look beautiful. I may have to rethink my assessment that you're not a girly girl."

"Thank you." Oddly, his compliment didn't embarrass her, though it did send a flare of warmth through her. "You look pretty spiffy yourself." The tailored suit fit his broad shoulders just right.

"You up for a dance, or are you too tired?" Levi studied his hands, looking sweetly uncertain.

"That depends. Are you asking me to dance?" Somehow, his uncertainty made her bolder.

He looked up with a grin. "As a matter of fact, I am." He held out a hand. "Grace Calvano, may I have this dance?"

She set her hand lightly in his, ignoring the trickle of joy in her fingers. "As long as you don't make me put my shoes on." She nudged them under the chair. She'd come back for them later.

Or not.

Levi led her to the dance floor and wrapped his other arm around her waist, letting his hand come to a rest on the small of her back.

She had never been a terribly skillful dancer, but he made her feel graceful as he led her naturally around the dance floor.

"You're a good dancer." She didn't mean to sound surprised. "Did you have to learn for football?" She'd heard of that—football players doing dance to improve their balance and flexibility.

Levi chuckled, pulling her closer. "Not this kind of dance, thankfully. My teammates didn't smell nearly as nice as you."

He tightened his arm, cinching her closer still, and she tentatively turned her head to rest it on his chest. The steady rhythm of his heart beat in her ear, and she closed her eyes, letting the rest of the room fade away.

They swayed silently until he leaned his lips close to her ear. "I didn't get a chance to thank you."

"For what?" She pulled back in surprise, needing to see his eyes.

"For last night. For talking to me. I had— It was . . ."

"I know," she whispered.

His throat bobbed, and with his eyes still locked on hers, he lifted one hand to her cheek.

He was going to kiss her. She could feel it.

And she wanted him to. She raised onto her toes.

Their lips touched for only the sweetest, briefest moment before Levi pulled back.

"Sorry," he whispered. "I just realized your whole family is watching."

"Oh." Grace swiveled to look around the room. Sure enough, three of her brothers, not to mention one very unhappy looking Mama, were staring in their direction.

Before she could tell Levi she didn't care who was watching, the lights in the room came up.

"It's time for the bouquet toss," a man's voice announced.

Grace scurried off the dance floor, followed by Levi.

"Aren't you going to try to catch it?" a woman she'd never met asked.

Grace shook her head.

No, she didn't think catching a bouquet would do anything to help bring her back to reality.

And reality was where she needed to be.

Chapter 35

A smile tickled Grace's lips as she woke. She'd been having a dream—a pleasant one, though she couldn't remember what it'd been about. Only the feeling it'd left her with.

It was the same feeling she'd had last night when Levi had kissed her.

She'd hoped for a chance to try that again, without an audience, but they hadn't had a moment alone together.

She slid out of bed and opened the door, the scent of coffee and waffles delighting her nose. Those smells meant Mama was up—and that Grace probably wouldn't get a second alone with Levi now either. But that was okay. They flew out this afternoon, and then they could have all the time they wanted together in Hope Springs. Assuming Levi felt this was as real as she did. And assuming she had the courage to ask him.

She paused in the doorway to the kitchen, watching Mama mixing up batter. There were times the woman drove her batty. But then there were other times, like this, when Grace realized how fortunate she was to have parents who cared about her so much.

Especially when she considered that they'd almost lost Mama to breast cancer only a few months after the whole Hunter incident. The thought that Mama could have died with that as her last memory of Grace was still enough to send Grace to her knees to thank the Lord for sparing Mama's life.

"There's my early bird." Mama looked up with a tired smile. "The day you were born at the crack of dawn, I knew you would be one."

"Morning, Mama." Grace padded across the kitchen to drop a kiss on her mother's cheek. "Why didn't you sleep in? I'm sure no one else will be up for a while yet." She glanced out the French doors, past the chaise lounge, to the spot where the river had just started to soak up the golden hues of the new day's sun.

"And when they do get up, everyone's going to need breakfast before church." Mama ladled batter onto the waffle iron.

"Please tell me you're at least going to take things easy after this. You'll burn yourself out."

Mama waved off her concern. "I'm planning the women's retreat for next month. So unless you're going to stay here and help me with that . . ." Mama gave her a pointed look, drawing a sigh out of Grace. Not this again.

She moved to pour herself a cup of coffee. "Mama, you know I can't. I have the bed-and-breakfast."

"And Levi?" Mama's gaze hit her full-on. "Don't think I didn't hear the two of you sneaking inside at an unholy hour the other night."

Grace nearly spit out the sip of coffee that burned her tongue. "We fell asleep talking."

But there was no point in explaining. Grace could read in Mama's eyes exactly what she was thinking. Because that was the same way Mama had looked at her the night she'd caught Grace and Hunter at the pond.

A flood of shame—fresh as the day it had happened—rolled over her, and she set her mug down with a shaking hand.

She and Levi had done nothing wrong.

"Grace, let's be real." The tiredness on Mama's face seemed to have doubled. "Levi Donovan is not the kind of man you're going to marry."

Grace swallowed, ignoring the papery feel of her burnt tongue. "Marry? Who said anything about marrying?"

Mama pried the waffle maker open. "That's the whole point of dating, isn't it? If you aren't thinking about marriage, then I don't know why you're with him."

"Well—" Grace stammered. "We haven't been dating that long. It's too early to think about that." And then there was the fact that they weren't *actually* dating.

"Honey." Somehow, Mama managed to hit her with a pitying look and ladle batter at the same time. "It doesn't matter how long you wait. A man like Levi Donovan isn't ever going to make a good husband. You probably don't realize this because you're so sweet and naive, but I looked him up, and he dates *a lot* of women. Plus, he said he doesn't believe in God."

Indignation filled Grace. Mama thought she was too naive to judge a man for herself? "As a matter of fact, I did know that."

Mama pressed a hand to her chest. "Then why in heaven's name are you with him? I know he's good-looking, but I had hoped you'd learned your lesson about letting your head be turned by lust like with Hunter."

A high-pitched buzz filled Grace's ears, and the smell of the grass that night at the pond, the dampness of the dew under her back swept over her. Mama's face was pinched again, same as it had been that night, her eyes a pool of disappointment and regret.

Was this what the rest of her life was going to be like? Living under the cloud of the mistake she'd made as a teenager? Constantly worried about disappointing Mama and Daddy again?

Or was she going to be brave enough to stand up to them? To tell them she could make her own decisions? That she'd learned from her mistakes?

"This is nothing like Hunter. And it has nothing to do with lust. Levi—"

"Please." Mama shook her head. "I saw the way his hands were all over you last night."

"We were dancing, Mama."

"Grace, this man is experienced. Do I have to spell it out? He's going to expect—"

"Mama, stop." Grace slapped the countertop with her palm. "Levi isn't like people think. He's kind and generous and loving." The words were out of her mouth before she realized they were true. She had told herself a thousand times that Levi wasn't the right kind of guy for her. And he may be a football player and a star and ride a motorcycle, but that didn't change who he was inside—a fundamentally decent and loving guy. She'd seen it in the way he treated his family, treated his brother especially. And the way he treated her.

"And his faith?" Mama shook her spatula at Grace. "You know it would break my heart and Daddy's to see you with an unbeliever."

Grace blew out a long breath. She couldn't argue with Mama on this one, as much as she wanted to.

"We talk about it," she said finally. "And I can see God working in his heart."

"That may be, but it's easy for a man to pretend to be what you want him to be. Until you're in too deep."

"Levi's not pretending." Grace bit her lip as soon as she'd said it. Technically, that wasn't true. Technically, this whole relationship was pretend.

Mama scrutinized her. "I know men like him, Grace. He'll say whatever it takes to get what he wants from you. And then he'll leave. He's done it to plenty of women before you, and I know you want to believe this time is different. But I can tell by the way he looks at you, honey. He's not in this for the long haul."

A jagged lump formed in Grace's throat. Mama was right. Levi had no reason to be in it for the long haul. He was in it for the weekend, like they'd agreed. She'd just let herself get swept away by the fantasy they'd created.

Mama set her spatula down and hugged Grace. "I'm only trying to watch out for my baby girl. I don't want you to get hurt." She brushed Grace's hair off her shoulder.

"I know, Mama." Grace swallowed down that lump. She had wanted to come back to reality, and here she was.

"It sure smells good in here."

Even without looking at him, she could hear the smile in Levi's voice.

As his footsteps approached, she scurried to hide in the fridge, pretending to rummage. "Mama made waffles."

"You'll spoil us, Mrs. Calvano. Need help finding something, Grace?"

"Nope. Here it is." She grabbed the first thing her hand landed on.

"Mustard?" Levi raised an eyebrow.

"Oops." Back into the fridge.

This time she came up with the orange juice, which had clearly been at the front of the shelf the whole time.

"You seem pretty exhausted." Levi was watching her, she could feel it. "We'd better get you to bed as soon as we get home."

Grace choked.

Levi's comment had been completely innocent, and yet heat flooded her cheeks at Mama's pointed look.

"We're all on our way to church, Levi," Mama said. "Feel free to watch some TV while we're gone."

"That's okay." Levi took the orange juice from Grace, then moved as if to put his arms around her.

She sidestepped him and opened the drawer to pull out forks and knives.

"I was planning to come along," Levi added. "If that's all right."

"Of course. Everyone's welcome at church." Mama's voice was sweet as the syrup she was setting on the table, but under it, Grace could hear her warning from earlier: *It's easy for a man to pretend to be what you want him to be.*

Chapter 36

$\mathcal{H}$ e shouldn't have kissed her last night.

That had to be why she was acting so strange and distant today.

He should have waited until he'd had a chance to tell her the truth about his feelings, waited until she'd had a chance to tell him whether she felt the same way. Instead, he'd been selfish and impatient, his only thought that if he didn't kiss her right then and there, he would regret it forever.

Now, though, it seemed like the only thing worse than regretting something he hadn't done might be regretting something he had.

She'd sat next to him in church, rigid as the pews. And now that they were back at her parents', she was doing everything humanly possible to avoid being in the same room with him. He knew for a fact that she hadn't brought nearly enough luggage to warrant the half hour she'd been in her room, packing her bag.

If she didn't come out soon, they were going to miss their flight.

"Come on, Grace," Benjamin, who had volunteered to drive them to the airport, called down the hallway.

Finally, Grace emerged, pulling her carry-on behind her. She made a round of the living room, hugging each of her brothers and her father. Levi followed in her wake, shaking their hands.

"I hope we'll be seeing more of you." Grace's father clapped his other hand to Levi's shoulder.

Levi nodded. He did too.

When Grace reached her mother, the two women shared a long embrace.

"Promise me you'll think about what I said." Mrs. Calvano's voice was so quiet that Levi assumed whatever she was talking about was meant for Grace only. He tried not to hear.

Grace nodded, and then Levi was standing face-to-face with her mother.

He debated for a second: hug or handshake?

This was his last chance to make an impression on her. He stepped forward and wrapped his big arms around her small frame. "Thanks for everything."

A noise of surprise escaped her, but she lifted a hand to his back for half a second before pulling away.

They followed Benjamin out to the car, where Grace again insisted that Levi ride shotgun.

Benjamin kept up a steady conversation with Levi all the way to the airport, but the moment he drove away, silence fell.

"This was a nice weekend," Levi said as they stood in the security line.

She nodded.

"Your family is pretty cool," he tried as they sat in the terminal.

She nodded again.

"I think even your mom came around in the end." He gave it one more shot as they boarded. "It was probably the hug."

She pressed her lips together.

"Are we going to talk about it?" he asked as they settled into their seats.

"Talk about what?" She didn't look at him.

He angled his body to block out the other passengers filing into their seats. This wasn't the ideal place to do this.

"I kissed you last night, and I'm sorry."

She didn't say anything, so he pressed on. "I shouldn't have. I didn't mean to make things weird."

She slipped her hands under her legs. "It's fine."

"Obviously it's not. You can't even look at me."

"Can we not talk about it?" She tipped her head back against the seat, eyes closed. "I'm going to take a nap."

"Yeah." Levi gave up. "That's fine. We don't have to talk about it."

Where was she?

Strange sounds bombarded Grace's ears, and she struggled to open her eyes. The moment she did, she sat up straight. She must have fallen asleep—with her head on Levi's shoulder.

"Hey you." His smile was warm but tentative, and she prayed he wasn't going to bring up that kiss again. He'd already said it was a mistake. That was all she needed to know.

"I was just going to wake you." Levi pointed to the window on the other side of her. "We're about to land."

She slid closer to the window, watching a darkened Lake Michigan below them.

A jolt of turbulence sent the plane jostling, and Grace instinctively grabbed for Levi's arm but drew her hand back the moment she made contact.

When the plane landed with a bump, she forced herself to keep her hands in her lap.

Silently, Levi retrieved their luggage from the overhead compartment, then gestured her in front of him.

They were halfway through the airport when a woman in a shirt that plunged straight to her belly button snatched at Levi's arm. "Oh my goodness. You're Levi Donovan. I *have* to get your autograph."

An involuntary noise came from the back of Grace's throat, and she shuffled to the side.

Mom had been right. Levi was not the kind of man interested in a long-term relationship.

And Grace had been stupid to think otherwise.

But before she'd gotten two steps, a strong hand wrapped around hers and tugged her back.

"Sorry," Levi said to the woman. "My girlfriend and I are in a hurry."

The woman's face fell, and she sent Grace a wilting glare but moved on.

"We're home now, you know." Grace wriggled her hand out of his. "You don't have to pretend to be my boyfriend anymore."

Levi was watching her, but she refused to look at him.

"It got that woman to go away, right?"

Grace's smile was tight. He'd simply been using her to get what he wanted. Chalk another one up for Mama.

"I can drive if you want," Levi said when they reached her car in the parking garage.

Grace shrugged and passed him the keys. Maybe she could pretend to sleep on the drive too.

In the car, she closed her eyes and leaned her head against the passenger door.

Levi was silent so long that she started to doze for real.

"Actually, no, it's not fine," Levi burst out just as Grace felt herself sinking into sleep.

She bolted upright. "What's not fine?" She scanned the road, the car—everything appeared to be in order.

"Not talking about what happened last night. Our kiss. I'm not fine with that."

Grace turned to stare out the dark window. "It *is* fine. You already said it was a mistake. Apology accepted."

"What if I don't want you to accept my apology?"

"That would be kind of weird. You want me to stay mad?" She tried unsuccessfully to avoid looking at him, instead turning in time to see the way his face fell.

"Are you? Mad at me for it?"

She sighed. "No, not really."

"Good." He reached for her hand, threading his fingers through hers. "Because I wanted to ask if you'd be willing to go out with me sometime. For real."

He sounded so earnest, so sincere, so vulnerable. But Mama's words had been parading through her head all day, and no matter how she felt about Levi, there was one thing Mama had been right about. She could never be with a man whose first love wasn't Jesus.

She extracted her fingers from his. "I don't think that would be a good idea."

"You. Oh—" A muscle in his jaw worked, but he didn't say anything else.

"I think we both got a little swept up this weekend. With the wedding atmosphere and all. That's all it was."

"That's not all it was for me." Levi's voice was quiet.

"Levi—" She tried to be gentle. "You know you're not my type. And I'm definitely not yours."

"You know—" Levi cut a glance at her. "I'm getting a little tired of hearing that. Especially when we're obviously so good together. Everyone there saw it. Why can't you?"

"My mama didn't see it." The words slithered right past her lips before she could lock them in.

Levi's face darkened. "Is that what this is about? Your mama got to you?"

"No." She sounded too defensive. "I just think—"

Levi lifted a hand off the wheel. "Forget it. I understand. Don't worry, I won't bring it up again."

Chapter 37

"You're sure you'll stay home?" Mom's worried eyes peered up to Levi's face, as if searching for some sign that he was going to throw a party the moment she and Dad left. "Maybe we shouldn't go. That's a lot to ask of you."

"Mom, I promise." Levi leaned against the kitchen doorframe. "You two go. Get out of town for a few days. It's your anniversary."

"I know." Mom looked over her shoulder, toward the hallway. "But Luke's been feeling under the weather all week, and if you decide to go out—"

"Mom, I told you, I'm not going anywhere." Where would he go? Who would he go with? The one woman he wanted to spend time with would barely acknowledge him anymore. After spending all week tiptoeing around her at the bed-and-breakfast, barely speaking aside from an overly polite "good morning" or "excuse me," he was more than ready for a night at home. Just him and Luke—the bachelor brothers.

"Come on, Sandra. Luke will be fine. Levi will take care of him." Dad held Mom's purse out to her, giving Levi a look that said he'd better not let them down.

Mom sighed but took the purse. "I'll have my phone if you need me. And all the emergency numbers are on the fridge. I left a lasagna in there that you can heat up."

"Mom, you don't have to feed us. We're big boys. Now go." Levi leaned to give Mom a quick hug, then shoved her gently toward Dad, who steered her toward the door.

"We're counting on you." He didn't add, *So don't mess it up*, but Levi heard it all the same.

After Mom and Dad had finally left, Levi plopped onto the couch. He'd get some dinner going in a little bit, but first he needed to zone out in front of the TV.

Except he couldn't keep his head on the baseball game, not when thoughts of Grace kept invading it.

He had been so sure, after they'd fallen asleep talking under the stars, that they were right for each other. He'd never been able to talk to anyone else so easily and openly before. Had never felt so listened to—so *seen* and understood.

Grace had felt it too, he was sure of it. Otherwise, she wouldn't have snuggled close to him on the chair, wouldn't have fallen asleep tucked into his arm. Wouldn't have returned his kiss at the wedding.

But all it had taken was one word of disapproval from her mother—he was all but sure that was what had happened—and Grace was willing to forget about all of that.

She was willing to take the door of his heart that he'd started to open to her and slam it shut.

He'd been trying all week to convince himself that if that was how she was going to be—steered by her family's wishes instead of her own heart—then he didn't need her.

But that was a lie.

She had somehow coaxed out the best in him—parts of him he hadn't even known he had. And he wasn't sure how to hold onto them—how to keep being this new, true version of Levi Donovan—without her.

Levi reached for the remote control with a growl. What he needed was some food.

But he wasn't in the mood for lasagna. What he really needed was a big, cheesy, loaded-with-all-the-toppings pizza.

He pushed to his feet. Might as well ask if Luke wanted to get in on that.

But there was no answer when he knocked on Luke's bedroom door.

He checked the time. It was only seven. But maybe his brother had fallen asleep?

He knocked again, harder, then turned the doorknob and pushed the door slowly open.

"Hey, I was thinking pizza. You want—"

He froze as a low groan came from the bed, where Luke lay sprawled on his back, the low light streaming through the window illuminating the sweat beading his forehead. His lips were parted, and a low wheezing noise came from them every few seconds.

"Luke?" A current of panic went straight through his chest. This was not normal.

"Luke?" He shook his brother's shoulder gently enough to keep from hurting him but hard enough to wake him. "You okay, buddy?"

Luke's eyes opened, but it seemed to take him a moment to focus on Levi. "Yeah. I'm good." But he gasped around each word.

"You sure?" Levi crouched next to the bed.

"It's kind of hard—" Luke paused to gasp a few short breaths. "To breathe." He closed his eyes, wheezing as he fought for another breath.

Levi stared. His mind had gone entirely blank.

Luke opened his eyes again, making a pathetic sound, as if he were trying to cough but couldn't. Levi may not know much about Luke's condition. But he did know that the inability to cough and clear the lungs was one of the dangers. It was why Luke had the cough assist. But was it something he should use now? Or would that only do more harm at this point?

"Luke, buddy, do you want your cough assist?"

But Luke had closed his eyes again and seemed to be concentrating on just breathing.

What did he do?

Mom and Dad never should have left him home alone with Luke. They never should have trusted him. They knew from experience that he'd only let them down. After all, he wasn't the kind of person who could make them proud.

They needed to be here. They needed to take care of what he couldn't.

Levi whipped out his phone, dialing Mom's number with a shaky hand.

His heart raced painfully as he waited, his own breaths coming in short gasps.

When Mom's voicemail snapped on, he dialed Dad. But there was no answer there either.

Levi snarled as he hung up and sent them both a text. *Call ASAP. Something's wrong with Luke.*

He stared at the screen.

Please answer. Please answer. He wasn't sure if it was a prayer or an attempt to send them a telepathic message, but either way, it didn't work.

After a minute, he jammed his phone into his pocket and stood, sliding an arm under his brother's shoulder.

"All right, buddy. Hang in there. We're going to get you to the doctor."

Chapter 38

$\mathcal{G}$ race scrolled aimlessly through the list of bed-and-breakfast websites. She'd spent most of the week on the computer, ostensibly to get her own website done but mostly to avoid Levi. And to avoid noticing that he seemed genuinely hurt by her rejection.

She tried not to feel guilty. She'd only done what was best for them both. So why had a fissure opened in her middle? A fissure filled with longing and a wish that things were different. That *he* was different.

The thing was, it almost felt like everything about him was perfect for her—aside from the fact that he was the exact opposite of the kind of man she was meant to be with.

You have something against attractive, funny, caring guys?

That was the thing. He *was* all of those things that she'd ever wanted in a man. But he was also a player, a motorcycle rider, a bad boy.

Too much like Hunter, just like Mama had said.

Even if sometimes she thought maybe he really did want to date her—and not only for a week or two. Maybe he wanted to be with her long term.

But then she remembered what Mama had said—men like Levi Donovan weren't interested in long-term relationships.

Of course he'd been hurt when she'd said no. He wasn't used to being rejected. But he'd get over it soon enough.

She checked the time. Seven thirty on a Saturday night? He was probably out with another woman right now.

The thought churned her stomach, but she'd have to get over that. It wasn't fair to Levi to say she wouldn't date him but then expect him not to date anyone else either.

Her phone rang, and Grace dug through the pile of papers in front of her to find it.

When she did, she set it right back down.

Levi.

They'd been together all week and barely said a word to each other. *Now* he wanted to talk to her?

Whatever it was, it could wait until Monday.

But something made her reach for the phone, pick it up, answer it, even as her head screamed at her to put it down.

Heaven help her, for reasons she was at a loss to understand, she felt like she had to answer it.

"Hello?" She tried for a friendly but slightly disinterested tone.

"Grace. I'm at the hospital with Luke, and I can't get ahold of my parents, and I didn't know who else to call. He's having a hard time breathing, and I don't know what to do." His words all ran together, but Grace's heart caught on the fear in his voice.

"I'm on my way. Keep trying your parents. I'll be there in fifteen minutes."

"No. You don't have to. Sorry, I was being stupid to call you. I don't know what I was thinking you could do."

"I can be there with you." She shoved paperwork off the desk until her hands landed on her car keys. "Fifteen minutes, okay? Maybe ten if I speed."

Levi's laugh was strained, and if she could have, she would have reached her arms right through the phone to hug him.

"And Levi?"

"Yeah?" His voice was hoarse.

"I'll be praying."

The moment she hung up, she scrolled through her contacts, dialing May as she sprinted to the car. When May answered, Grace broke the news as quickly and gently as she could. Despite the younger woman's muffled cry, Grace pushed ahead. "We need you there, May. You know more about Luke's condition than we do. Do you think you could meet us at the hospital?" She started the car and sped down the driveway.

"What if he doesn't want me there?" May's whisper carried a load of heartbreak.

"He needs you there," Grace said firmly. "We all do."

"Okay." May's voice rang with a strength Grace had never heard in her before. "I'll be there as soon as I can."

"Good." Grace threw the phone onto the passenger seat and floored the accelerator, careful not to push her speed too much above the limit but desperate to get to Luke and Levi as fast as humanly possible.

Twelve minutes later, she pulled into a parking space and sprinted for the emergency room doors. Inside, it only took half a second to spot Levi in one of the hard plastic waiting room chairs, his shoulders hunched over his knees.

As she rushed toward him, he looked up, and when he saw her, it was like his entire face crumpled. He stood, and in two strides he was in front of her, pulling her against him, burying his face in her hair.

Her arms rose to his back, and she squeezed as hard as she could, trying to get his trembling to stop.

Finally, he sucked in a shaky breath and pulled away, clearing his throat. "Sorry— I didn't mean to—"

She waved off his apology. "How's Luke?"

"They haven't told me anything yet." He raked both hands through his hair. "I'm going a little crazy here."

"Okay." Grace led him to a chair. "Have you gotten ahold of your parents yet?"

Levi shook his head, despair written across his face.

"We'll keep trying them. In the meantime, I called May."

"You what?" Levi's eyes went hard. "She left him. He doesn't need that right now."

"She's exactly what he needs. She knows his condition and his needs better than anyone other than your mama."

The swish of the emergency room's automatic doors drew their attention. May walked through, her stride purposeful in spite of the fear on her face.

Levi swallowed, then gave a grudging nod. "Fine. But she doesn't see Luke." He said it loudly enough for May to hear. Her footsteps stuttered for a second, but she closed the distance to them.

"What are they doing so far?" Her hands were shaking, but her voice was clear and efficient, and Grace marveled at her strength. She'd seen the way May still looked at Luke—that woman's feelings for him definitely had not diminished.

"I don't know." Levi glared toward the desk, where a woman in scrubs sat typing on a computer. "No one will tell me anything."

"Did you tell them about his BMD?"

"Of course." Levi's answer was scathing. "I'm not as useless as everyone thinks."

May ignored the comment. "Did you tell them not to give him oxygen unless absolutely necessary?"

"He couldn't breathe. Why wouldn't they give him oxygen?"

May spun and sprinted for the desk, leaning over it to catch the woman's attention. The woman immediately stopped typing and picked up the phone next to her.

Grace turned to Levi to see if he understood what was going on. But he looked as baffled as her. And a lot angrier.

The woman behind the desk hung up the phone, and after a short conversation with her, May started back toward them.

"Be nice," Grace said just loud enough for Levi to hear.

But his jaw was hard. "Mind telling me what that was about?" he shot at May.

"Luke's BMD affects his respiratory muscles, so he breathes more shallowly than most of us. His body is still able to keep the right balance of carbon dioxide and oxygen, but if you add oxygen, his body could think he has enough, and he'll stop breathing, which makes the carbon dioxide levels spike." Now she was the one giving Levi the hard look. "It could kill him."

Levi dropped onto the chair behind him with a thud. "I didn't know."

His face had gone chalky, and Grace sat next to him, placing a hand on his arm. "How could you have?"

"I'm his brother." His voice was tortured. "I'm supposed to know these kinds of things. Supposed to look out for him."

"It's okay." May spoke gently, her tone soothing. "I asked them to monitor his carbon dioxide levels. He'll be fine. You did the right thing bringing him here."

Her words didn't seem to have any effect on Levi. He dropped his head into his hands, and Grace rubbed his back, fighting off a wave of helplessness.

What can I do, Lord?

But the moment she asked, she knew the answer.

"Would you like to pray together?" she asked softly, still rubbing her hand up and down on Levi's back.

He turned red-lined eyes on her. "If you think it will help."

She nodded and closed her eyes, letting her hand still on his back but not lifting it off. She felt May settle into the seat on the other side of her.

"God, our loving Father," she started. "We know how much you love your children. Please be with Luke right now. We don't know what he needs, Lord, but you do. Give the doctors wisdom, give Luke healing, and give us trust. In Jesus' name we ask this. Amen."

Levi had played football for hours at a time, he'd taken hits so hard they made his head spin, he'd worked himself to the point of exhaustion, but his limbs had never felt as heavy as they did in this moment. He rubbed at his bleary eyes. He'd finally gotten ahold of Mom and Dad an hour or so ago. They'd had no cell signal for part of the drive. Which meant they now had to turn around and make the three-hour drive home.

In the seat next to him, Grace stirred, then stood. "I'm going to go get us some coffee."

He nodded, trying to work up a grateful smile, though his face was too tired to move.

In the next chair, May nodded too. As Grace walked off, May bent forward, bowing her head over her hands. She'd been doing that periodically all night. Praying, Levi assumed.

He hadn't quite been able to bring himself to do that, though Grace's prayer earlier had brought some small measure of comfort. Now what he wanted was an answer to that prayer. Sooner, rather than later.

As if she sensed his gaze on her, May raised her head and looked at him, her dark eyes filled with both strength and pain.

"Do you love him?" He didn't know why he asked, didn't know why it mattered to him, but it did.

May's eyes met his. "Yes." Her answer was simple and direct, but somehow it was more powerful than a profession of hundreds of words could have been.

"Then why did you leave him?" Let her try to explain that.

May watched her foot trace a line on the floor. "You're his brother. I couldn't stand coming between you two."

Levi gave a disbelieving laugh. So she was going to pin this on him. "It seems if you loved him so much, you wouldn't let an idiot like me stand in the way."

May stood and stepped in front of Levi. "Sometimes when you love someone, you do what's best for them. Even if it hurts you." She walked off in the direction Grace had gone.

Was that true? Could you love someone so much that you would leave them if you thought it was best for them?

A doctor in blue scrubs approached Levi, and he put the question out of his mind. He had more pressing concerns right now than theoretical questions about love.

"Luke Donovan's brother?"

Levi grimaced and stood, trying to brace for the worst, though he had no idea how to do that.

"Looks like it's pneumonia," the doctor said.

Levi allowed himself a quick, relieved breath. Pneumonia wasn't so bad.

"He's relatively stable right now, and we're pumping him full of antibiotics, but of course for someone with Luke's condition, pneumonia is quite dangerous."

Levi tripped against the seat behind him. It was?

"Could be touch and go for a few days," the doctor continued. "But it's good that you were able to alert us to monitor his carbon dioxide levels. Nice work. Your brother's lucky to have you watching out for him."

"Yeah." Levi grasped for the chair and sat.

If things had been left to him, his brother could have died.

Could still die.

And it would be all his fault.

Chapter 39

$\mathcal{G}$ race rubbed her grainy eyes and checked the time.

Six a.m.

She must have dozed off, thanks to the slightly more comfortable chairs in the ICU waiting room. Luke had been transferred to the unit a few hours ago, and now she, Levi, May, and Mr. and Mrs. Donovan—who had arrived shortly before that, looking distraught and disheveled—were piled into the small waiting room. Levi had tried to insist that she go home, but she refused.

She may not have any intention of dating him. But she was still his friend, and she wasn't going to make him go through this alone.

"Good morning," he whispered from next to her.

"Morning," she whispered back, letting her eyes travel over the others. Next to her, May was curled up in her chair, feet up, eyes closed. On the other side of the room, Mrs. Donovan's head rested on her husband's shoulder, while Mr. Donovan stared blankly at a spot on the ceiling.

"Did you sleep at all?" she asked Levi.

He shook his head. His eyes were bleary and bloodshot, the skin beneath them a gray-blue.

"Close your eyes," she whispered. "I'll wake you if there's any news."

"I'm fine. You should go."

She tucked her hand into his. "How many times do I have to tell you I'm not going anywhere?"

Levi looked from their linked hands to her face. "Thank you."

"For what?"

He shrugged. "For being a friend."

"Always. Now close your eyes."

He shook his head, but when she glanced over a few seconds later, his eyes were closed, and his head lolled to the side.

She scanned the room for something soft to tuck under it for a pillow. But there was nothing.

Slowly, so she wouldn't wake him, she reached up and drew his head closer, until it rested on her shoulder.

Then she pulled out her phone and opened her Bible app.

For the next few hours, she alternated reading, praying, and dozing, her hand still resting in Levi's, his head still on her shoulder.

When he finally stirred, she craned her neck to smile at him. As if just realizing he'd fallen asleep, he bolted upright.

"Sorry. I didn't mean to fall asleep on you." He scrubbed his hands over his cheeks. "What time is it?"

Grace checked the phone in her hand. "Almost ten o'clock."

Levi blinked. "I can't believe I slept that long. You'd better get going."

"Levi, I told you—"

"You're going to be late for church."

Grace blinked at him. That was incredibly thoughtful, but also—

"Church started half an hour ago."

"Oh, I'm sorry. I didn't mean to make you miss it."

"Levi—" Grace took his hand back. "I wasn't planning on going."

"You weren't?" Levi's brow wrinkled. "I thought you liked church. You always go. You probably have perfect attendance."

"I do enjoy church, and I go every opportunity I can. But not to check off some attendance card. I go because I love to hear God's

Word and sing his praises with my fellow believers. But right now, I think I can best serve God by being here for my friend in need."

As Levi watched her, something shifted in his eyes. "Will you sing for me?"

"Here?" Grace glanced around the room. May and the Donovans were awake but silent, and another woman who had come into the waiting room about an hour ago was crying quietly into her hands.

It wasn't a big audience, but it was an audience all the same. "I don't think . . ."

"Please. That song you sang in church?" Levi's eyes held hers, and there was no way she could say no.

She swallowed and closed her eyes, taking a deep breath. "Great is thy faithfulness . . ."

Levi's hand gripped hers, and she squeezed it, trying to pass the peace the song always brought her on to him.

When she got to the refrain, another voice joined hers. She opened her eyes to see May singing even as tears ran down her cheeks.

Grace kept singing, swaying to words that promised God's faithfulness no matter the circumstances.

When she sang the refrain a second time, Levi's parents joined in, as did the woman on the other side of the room. And on the final refrain, another, deeper voice joined theirs.

She turned to Levi, her mouth widening into a smile.

The man could *sing*.

And to hear the words coming out of his mouth—God was so, so faithful.

When the song was done, they all sat there, a sort of holy awe hanging over the room.

"Thank you," the woman across the room finally said. "I needed that reminder right now. My husband is in a coma. They don't know . . ." She brought a tissue to her eyes. "Sorry, I just— I really needed that."

Mrs. Donovan patted her husband's arm, then moved to sit next to the other woman. As they began to talk in low voices, Grace leaned toward Levi.

"You tricked me," she murmured.

His eyes shot to hers. "About what?"

"You can sing."

"When did I say I couldn't?"

"In the airport." She pointed a mock accusing finger at him. "You didn't say. You showed. In front of all those people."

He chuckled. "Got you to forgive me though, didn't it?"

She swatted at his arm, but he caught her hand and held tight to it. "Thank you for being here. It means a lot to me."

She nodded. "It means a lot to me too."

"Donovan family?" A doctor entered the waiting room, and everyone froze.

Grace clutched Levi's hand tight enough that she was surprised he didn't cry out.

"Luke's lung function has improved slightly," the doctor said. "We'll still have to be careful of infection, but I'm cautiously optimistic at this point. He's awake and can have visitors now, but I'd ask that you limit it to three at a time."

"Thank you, Jesus," Mrs. Donovan murmured. "Thank you, doctor."

Mr. and Mrs. Donovan rushed to the door, and Grace let go of Levi's hand and nudged him forward.

But he looked at the spot where May had collapsed onto her chair. "May should go."

May looked up at him, her mouth opening.

"Levi—" Mrs. Donovan started.

"It's what Luke would want," Levi said. "Trust me, he's been waiting a long time to see her again. Go, May. I'll visit with him later."

May gave him one more dumbfounded look, then jumped out of her chair and threw her arms around him.

Then she followed Mr. and Mrs. Donovan out of the waiting room.

"That was sweet of you." Grace bumped his shoulder as she took her seat.

Levi shrugged. "They love each other. I don't want to get in the way of that."

Chapter 40

Levi stood over Luke's bed, hand over his mouth to stifle the anguish that threatened to find its way out.

His brother had been doing so well yesterday—Levi had been in here talking with him—and overnight he'd taken a turn for the worse. The doctor said it was an infection in his lungs.

"Hey, bro." He barely managed to scrape up the whisper. "We're counting on you to fight this."

He pulled a chair up next to the bed. Luke's face was gray and slack, his eyes closed, his body still.

"I know you said you're ready to go home—" When Luke had said that to him two days ago, Levi had assumed he'd meant back to Mom and Dad's. He'd promised they were doing everything they could to get him healthy and back in his own room as quickly as possible.

But Luke had given his customary smile. "I mean *home* home. Whenever God calls me, I'm ready."

It had taken Levi a moment to realize he was talking about dying. About going to heaven.

It'd left Levi more than a little shaken.

"But I really need you to hang around here a while longer," he said now. "I need more time with my little brother." He looked down, rubbing at his forehead. "May needs you too. I see now that she loves you. She's going to stick around for the hard parts. Do you know she hasn't left this building once in four days?" Even Levi had gone home to shower and change yesterday, and he'd convinced Grace to do the same. He'd told her to stay home and sleep in her own bed too, but that part she hadn't listened to.

"Not to sound selfish," Levi said to Luke's still form. "But I really need you to pull through this because I need some advice. About a girl."

He waited for Luke's laugh—but the only sound was the whir of the medical equipment.

Levi wasn't sure how much more of this they could all take.

They'd been sitting vigil at the hospital for a week now. He hadn't seen Mom eat an actual meal since Wednesday. Dad seemed to age by the day. And even May and Grace were looking worn and disheartened.

Next to him, Grace read her Bible. Whenever he looked at her, she sent him an encouraging smile. But it didn't hide the worry in her eyes.

Restlessness driving him to his feet, Levi began to pace the room. His new hobby.

His eyes scanned them all. What good were they doing here?

"I think we should go to church," he announced, catching even himself by surprise.

"You do?" The question seemed to come from Grace, Mom, Dad, and May all at the same time.

"Grace says—" He looked at her for confirmation. "Church is a place of hope and encouragement, and I don't know about y'all—" He slipped the word in with a quiet smile at Grace. "But I could use some of that right now."

Grace stood. "I'll come with you."

"Me too." May stood as well.

He looked at Mom and Dad. "If you want to stay here with Luke . . ."

"We'll come." Dad held out a hand to help Mom up. "We have two sons, and we want to be there for both of them."

All Levi could manage was a short nod.

He didn't know why it meant so much to him that they all go together, but it did.

Dad drove everyone in the van, and Levi and Grace sat in the far back. Halfway to church, she reached for his hand. "This was a good idea."

He clung to those words—and to her hand—as they walked into church together a few minutes later. Dozens of people stopped to ask after Luke and say they were praying for him. So many of them had visited the hospital this week that Levi was beginning to think that though he was the famous brother, Luke was the popular one.

Instead of filling him with jealousy, as it may have once, the knowledge heartened him. Luke deserved their good opinion and their prayers. He was a part of their community, and he cared about each one of them.

By the time they'd spoken to all the well-wishers, the service had already begun. Levi glanced toward Dad—he must be having a heart attack at the prospect of walking in late. But instead, Dad looked more optimistic than Levi had seen him in days.

They filed into the sanctuary as the first song ended.

Last time he'd been in this church, he'd tried hard not to listen to the message. But today he wanted to soak up every word. If there truly was hope to be found here, he wanted to find it.

By the time Dan stood to deliver his sermon, Levi was starting to feel some of that hope. He leaned forward, ready to take in more of it, greedy suddenly for this message.

"Many of you know that I'm now a father of two," Dan began. He scrubbed his hands over his face. "Can I be honest with you? It's exhausting."

A laugh rippled through the congregation.

"With the newborn, there are the diaper changes and the feeding and the refusing to sleep at night. And with the preschooler, there's the temper tantrums and the constant questions and the refusing to sleep at night."

Sounded fun. Maybe Levi should advise Dan never to make a parenting commercial. But he'd seen Dan with his kids, and he knew that man loved his family fiercely. Which meant all of this was to make some sort of point.

"But you want to know what the hardest part of parenting is?" Dan looked directly at the spot where Jade sat with their children. "Saying no. When Hope comes to me and looks at me with those big eyes and asks me for something in that sweet voice, I want to say yes every time. But of course I can't. Because sometimes what she asks for might be something I know isn't what's best for her. Something that might even hurt her or be dangerous for her. Or what if she asks me for something good, but it's something I don't think she needs or should have yet? Or maybe she asks for one thing, but I have something even better planned for her? So I say no. And she may not like it, may not understand it, may throw a tantrum about it. But still my answer stands. No."

Dan looked down for a moment, as if searching for the words to express what he wanted to say next. Levi stilled as he waited. He had no idea where Dan was going with this, but he had the strangest feeling Dan's musings on fatherhood were somehow relevant to his own life, even if fatherhood didn't appear to be anywhere near the horizon for him.

"The hard part of being a human father," Dan said as he looked up, "is that I don't always *know* what's best for my kids. I do my best. I try hard. But sometimes I make mistakes. But God—" He smiled and shook his head, as if he could hardly contain what he was about to say. "God doesn't have that problem. He knows exactly what's best for his children. What's best for us."

Dan paced to the far side of the sanctuary, and Levi's eyes followed him.

"The hard part for us," Dan continued, "is that sometimes doing what's best for us means God says no to our prayers. Even when we think those prayers are exactly what we need. Maybe they're prayers for a job or prayers for a wounded relationship or prayers for a sick loved one. And we can't see any way God wouldn't answer those prayers with a yes. Because they're obviously for our good. But here's the thing—" He spread his arms wide. "We may think we know what's good for us—but God knows what's *best* for us."

Levi sat back hard against his seat. He needed God to answer his prayers for Luke. He had come here to hear that God was going to do that. And now Dan was telling him that wasn't going to happen?

Grace's hand, which was still in his, squeezed tight. Levi wanted to tune Dan out, but he forced himself to keep listening. Maybe he had misunderstood what Dan was saying. And Dan would clear it all up right now—tell him that as long as he prayed hard enough, God would do what he wanted.

"You know," Dan continued, "we tend to focus on those places in Scripture where God answered prayers—enabling David to slay Goliath, sending down fire on Elijah's offering to prove he was the only true God, healing the lame and giving sight to the blind. But there are plenty of examples in here"—he picked up his Bible—"of God saying no to his people's prayers too. And these weren't just any old Joe Schmoes God said no to—they were some of his most faithful servants. We might think if God was going to grant anyone's prayers, it would be theirs."

He paged through the Bible. "There was David, who prayed for God to spare his son's life. God said no. There was Paul, who prayed for God to take away the thorn in his flesh. God said no. And there was Jesus. Yes, Jesus, God's Son. On the night before his crucifixion, Jesus went into the garden and prayed, not once, not twice, but three times: 'My Father, if it is possible, may this cup be taken from me. Yet not as I will, but as you will.' And, well, we all know how God answered that prayer: that cup—the suffering he was about to experience—wasn't taken from Jesus. The very next day, he went to the cross for our sins."

The words rang in Levi's ears. Jesus? God had said no to Jesus' prayer? Then what hope did Levi have that God would answer his?

"So what good is prayer then?" Dan moved toward Levi's side of the sanctuary. "If God didn't give his own Son a yes, then what good does it do for us to pray?"

Dan's face broke into a smile again, and Levi had to resist the temptation to stand up right here in front of church and punch the guy. He didn't see what there was to smile about.

"So much good." Dan's smile widened. "It does so much good to pray. Because God hears every one of our prayers. It doesn't matter if you're Jesus or Joe Schmo. It doesn't matter how hard you pray or if you say the words just right or how much faith you have. Because prayer isn't about *you*. It's about God. About how he listens to you and how he, in his infinite wisdom and mercy, answers you, every time, whether that's with a yes, a no, or a not right now. His answer is always, *always* what is best for us. Even when it doesn't feel like it."

Levi wanted to believe that, he really did.

"How do we know that?" Dan seemed to pull the question out of Levi's head.

This time when he smiled, Levi felt a little less like punching him. "Because he tells us. Romans 8:28: 'And we know that in all things God works for the good of those who love him, who have been called according to his purpose.' Notice it doesn't say most of the time or sometimes or once in a while. No. *In all things*, God works for our good. That's why we can confidently pray, like Jesus did, 'not as I will, but as you will.' Praying for God's will to be done isn't a cop-out. It's not leaving some wiggle room for God, in case he can't do what we asked. It's saying, 'God I trust you. I trust that you know what's best for me. Please do *that* in my life.'"

Levi took a deep breath. That sounded like a big step. What if he prayed for God's will to be done, and God's will was to let Luke die? How would that be for his good?

He thought of Luke's words the other day: *God has a glorious home prepared for me, Levi. I'm ready to go there when he calls me.*

As the sermon ended and he stood with the others, Levi closed his eyes. *I want to want your will, Lord,* he prayed. *But I'm not sure I'm there yet. Please heal Luke.*

He opened his eyes.

That was the best he was going to be able to do for now.

Chapter 41

That had been intense.

Grace could almost feel Levi absorbing the sermon this morning, though as they walked to the car now, she wasn't exactly sure what his final verdict had been.

Mr. Donovan opened the door of the van, but Levi stood staring at it.

"I can't go back there right now," he choked. "I just— When I see him like that—" His hand fisted around the front of his shirt. "It's like I can't breathe. I need to go for a ride or something."

It was all Grace could do not to throw her arms around him. Instead, she slipped her hand quietly into his.

Mr. Donovan studied his son, and Grace held her breath. She'd gotten the feeling over the last few days that something was improving in Levi's relationship with his dad, but she felt like Mr. Donovan's response now might have the power to undo all of that.

After a moment, Mr. Donovan nodded. "I'll drop you off at home."

The tension in Levi's jaw eased. "Thanks." He ducked into the van, and Grace climbed in behind him.

All the way to his house, she debated. She didn't want Levi to be by himself right now. But he didn't necessarily seem to want company. And she had promised herself never to get on that bike.

By the time Mr. Donovan pulled into his home's driveway, she'd made up her mind. She'd go to the hospital and sit with the family.

Levi would be fine on his own.

"Be careful," she whispered as he unfolded himself from the van. But he didn't respond, and she wasn't entirely sure he'd heard her.

He shuffled toward the garage, shoulders hunched forward, head down.

Mr. Donovan backed the car out of the driveway.

"Wait." Grace unclicked her seatbelt as Mr. Donovan shifted into drive. "I'm going with him."

Mr. Donovan nosed the van back into the driveway.

"Thank you." Mrs. Donovan squeezed her arm as she clambered out of the van. Mr. Donovan nodded to her, and May added that she'd be praying for them.

As she stepped to the ground, Levi's Harley roared to life. Grace sprinted up the driveway as the Donovans drove away.

Levi was already sitting on the bike, helmet on, visor over his eyes, but she waved her arms wildly as she charged toward him, and he cut the engine.

Slowly, he pulled his helmet off. "What are you doing?"

Grace reached his side. "I'm coming with you. Where's that extra helmet?"

Levi's stormy eyes slid over her face in a long, searching look. She put on her most determined expression, and he finally gestured to the hard-sided case behind the seat. She popped it open, grabbing the helmet and pulling it over her head.

"So where to?" She pushed the visor up to watch him.

He shrugged. "I was just going to drive around. You're sure you want to ride? You don't have to, you know. I'll be fine."

"I know you will. I want to come. But I have a better idea than just wandering. You ever been to Rocky Point?"

Levi shook his head.

"Good." She lowered her visor and threw her leg over the bike. "Head out of town on highway twelve."

Levi nodded, put his helmet back on, and started the bike. Grace moved her hands easily to his waist, leaning with him as he gently steered out of the driveway and onto the street.

As they rode farther out of town and into the more sparsely populated countryside dotted with corn fields and orchards, she could feel the knots in his back loosen.

She liked to drive out this way whenever she had a problem. Seeing the wonders of God's creation always restored her soul—and Levi hadn't even seen the best part yet.

After over an hour on the bike, she pointed him down a nearly hidden road with thick forest on either side. Levi turned onto it, and they wound uphill through the trees until the road dead-ended at a parking lot. Levi pulled into a spot and shut the motorcycle down.

They sat in the abrupt silence for a few moments before Grace swung her leg off the bike and removed her helmet.

Levi followed, his eyes landing square on her. "That was *not* your first time on a bike."

"No." She tucked her helmet into the case on the bike. "Hunter had a bike."

"Oh." He didn't press the point. "So what is this place?"

"You'll see. You up for a hike?"

"Do I have a choice?" But he fell into step next to her with a soft smile.

She led him to a trail just wide enough for the two of them to walk side-by-side.

"Do you want to talk or just walk?" The thing she always appreciated about this place was the stillness—the chance to be alone with God—and she didn't want to take that from Levi. But if he wanted to talk, she was here to listen.

"Let's just walk for now." He offered her a grateful smile, and they lapsed into a silence so full and meaningful it almost felt as if they were talking without words.

Half an hour later, they emerged from the trees, right at the edge of a hill that sloped steeply down to Lake Michigan below, and Grace caught Levi's hand to stop him.

"There." She pointed to the right where, halfway down the hill, an arch of rock framed the view of the water below. The center of the arch was so impossibly narrow that there was no way the whole thing shouldn't crumble to the ground.

"How on earth?" Levi walked down the trail that led toward the arch. "That should not be possible."

Grace stepped to his side. "That's what I love about this place. It reminds me that things that are impossible with man are possible with God."

Levi's sigh was long and labored. "If God *wants* to do those things." He turned to her, looking completely broken. "Do you think God's answer to our prayers for Luke is going to be no?"

"I don't know." The whispered words were maybe the hardest she'd ever said. She so wanted to tell him that of course God would heal Luke. But she couldn't know God's will in this any more than the next person.

"I don't understand. Why would he say no?" Levi's voice cracked.

Grace moved closer to wrap her arms around him. "I don't know," she murmured. "There are so many things we'll probably never understand this side of heaven. But I do know God is the Great Physician. If it's his will, he can cure Luke of this infection. But more than that, he's already cured him of the infection of sin. He has a perfect home waiting for Luke in heaven."

Levi nodded into her hair. "That's what Luke said. But I'd rather if he stayed in his home here. Is that wrong? For me to want that?"

"Of course not." Grace rubbed her hand up and down his back. "Just remember that God might have something better planned. For Luke. And for you."

"I'm trying to trust that. But it's hard."

Grace held him like that for another minute, her heart giving way when a teardrop fell onto her shoulder. She sniffed and failed to hold back her own tears.

Finally, Levi cleared his throat and pulled away, passing the back of his hand over his cheek. "I'm sorry. I wasn't trying to take advantage of you."

She laughed, wiping at her own eyes. "If you recall, I'm the one who hugged you."

"Thank you." He turned to walk down the trail toward the arch. "For being honest about the fact that God might say no. I think I can accept that." He gave a dry, mirthless laugh. "Or at least I'm trying to."

Chapter 42

Over the past two hours, the weight of worry that had oppressed Levi since the moment he'd taken Luke to the hospital had lifted little by little.

He and Grace had hiked all the way to the rock ledge that passed within a few feet of the arch, followed the trail down to the beach, and splashed along the shore.

Every once in a while, the thought would creep back in: *What if God says no? What if Luke dies?*

And each time, he prayed silently: *Lord, please heal him.* And then added, painfully, *Not my will but yours be done.*

He couldn't remember a time ever before in his life that he'd prayed for God's will to be done—or at least not and really meant it—and it was slightly terrifying to put that much trust in a God he'd only recently started to see as relevant again. But it felt freeing too, to know that whatever happened was in God's hands. And if Grace and Dan were to be believed—if God's Word was to be believed—that was the best place for it.

"Here. This is for you." Grace held out a seashell in deep shades of orangey-red. "It reminds me of the sunset that night on the parasail. Remember how vibrant the colors were?"

Remember?

Of course he remembered. Just like he remembered how vibrant her smile was, how joyful her laugh was, how sweet everything about her was.

He cradled the shell in his hand.

Maybe after all of this was over, he'd start praying for his relationship with Grace. Because after all they'd gone through in the past week, his feelings for her had grown—not only stronger, but deeper, like there was a well in his soul that she was filling.

Her compassion, her faithfulness, her willingness to be there for others at her own cost—all of that had him more convinced than ever that she was the perfect woman.

What he wasn't quite so sure of was whether he was the perfect man for her. And he didn't want her to have anyone less than the one who was God's will for her.

So if—when—he prayed for their relationship, he'd pray for God's will to be done in that too.

"What's that?" She pointed toward something glinting in the sand down the beach.

But before they could check it out, Levi's phone rang.

They both froze.

After a moment, he pulled it out of his pocket, staring at it, every care, every worry, slamming back into his soul with a force that nearly bowled him over.

"It's my mom." Levi's vocal cords were too tight.

Grace took his free hand in hers, squeezing it around the seashell he still clutched.

Your will be done.

He lifted the phone to his ear.

"Levi?" Mom's voice was nearly hysterical, and Levi stepped closer to Grace, letting her hand around his anchor him.

He couldn't say anything. All he could do was wait.

"He's awake. He's awake." Mom's sobs drowned out the rest of her words, but it didn't matter. Levi's heart had taken off for the clouds.

He gathered Grace to him in a monumental one-armed hug, burying his face in her hair. "He's awake."

"Thank you, Lord," Grace murmured, wrapping her arms around him.

He turned his attention back to the phone. "So he's going to be all right?"

He barely heard as Mom explained that it was too soon to tell but that the infection seemed to be clearing, and Luke's lung function was improving. All he could think about was how he'd prayed for God's will to be done.

Was this God's answer? Was this his will? To bring Luke back to them?

When he hung up the phone, his arm was still around Grace, and hers were still around him.

Her eyes met his, and her smile was as big as his.

Slowly, she raised onto her toes, tipping her face toward him.

Levi almost bent down. Almost brought his lips to hers.

But she didn't know what she was thinking. She was just happy that Luke would be okay.

Gently, he took a step backwards. "We should probably get back."

"Yeah." Grace's eyes were still on his, their mocha color deeper and warmer than ever. "Let's go."

Chapter 43

There was something in the air tonight. Grace couldn't put her finger on what it was. But everything around her seemed to crackle with life: Her friends milling in Jared and Peyton's backyard. The birds calling from the trees. And Luke, seated in the wheelchair he'd use until he regained his strength, May at his side, both of them smiling so widely she wasn't sure they noticed the rest of the group surrounding them.

And then there was Levi, playing catch with Jackson, occasionally offering him pointers, but mostly just seeming to have fun. Every once in a while, he stopped to toss a Nerf football to little Hope.

And he never once stopped smiling.

Which had, in turn, put an impossible-to-erase smile on her lips too.

The change that had come over him in the two weeks since that day at Rocky Point—Grace had never seen anything so profound, and she wasn't sure what to make of it. Aside from the fact that it made her long even more for what she couldn't have.

She'd almost kissed him that day on the beach, but he'd pulled back.

He'd been right to do it—she knew he had. And yet, working with him for the past two weeks, it had been impossible not to wonder what it would be like to walk over to him, grab the hammer out of his hands, wrap her arms around his neck, and taste his lips on hers.

"He's good with kids." Jade settled into the chair next to Grace.

"Who?" Grace tried to sound surprised, innocent, confused, though her face felt as if it had been stuffed into an oven.

"Do you have feelings for him? Never mind. That was a dumb question. Let me rephrase: What are you going to do about your feelings for him?"

Grace leaned her head back on the chair and closed her eyes against the image of Levi in front of her. But that was no good because the image in her mind was of him kissing her.

She let her lids spring open in time to catch Levi fist bumping Jackson. "I'm not going to do anything."

"Why not?" Jade fixed her sharp gaze on Grace.

"Because—" Grace spluttered. "Because he's obviously not my type." Though it was taking more and more work to convince herself of that every day.

"The same way Dan wasn't my type? And I definitely wasn't his?"

Grace tucked her feet under her and shook her head. "That's different."

"How?"

"Because . . ." She harrumphed. "It just is. I have a plan for what my future husband will be like. And it's not Levi."

Jade gave her a probing look. "You know what I think? I think God takes one look at our plans, and he laughs and shows us how much better what he has planned for us is."

"You're saying you think God wants me to be with Levi?" The thing was, Grace had been feeling more and more lately like that might be true. But she'd chalked it up to her own desires.

"I'm saying you need to trust God. Even if he leads you somewhere you never would have thought of going on your own."

That may be true. But it didn't mean it wasn't terrifying. "How will I know?"

"Trust me, you'll know." Jade patted her hand. "Now, I'm off to get a cupcake. You want anything?"

"No thanks." Grace closed her eyes and leaned back against the chair again.

She would just know, would she? A sign or a roadmap or something would be much more helpful.

"Hey you." How was it that the sound of his voice was enough to make her limbs tingle? She let herself open her eyes a crack.

Levi stood a good five feet from her chair.

He'd been careful about that lately. Careful to leave enough distance between them. Careful not to enter her personal space. Careful not to so much as brush his hand against hers.

And after sitting by his side, holding his hand, every day for a week while Luke was in the hospital, she missed Levi's touch with a fierceness she couldn't explain.

"Mind if I sit?" Levi's voice was adorably hesitant.

"Of course not." Thankfully, the acceleration of her heart rate didn't come through in her words.

He lowered himself into the chair Jade had vacated but instead of relaxing back into it, leaned forward, bracing his elbows on his knees, clasping his hands in front of him. He looked at her, then looked toward the spot where Jackson and Hope were now tossing the Nerf ball.

Grace sat up a fraction. What was he thinking? She wanted to ask, and yet she didn't want to know.

"Hey, I didn't get a chance to thank you." She let herself touch his arm, but only for a moment.

"Oh yeah? And what do you have to thank me for this time?" His grin was joking, but there was something under the surface of his gaze that sent her heart skipping.

"I saw Tori's interview today. You called her, didn't you? There were things in there we didn't talk about that day. Things about the bed-and-breakfast. And about me."

Levi shrugged. "I told you, Tori's good at what she does. Good researcher."

"Is that so?" Grace pulled out her phone and scrolled through the article, which she had left open. She read: "Former Tennessee Titans quarterback Levi Donovan, whose family's company is involved with the renovation, offered high praise for Ms. Calvano: 'Grace is joyful and passionate, and she loves people. That comes through in everything she does, including preparing this place for guests. I know she will touch the lives of everyone who stays here.'"

She swallowed. She'd been just as moved all sixteen times she'd read it. "Where do you suppose Tori researched that?"

"I thought people should know about you, that's all."

That urge to kiss him came over her again, and Grace stood abruptly so she wouldn't act on it. "I think I'm going to . . ."

"I wanted to ask you—" Levi stood too. "There's this thing next weekend. A fundraiser for muscular dystrophy. I go every year. But I thought maybe this year you might want to . . ." His voice trailed into uncertainty.

"Levi, I—"

"Excuse me, everyone." Luke's voice sounded over the hubbub of conversations taking place across the patio, and everyone turned to him.

"Sorry to interrupt." He had pushed up out of his wheelchair and was leaning heavily on his cane, the effort of remaining upright clear on his face.

"What is he doing?" Levi muttered. "He's not strong enough yet." He left Grace staring after him as he strode across the patio toward his brother.

"I wanted to say thank you to all of you for coming to visit while I was in the hospital and for your prayers," Luke said. "I can't tell you how much that meant to me. And to my family." He nodded to Levi, who had reached him but hung back. From his alert expression, Grace could tell he was ready to step in and plunk his brother back in the wheelchair at the first sign of trouble.

"Growing up, I didn't always have a lot of friends, and I thought that was just the way my life was always going to be. And I was fine with it." Luke looked around at the group gathered there, smiling at each one of them. "But now I know how much richer life can be with people in it. People who love you and support you and pray for you." He wobbled a little, and Levi took a step forward, but Luke waved him off.

"And that's why I wanted to do this here. With all of you." He let out a quick breath. "May, could you come here a second?"

May looked surprised, but she stood and took the hand he held out, her smile quizzical but tender.

"My plan was to go through life alone," Luke said, and Grace felt a lump solidifying in her throat. Was he about to do what she thought he was about to do?

"And I was so certain that was God's plan for me too. He wouldn't want me to burden anyone with my illness."

May shook her head, looking like she had something to say about that, but Luke kept talking. "But you showed me that I wasn't a burden. You made me feel like a . . . like a gift. I mean, I knew my mom and dad felt that way. And probably my brother—" He threw a look over his shoulder at Levi, who gave him a tight smile that anyone who didn't know him might mistake for tension. But Grace knew it hid a well of emotion he was working to hold back.

Luke turned to May. "Aside from my salvation, you are the greatest gift God has ever brought into my life. And I don't ever want to lose you."

He adjusted his grip on her hand and moved one leg back, his cane shaking roughly. Grace raised her hands to her mouth. He was going to fall trying to get down on one knee.

But then Levi was at Luke's side, supporting his arm, slowly helping him lower into position.

Grace pressed a hand to her chest, her eyes following Levi as he patted his brother's shoulder, then took a step back.

That man might not be right for her, but he was something special.

"May."

Grace forced her attention back to Luke, so she wouldn't miss his big moment.

"I don't know what God has planned for the rest of my life. I don't know how long it will be. I don't know how long I'll be able to walk or how my disease will progress. But I do know that I want to spend the rest of my life with you. Will you marry me?"

May was crying too hard to answer, but at her emphatic nod, the entire group broke into cheers.

Grace wiped a tear from her own cheek as Levi rushed forward to help Luke back to his feet. The moment Luke was upright, Levi clapped him into a strong hug.

"Thanks, bro, but I'd like to hug my fiancée now if you don't mind." Luke's voice was loud enough for everyone to hear, and Levi let go of his brother, not a hint of embarrassment on his face as he moved out of the way.

May instantly stepped into his spot, her arms going around Luke in a long embrace with a sweet kiss that elicited more cheers, before she and Levi helped Luke back into his wheelchair.

Levi turned to May and held his arms out to her, wrapping her into a quick hug that brought another lump to Grace's throat.

She gave her eyes a determined swipe, then approached to congratulate the happy couple along with everyone else.

An hour later, as the group started to disperse, Grace found herself alone in the kitchen, where she'd offered to load the dishwasher. Mostly, she'd needed time to think.

The patio door slid open.

"Hey you." There was something about the way he said it that always made her smile.

"Hey yourself."

"Want some help?"

"Just finished." Thank goodness. She wasn't sure she could handle being alone with him right now. Not when her feelings were more mixed up than ever.

She couldn't be with him. And yet she wanted to be.

She knew he was Mr. Wrong. But he felt so much like Mr. Right.

"I think I'm going to head home, actually." She dug her keys out of her pocket. "You?"

He shook his head. "I'm Luke's ride, so I'll stay until he's ready to go."

"He's over the moon. I'm happy for him."

Levi gave her a thoughtful look. "Me too."

"I'm glad about that. I wasn't sure you would be."

"Guess I've learned a few things lately."

"Like?"

"Like I'm fortunate to have a brother like him. And like I didn't have a right to make assumptions about May based on what other women had done. And like—"

But she was stuck on that last one. Was that what she'd been doing to Levi? Making assumptions about him based on what Hunter had done? On the kind of person Hunter had been? Because, when she really thought about it, Levi wasn't anything like Hunter at all.

"I didn't answer your question from before." She didn't mean to interrupt what he'd been saying, but she had to do this right now. "About the fundraiser."

"Oh." Levi dropped his head. "Don't worry about it. I shouldn't have asked."

"No. I mean yes." She took a breath. "I mean, I want to go. With you."

Chapter 44

"*I* need your advice." Levi stood in the doorway of his brother's room.

Luke was in his wheelchair, reading a book, but he closed it and looked up with a smirk. "That's a first."

"Yeah well. There have probably been plenty of times that I should have asked you for advice, but I was too stupid to realize it."

"True." Luke gestured for Levi to come in, and Levi took the opportunity to snatch the pillow off Luke's bed and chuck it at his brother. Luke caught it easily. "So how can I help the great and mighty Levi Donovan?"

"Knock it off. If anything, you're the great and mighty one. Coming back from death's door like that." He pointed a finger at his brother. "Don't ever do that to me again, by the way."

"I'm only great and mighty because of the One who makes me great and mighty. Same for you. You know that, right?"

"Yeah. I do." Levi had continued to go to church ever since that day when Luke was sick and he hadn't known what else to do. And every time, he was sure he was going to hear something that would bring back all the old doubts. But instead, every time, his certainty that God was real—that God loved him—only seemed to grow.

"Anyway, this advice you desperately need . . . I assume it's about Grace?"

"I don't desperately need it." That wasn't true. "Okay, I do. And yes, it's about Grace." He was supposed to pick her up for the fundraiser in an hour, but he was petrified.

"I'm afraid I'm going to screw this up," he admitted to Luke. "She's already made it clear that she doesn't want to date me."

Luke eyed him as if he were a simpleton. "You're about to go on a date, so I think you can conclude that you've passed that hurdle."

Levi shook his head. "As a friend. I asked her to the fundraiser as a friend. But the truth is—" He swallowed. Even thinking the words felt monumental.

"The truth is you're in love with her," Luke filled in.

Levi watched his hands. It would be safer to deny it.

But he nodded. "Madly in love, actually."

"And have you told her that?"

Told her that? Was his brother crazy? "Of course not."

"What are you waiting for? A personal invitation?"

Yeah. Sort of. Shouldn't he be?

"Look." Luke maneuvered the wheelchair to the bed. "You said you wanted advice. So here's my advice: Love isn't always easy. Sometimes it's scary. But it's what we were created for. And you have the best example out there to follow."

"What? You and May?" His brother did seem to have things figured out in the love department.

"No, you doof. Jesus. He's your example of love."

Levi thought about that for a minute, then stood. "Thanks for the advice, man. And for, you know, being my brother." He moved toward the door.

"You're welcome. And Levi?"

Levi looked over his shoulder.

"Let's have these talks more often."

"You're sure everything's all right?" Grace must have asked the question half a dozen times on the drive down to Chicago. She threw in one more now as the limo Levi had rented traveled toward Navy Pier.

"Of course. Why do you keep asking?"

"You seem different tonight." Quieter than usual, with a sort of nervous energy cascading from him—which, in turn, was making her nervous.

"Sorry. I've just been thinking."

"About what?" She craned her neck to look at the skyscrapers towering over them. Ahead of them, a line of limos crept toward what she assumed was their final destination.

"You." He said it quietly, but it drew her eyes to him.

"What about me?" She bit her lip against the words, but they were already out.

"I was thinking," Levi said, sliding forward on the seat and taking her hands in his, "that you look beautiful."

"Oh." Grace glanced down at the floor-length silver evening dress she'd borrowed from Jade. "Thanks."

Why was she disappointed? The man had complimented her. She shouldn't have expected something more substantial—something deeper.

"You look nice too." Nice was putting it mildly. Levi looked like a celebrity in his tailored suit coat with a white t-shirt underneath. Then again, he *was* a celebrity.

Too often, she forgot that.

Levi cleared his throat. "And I was also thinking—"

"Sir, we are next in line." The driver's voice came over the intercom. "Please be ready to exit."

Grace's eyes tracked to the window, catching on a beautiful couple walking down a red carpet surrounded by a sea of people and flashing cameras.

"Wait. We're not going to have to do that, are we?" Her stomach seesawed. There was no way . . .

"It'll be fine." Levi scooted toward the door, pulling her with him. "I'll be right at your side the whole time. But maybe—" He lifted a hand toward her face and pushed the corners of her lips up. "Try to look like you're not mortified to be seen with me. Ready?"

Before she could say no, the door of the limo opened, and he stepped out, then reached back to help her out.

Grace had no idea how she was supposed to walk in these heels, let alone walk in front of all these people, but Levi wrapped a firm arm around her back and steered her toward the glass doors.

Every few seconds, another camera flash went off, and Grace heard a few people call Levi's name. He waved and smiled, and she turned to marvel at him. How did he do this all so naturally?

Finally, they reached the building and slipped inside.

Levi's arm remained tightly around her—and she was in no rush to step out of it.

"You did great." His smile made her want to cinch up closer to him. "You can relax now. That was the hardest part of the night."

But Grace knew she couldn't relax. Because the hardest part of the night was going to be denying her undeniably real feelings for Levi Donovan.

Chapter 45

Coward.

The word had been ringing in Levi's head since in the limo when he'd told Grace she was beautiful instead of saying what he'd meant to say. Luke had told him he needed to tell her. He *knew* he needed to tell her.

But he'd taken one look into those deliciously warm eyes and realized—if she didn't feel the same way, he would be devastated.

All through dinner, all through the speeches, all through the auction, and even now, holding her in his arms as they danced, he'd been trying to convince himself to go through with it.

Man up, he scolded himself. *If you can take a hit from a three-hundred-pound defensive tackle, you can tell this woman you love her.*

He gulped in a breath. "Hey, Grace?"

"Mmm hmm?" Her head was pressed to his chest, but she picked it up to look at him.

Oh man. He was a goner.

Again.

His mouth went dry. "You want to get some air?"

"Sure." She dropped her hands from his shoulders and slipped out of his arms.

Nice move. Wouldn't it have been easier to tell her while you held her?

But he led her toward the glass doors that led out onto a wide balcony overlooking the lake. The late August night had started to cool, and a sharp breeze blew in off the water. Levi let the fresh air fill his lungs. Much better than the stifling air inside. He peeled off his jacket and settled it over Grace's shoulders.

She wiggled her arms into the oversized sleeves, and he had to laugh.

"What?" Grace grinned at him. "Do I look silly?"

"Nope." Levi stepped closer, daring to press a hand to her cheek. "You look perfect."

Her eyes came to his, and he knew. He *had* to do this.

"Grace, there's something I've been wanting to tell you all night. But I haven't known how."

"Oh no. Do I have spinach in my teeth?" She lifted a hand toward her mouth, but he caught the hand.

"Your teeth are perfect. Your eyes are perfect. Your face is perfect. Your heart and your mind and your soul are perfect."

"Levi I'm not perfect. You know that I—"

"Fine. You're not perfect."

Grace looked satisfied.

"But you're perfect for me." He lifted her hand to his lips and brushed a gentle kiss over it. "What I'm trying to say, Grace, is I love you."

"Oh." Grace didn't move.

"It's okay." His heart was somewhere down below in the lake, drowning. But he could take it. "I realize you probably don't feel the same way. I just wanted you to know."

Still she stood, frozen.

"I'm sorry." He dropped her hands. "I shouldn't have said it. I didn't mean to make things awkward for you. I'll call the driver. We'll go home and pretend this never happened." He pulled out his phone, fumbling at the screen.

What had he been thinking, taking Luke's advice?

Tell her, his brother had said.

Well, now he'd told her—and had likely completely destroyed their friendship in the process.

Grace's fingers covered his phone screen, and she gently tugged the device away from him.

"Grace, what—"

But when he looked up, her face was raised to his.

Before he could figure out what was happening or how to react, her arms were around his neck, and her lips were on his.

He almost fought it.

He didn't want her to kiss him because she felt obligated.

But the feel of her lips on his was so right.

This was no kiss of obligation.

It was a kiss of sheer delight.

Grace pinched her lower lip between her fingers as she stood alone on her porch in the early morning mist. That kiss with Levi last night had been . . . sensational.

Which one? She giggled to herself. They may have kissed a few more times as they'd danced. And in the car. And when he'd walked her to her door.

Each one had felt more right than the last.

Until she couldn't deny it anymore.

Levi Donovan loved her.

And she loved him.

She giggled again.

All right, God. You may have known what you were doing when I prayed for you to send Mr. Right to my doorstep.

She'd been too blind to see it at first, since Levi had come in a different package—a motorcycle-riding, football-playing package—than she'd expected.

A familiar tickle went through her tummy as she spotted his truck at the end of the long driveway. The faintest glow of sunlight dusted the leaves that arched over the driveway, and it gave the whole scene a golden glow.

Or maybe that was the joy in her heart.

Levi sprang out of the truck, and before she could even say hello, he had taken the steps two at a time and caught her up in his arms.

"I missed you," he murmured into her hair.

"It's been less than eight hours." But she knew what he meant as she brought her hands to his broad back. That was about eight hours too long.

He lowered his face, catching her lips between his in a long, drawn-out kiss that left her breathless when he pulled away.

Breathless and tugging him closer for another.

"Sorry I called you so early," she said when they finally pulled apart.

"You can get me up early to do that anytime." Levi brushed a hand over her cheek, sliding his fingers into her hair.

"There's another reason I wanted you to come too."

"Yes, boss." Levi gave her a mock salute with the hand that wasn't in her hair. "We have cabinets to install today."

"True." She laughed but then wrapped her arms around his waist. "But also, I love you."

Levi's exhale was loud enough to be comical. "You do?"

She lifted her face to his and answered with another kiss.

Chapter 46

This was going to drive Grace crazy. She was supposed to open this place in less than three months, and she still didn't have a name for it. Which made it impossible to advertise.

Fortunately, Tori's blog had drummed up so much interest that she already had a handful of reservations, even without a name, but this was getting ridiculous. She didn't know why the decision was so paralyzing.

"Hey you." Levi came straight to the desk she'd set up to the side of the stairway so that she'd be able to greet guests the moment they arrived. He swiveled her chair and nuzzled his face into her neck. "Want to take a break for some lunch?"

"Yes, please. I'm not getting anywhere here."

"Still?" Levi pulled her to her feet. "How about The House Without a Name? Then you don't have to worry about it."

"That's helpful." She brought her lips to his. "What would I do without you?"

"I don't know." He drew her closer, kissing her again. "Good thing I'm not going anywhere."

Grace's eyes met his. Though the past week had been blissful, filled with kisses and long conversations, one thing had hung at the back of her mind—Levi had never made a secret of the fact that he had no intention of staying in Hope Springs.

"You're not?"

He brushed her hair off her shoulder. "You're here. Why would I want to be anywhere else?"

There was only one way to respond to that. She twined her arms around him and concentrated on putting the depth of her feelings into the kiss.

His kiss said he was doing the same.

When she pulled away from him, she studied him. "You're sure you'll be happy here?"

"Like I said, you're here."

"Yes, but Levi—"

"And my dad asked me to stay and partner with him—help him expand. Plus the football team needs a coach, so . . . I'll have plenty to keep me busy."

"In that case—" She gave him a playful smile. "It just so happens that I have an announcement too."

"Yeah? What's that?"

Another kiss distracted her from answering for a moment.

"I've decided to include TVs in at least some of the rooms. I realized that night we watched the movie was the start of things for me . . ."

"Really? That early?"

"Yes. Why? When did you start to realize you had feelings for me?" Not that it mattered that she'd liked him before he'd liked her.

"Oh, way before that. The first day I met you."

"You did not." She slugged him.

"Want to bet?" Levi brought his lips to hers again.

Grace considered taking him up on that bet but decided she liked the kissing better. Her fingers played with the ends of his hair.

The sound of a throat clearing from the doorway had them jumping apart.

"I'm so sorry. I didn't hear the—" Grace choked on her own words as her eyes fell on the open door.

"Mama?" Grace smoothed her shirt, though it wasn't rumpled, then rushed forward and pulled Mama into a quick hug. "What are you doing here?"

"I wanted to surprise you." Mama squinted toward Levi, who had stepped forward as well. "Looks like I succeeded."

Grace ignored the comment, as well as Levi's half-amused smirk.

"It's nice to see you again, Mrs. Calvano." Levi held out his hand, and Mama gave it a halfhearted shake.

"Would you like a tour, Mama?"

Mama's eyes traveled over the freshly finished fireplace, the newly laid floors, the recently hung window treatments, and Grace held her breath. Mama had grown up in this house—what would she think of the changes Grace had made?

"Actually, I could use a little rest."

Grace nudged her disappointment aside. She didn't need Mama to approve of this place in order to be proud of it herself. She led Mama upstairs to the Garden Room.

"Hmm." Mama stopped in the doorway. "This was my old room."

"I know." Grace moved to close the curtains so Mama could sleep, but she couldn't resist asking, "Do you like it?"

"I sure wouldn't have minded having my own bathroom as a kid." Mama laughed and sat on the bed.

Grace smiled. That might be the closest thing to a compliment she was going to get, but she'd take it.

"So what does bring you here, Mama?"

"Can't a mama want to spend some time with her only daughter? We didn't get a lot of time together at Simeon's wedding. Everything was so crazy."

"Of course you can, Mama. I'm glad you're here. But I'm not sure how much fun I'm going to be. We only have a couple months until the grand opening, and there's a lot to do yet."

"That's what you hired Levi for, isn't it? Or do you pay him simply so the two of you can stand around and kiss all day?"

There it was.

"Mama, we don't—"

Mama held up that finger that always quieted her. "You're a grown woman Grace. If you want to kiss a man, that's your business. I thought I made my feelings about that man being Levi Donovan clear. But if you want to ignore my advice, that's your choice."

"Mama, I'm not ignoring you. I just think—"

But Mama waved her off. "We'll talk about it later. Right now, I really do need to rest."

"Your mom all settled?" Levi looked up from the sandwiches he'd been preparing as Grace returned to the dining room. With the kitchen pulled apart, they'd moved the refrigerator in here.

She nodded but didn't say anything.

"You want mustard on your sandwich?"

"Sure."

He set down the cheese he'd been about to slice. She never had mustard. He'd only asked to see if she was paying attention.

Guess he had his answer.

He stepped around the table to stand directly in front of her. "Hello?"

"Huh? Oh." She shook herself. "Sorry. What'd you say?"

"I asked if you wanted mustard."

"Oh. No thanks."

"I know." He wrapped her in his arms, but she squiggled out of his grip after a quick hug. He frowned at her as she knelt and rummaged in a box full of dishes. "What's wrong?"

"Hmm? Nothing."

"Grace, do you really think I don't know when something is wrong?" He moved to her side and rested a hand on her shoulder. "Are you embarrassed that your mom saw us kissing?"

"What? No." But she kept her eyes on the cups in her hand.

"We weren't doing anything wrong, you know. Anyway, you've been meaning to talk to your mom about us, right? This will give you the perfect opportunity." Grace had confessed the other day that one of the things that had been holding her back from giving in to her feelings sooner was her mother's disapproval. So now they could get that all squared away.

"Yeah." But she still wasn't meeting his eyes.

"Grace? You *are* going to talk to her, right?"

She sighed, and his heart dipped.

"You don't understand," she said. "It's not that easy."

"No." He pulled her to her feet and turned her to face him. "I don't understand. I love you. You love me. What does any of that have to do with your mother?"

She wiggled out of his grip and retreated to the other side of the table. "Just give me some time. Please. I promise I'll tell her. But until then, maybe you should lie low."

He blinked at her. "That's what you want?"

She bit her lip, then nodded.

"Okay." He passed her the plate with her sandwich. "Then I'll lie low. Just don't take too long. I'll miss you."

He picked up his own plate and carried it to the front porch to eat.

Chapter 47

*W*hy was this so difficult?

Grace had had three days to talk to Mama about Levi.

She and Mama had gone shopping and out to eat. They'd walked along the beach and gone to church. But never once had Grace worked up the courage to say Levi's name to Mama.

And aside from across church this morning, she hadn't seen him all weekend. He was keeping up his part of the bargain, lying low. Now it was time for her to do her part. And since Mama was leaving tomorrow, this was her last chance.

"Mama?" Grace settled onto the love seat in her sitting room, where Mama was resting with her feet up and eyes closed.

Mama had been napping a lot since she'd gotten here, which wasn't at all like the energetic woman Grace knew. Then again, she was getting older, and she'd just organized a huge women's retreat. She deserved some rest.

Mama opened her eyes. "This has been a nice visit, hasn't it?"

"It has, Mama." Grace licked her lips. "I was wondering if we could talk about something. About Levi, actually."

There. She'd brought him up.

Mama sat up, giving her a cautious look. "I noticed he hasn't been around the last couple days. I took that as a good sign."

"That's because I asked him to lie low. Until I could talk to you." When she said it out loud, it sounded horrible. She was fortunate Levi hadn't written her off then and there.

"I see." Mama's mouth went tight.

"Why don't you like him?"

Mama sighed. "If you must know, I do like him. I just don't think he's the right man for you."

"And you don't think I can decide that for myself? Did you choose Simeon's spouse for him? Or Zeb's?"

"Of course not. But this is different. You're my little girl. And—" She folded her hands in her lap, looking suddenly afraid and vulnerable.

It was enough to scare the indignant comment right off Grace's tongue and back down her throat. She waited.

Mama's exhale was long and drawn out and seemed to carry the weight of her years. "And I know what it's like to have your head turned by the wrong man. To be so in love with the idea of a man that you fail to see his shortcomings. Until it's too late."

A truck running her over couldn't have hit Grace harder. She clutched at the couch cushion. "What are you talking about? Daddy is—"

"I don't mean your daddy," Mama rushed in. "He's a wonderful, loving, God-fearing man."

"Then what are you talking about?"

Mama's hands twisted in her lap, and she refused to look at Grace. "There was a boy in high school. Ezra Talbot. I was so in love with him." Wistfulness and pain twined in Mama's voice. "But he never noticed me. Not until the end of senior year. And then, for whatever reason, he swooped in and swept me off my feet. I was blindsided. But I thought I was so, so in love." She blinked and let her eyes come to Grace's. "So in love that I conceived a child with him."

Grace's lips parted, but there were no words. She stared at Mama, and Mama stared back at her.

Finally, Grace found her voice. "What happened?"

Mama shrugged. "Soon as Ezra found out, he didn't want anything to do with me. I couldn't bear to tell my parents, so I arranged for my cousin Mary Beth in Tennessee to invite me for the summer. Her parents helped me arrange for the baby to be adopted." She drew in a shuddering breath, dropping her face into her hands.

Grace stared. She'd never seen Mama like this. She rested a tentative hand on Mama's shoulder. "You're saying I have another brother somewhere?"

"A sister." The word came out strangled.

Grace clutched Mama's arm. "I have a sister? Do you know where she is? What happened to her?"

Mama shook her head. "I didn't want to know."

"Does Daddy know? About the baby?"

"No one else knows." Mama brushed a piece of hair off Grace's forehead. "Now do you understand why I don't think Levi is right for you? I don't want you to go through the same thing I did. That night we found you and Hunter at the pond . . ."

The shame Grace had always experienced at the memory of what she'd nearly done with Hunter washed over her, but so did a new feeling. It was like being freed from a heavy weight that had chained her in place for years.

"Hunter was a mistake, Mama. One that I deeply regret. But one that I know I'm forgiven for. And you're forgiven for your sin too."

Mama pressed her lips together. "I know. But I also know how tempting it can be—"

"Mama," Grace said firmly. "I have no intention of ever making that mistake again."

Mama clutched at her hand. "I know *you* don't want to make that mistake again, Grace. And I trust you. But men like Levi—"

"Mama, Levi is—"

"There's something else, Gracey," Mama interrupted, her voice oddly quiet.

Grace froze. Mama only used that nickname when she had to deliver bad news.

Mama sat up straight and tall, the same way she'd taught Grace to, but she looked frail and older than her fifty-six years. She patted Grace's hand. "It's back."

"What's back?" But Grace knew the answer before Mama spoke, and already tears were gathering at the back of her throat.

"The cancer." Mama's voice was matter-of-fact, as if she were remarking on the return of the geese at the end of winter.

"But you had a mastectomy. You had radiation. You went through all that—" That year had been horrible and hard on all of them, but they'd come through it. Mama had survived. She was still here. She had so many years ahead of her yet. Work to do here on earth yet. That's why God had spared her. That's what she'd always said.

Mama reached over and pulled Grace into her arms. But Grace pulled away. She didn't want Mama to hold her. Mama only held her when something was wrong.

"It's everywhere this time." Mama took Grace's hand. "The doctor says there's nothing they can do. I probably have a couple months at the most. That's why I came. That's why I have to know you'll be okay. That you're not going to yoke yourself to the wrong man. Promise me, Gracey. You won't marry Levi."

This time when she reached for Grace, Grace fell into her arms, the first sob erupting into Mama's shoulder.

Forgive me, Levi.

"I promise." The words nearly tore her heart in two. But as much as she loved Levi, she couldn't deny Mama's last request. Couldn't let Mama die disappointed in her.

Chapter 48

After three days of lying low, Levi had to face it—Grace wasn't going to talk to her mom about him. She'd rather sacrifice her own happiness—and his—than risk disappointing her mother.

He rolled over and punched his pillow. He'd known, hadn't he, when he started to have feelings for Grace, that it was a mistake? Known that he couldn't live up to the ridiculous checklist she'd created for her future husband. Known that as soon as she realized that, she'd be done with him.

He just hadn't expected it to happen so quickly.

Nor had he expected it to hurt this much.

He tried to be thankful. He'd dodged another bullet. This one stung a whole lot more than Rayna, he could admit that. But he'd get over Grace—maybe not today or tomorrow, but someday.

And this time, he'd keep his pledge to remain a bachelor. Maybe date casually every once in a while. No strings. No obligations. No love.

That was what he'd wanted once, wasn't it?

He rolled to his other side, trying to shake the feeling that he'd changed. That he'd gotten a taste of what life could be like with genuine love. And he wanted more of it.

It would pass soon enough.

He closed his eyes. But the inside of his eyelids became a movie screen, playing images of Grace—Grace laughing with him, Grace mock scolding him, Grace kissing him.

Levi opened his eyes, growling into his pillow.

He wasn't going to get any sleep tonight. He slid out of bed, pulled on a t-shirt, and eased his bedroom door open.

He didn't know where he was going. Just that he couldn't stay here right now. Couldn't hold still.

A run.

That was what he needed.

He tiptoed through the house, careful not to wake Luke and his parents, and slipped out the front door. The night was darker than he'd expected, cloudless and filled with stars but no moon.

He tilted his head up, remembering the night he and Grace had spent lying on that chair under the stars, talking about everything under heaven. Talking about heaven itself, even. That was the night he'd first seen God's love in such a real and tangible way. And it was the night he'd known—she was the one.

Clearly that had been wishful thinking.

What would happen, he wondered, if he marched over there right now, told Mrs. Calvano that he didn't care what she thought, and asked Grace to marry him?

He laughed at himself. He already knew what would happen.

Grace would say no, and he'd end up more broken than he was right now.

The sound of a car drew his gaze to the street. It had to be after one in the morning. And Hope Springs was the kind of town that turned in by ten o'clock every night.

The car pulled to the curb in front of the house. For half a beat, Levi prepared to defend his family's home from an intruder.

And then his eyes picked out the silhouette behind the wheel. It was dark, but not dark enough to keep him from recognizing her.

In spite of himself, his heart sped up as if he'd gone on that run he'd been planning to take.

He waited for her to get out of the car, to explain what she was doing at his house in the middle of the night. But she just sat there, staring straight ahead, her hands still gripping the steering wheel, even though she'd shut off the engine.

After a minute, she dropped her head to the wheel, and then her shoulders started to shake.

Levi was across the yard in an instant, knocking on the passenger window.

Grace shot upright with a quiet scream, but when her eyes fell on him, she pressed the unlock button.

Levi didn't wait for a further invitation but slid into the car.

Angry. He wanted to be angry with her.

But one look at her face, and he was reaching across the seat and pulling her to him. He didn't know what was wrong, but he did know he couldn't bear to see her hurting like this.

She clutched at his shirt, her tears wetting it, as she drew in deep, shaky breaths. He stroked her hair, not saying anything, trying to just be there for her the way she'd been there for him through everything with Luke.

"I'm sorry," she said finally, letting go of his shirt and pushing herself out of his arms. "I had no right to do that."

"Of course you have the right." He skimmed a hand over the tears still tracking down her cheeks. "Do you want to talk about it?"

"Mama has cancer. She's probably not going to make it much longer."

"Ah, Grace." Levi tugged her back to him, tucking her against his chest and cradling the back of her head in his hand. "I'm so sorry."

She nodded into his chest. "I wanted to talk to her, Levi. About us." Her swallow was audible, and he rubbed her back.

"It's okay. I shouldn't have asked you to."

"No. You were right. And I did try. But she's dying, Levi." She shuddered against him. "I just can't have her last memory of me be disappointment that I didn't listen to her. Even if I know she's wrong. I'm sorry."

He ducked his head to kiss the top of hers. His heart was breaking for her. And he wasn't so unselfish that it wasn't breaking for himself too. "I understand."

She tilted her head to look up at him. "You do?" Her eyes were dark and surprised and grateful.

He thought of what May had said in the hospital. *Sometimes when you love someone, you do what's best for them. Even if it hurts you.*

"Yeah." Oh, he wanted to kiss those lips. But he resisted. "I love you, Grace. Enough to let you go."

She dropped her head to his chest again, silent tears soaking his shirt and shaking her shoulders. But after a moment she slid gently out of his arms. "I'm going to go back to Tennessee with Mama. To be with her until the end. I don't know if I'll be back. Daddy might need someone to stay and take care of him—afterward."

"What about the bed-and-breakfast?" Her life's dream. But he knew she loved her family enough to give it up for them. And he only loved her more for it.

"I guess we'll have to put a hold on things for now." Her voice broke. "I may have to look into selling at some point."

"You go. Do what you have to do. I'll take care of things here. Whenever you're ready, it'll be in shape for you to either open up or sell."

Grace studied him. "You'd do that for me?"

"I thought you already knew." Levi picked up her hand and kissed her palm, then closed her fingers around it. "I'll do anything for you. Even this." He opened the car door and stepped out. "Goodbye, Grace."

Chapter 49

"Can I get you anything else, Mama?" It took Grace's breath away, sometimes, how quickly Mama's health had deteriorated. When Grace had returned home with Mama a month ago, Mama had insisted on taking Grace out shopping or to make the rounds of the church's shut-ins she continued to minister to. But within two weeks, Mama had weakened so that they'd had to order a hospital bed for her. They'd pushed the large oak dining table aside to make room for it, and there was a constant stream of people in and out to visit Mama.

Grace's favorite times were in the evening, when she and her brothers gathered around, laughing and telling stories like it was a party. And in a way, she supposed it was. A party to celebrate Mama's life—and to rejoice in the eternal life waiting for her.

But then there were moments like this, moments when the house quieted and she had a second to just look at Mama, lying there in bed, still so spunky in spite of her weakness, that a wave of sadness nearly knocked Grace over. She knew it was selfish. Though Mama would never admit it, she was in more and more pain by the day, and she was ready to go home to her Father. But Grace wanted to keep her here. Wanted to have her Mama there on her wedding day—though without Levi, she wasn't sure she ever wanted that day to come.

He'd texted every few days, usually with questions about the finishing touches for the bed-and-breakfast. And he'd called a couple of times as well, just to see how she was doing. How Mama was doing. But as much as she appreciated the calls, appreciated the fact that he never crossed the boundaries of friendship, they always left her hurting, aching for more.

She'd thought Levi was selfish. But she was the selfish one. Because as much as she knew she could never be with him, not after she'd promised Mama, she also wanted him to still love her. The way she still loved him.

Mama held out a hand to Grace. "I'm fine, Gracey. Are you okay?"

Grace half-laughed. "Don't you go worrying about me now, Mama."

But Mama shook her head. "Until I draw my last breath, I'll still be your mama. And I know when something's bothering you."

"Of course something's bothering me, Mama." Grace took Mama's hand, then settled herself onto the edge of the bed. "I don't want to say goodbye to you."

"Oh hush." Mama frowned at her. "You know our goodbye is only temporary. I'll see you again soon enough. I think what's really bothering you is Levi Donovan."

"What? Mama, I—"

But Mama raised her index finger, and Grace closed her mouth. "I've been your mama for twenty-nine years, so don't you go thinking you can pull something over on me. I know that look in your eyes when you think of him. It's the same look your daddy gives me, same look I give him. You're in love with Levi Donovan." Though her features had grown gaunt, Mama's eyes were as sharp as ever.

Grace couldn't hold her gaze. She didn't want to lie to Mama, but she didn't want to disappoint her either. "I'm trying not to be," she whispered.

"Oh Gracey." Mama's weak arms pulled Grace closer. "I didn't know. I thought it was ..." She shook her head. "Never mind that. Does he love you too?"

Tears stabbed at the back of Grace's eyes, but she blinked them away. Now was not the time to make Mama feel bad. "Enough to say goodbye. I told him I couldn't be with him, Mama, and he understands." Oh goodness, she was going to cry after all. She sniffled, and Mama fell silent so long that Grace thought she'd fallen asleep.

She moved to stand up, but Mama reached for her again. "Does he make you happy, Gracey?"

"Levi?" Grace gave a soft laugh. "Yes, Mama. Happier than I've ever been before. But it's more than that. Deeper. It's like . . ." She searched for a way to explain it.

"Like your souls are connected."

"Yeah." Grace's voice caught on the word. "But that doesn't change anything. I made a promise to you, and I intend to keep it."

"I thought you were smarter than that." Mama's voice was flat, and Grace looked up to find a wan smile on Mama's lips. "If you love him, you shouldn't let me stand in the way."

"But you said . . ."

"I was wrong."

Grace was pretty sure she'd never heard those words from her mama before.

"It's okay, Mama. We already agreed—"

"Grace, you listen to me." Mama raised her finger yet again. "I've made plenty of mistakes in my life. But I'm not going to let keeping my daughter from the man who loves her with a sacrificial love be one of them. I'm sorry I interfered."

"You didn't interfere, Mama."

But Mama gave her a look.

"Well you did. But I know it's only because you want what's best for me. And I'm thankful for that."

Mama closed her eyes, her hands settling over her middle. "All I ever wanted was to know you'd be okay, Grace. That you'd be taken care of when I'm gone. I thought I had to be the one to set that up. But it turns out God had a better plan than I did all along. You'd think I would have figured that out by now, after all these years, wouldn't you?" Mama sighed. "Better late than never I guess."

"Get some rest, Mama." Grace brushed a kiss over Mama's forehead. "We can talk about it more later."

"There's nothing more to talk about." Mama smoothed Grace's cheek. "We both know I'm right."

Chapter 50

A we.

That was the only word that could describe how Levi felt right now, as he sat in church.

Awe that two months after doctors had been sure Luke was going to die, his brother was sitting next to him this morning, his wheelchair a thing of the past. Awe that though he'd had to let go of Grace, he felt more alive and complete for having loved her—for still loving her, even if he could never be with her.

But most of all, awe at the love of God that seemed to bounce off the walls and hang in the air this morning. Every song seemed to point to that love, to call it out, to surround him with it, and to his own surprise, he was soaking it up, basking in it, wanting to hold onto it.

He'd grown up in the church, had known about God since he was a young boy. If he was honest, it wasn't only that he'd questioned whether there *was* a God over the last few years. It was that he'd wondered how God was relevant to his life, whether God cared about him, loved him.

His dad had been right—as he'd become successful, he'd made himself into his own god. Thought he could earn his own way through life. And maybe he could—if life was only about football and money and chasing after fleeting pleasures. But the past few months had shown him that there was more at stake than life itself. There was eternity.

And he couldn't earn that himself. Not with all the skill or money or fame in the world.

He was about as unworthy of heaven as a person could be.

And yet, Jesus had saved him anyway.

Grace. That was what that was called, he remembered. Grace.

He'd been so sure that what he needed was Grace, the woman.

When what he really needed was grace, the undeserved love of God.

When I was lost, stumbling in the dark, Nate's worship band sang from the front of the church.

You came, you lit a fire in my heart.

A fire so bright that now I can see,

And darkness no longer has a hold on me.

I am free. Free in Jesus.

Levi closed his eyes. Those words. That was exactly how he felt.

Like he'd spent years stumbling in the dark, crashing into obstacles, bouncing off of walls, careening toward nothing. But now he could see. Now he knew the fire of Christ's love. Maybe for the first time in his life, he knew what it really meant. It meant he was free.

By the time church was done, Levi was buzzing with energy. He declined Jade's invitation to join the group for lunch. He was nearly done with things at Grace's bed-and-breakfast, and he wanted to wrap them up, both because he wanted it to be ready for whatever she decided to do with it and because Dad had a new job he wanted Levi to get started on.

When he reached the bed-and-breakfast, he headed straight for Grace's private sitting room. He knew she hadn't been planning to do any remodeling in here, but he couldn't resist making a few updates for her.

He told himself that it was because he wanted to do something nice for her, to thank her for helping him find his way back to what was important—his family, his friends, and his faith. But he knew it was also at least partly selfish. Being in this part of the house made him feel closer to her. And he maybe secretly hoped that every time she looked around at the walls he'd painted her favorite shade of lavender, she'd think of him. Unless she decided to sell—in which case having this area spruced up should help.

The thought of not coming here every day—of not seeing Grace every day—made his heart ache. But it wasn't the sharp ache of disappointment. More the sweet ache of knowing he was doing what was best for her.

It was what he prayed every day—that God's will be done in her life.

Not that his thoughts hadn't been filled with her every minute for the past month. Or that it didn't nearly kill him every time he texted or talked to her not to say those three words that flashed in his head the whole time. Not to beg her to please, please ignore the wishes of her dying mother and say she'd be with him.

But even he wasn't *that* selfish.

His phone buzzed in his pocket, and though he didn't recognize the number, he answered—just in case.

"Levi?" The voice was familiar, but he couldn't place it.

"Yes?"

"This is Heather Calvano."

"Mrs. Calvano." Levi snapped to attention, as if he'd just been caught snooping through Grace's private things. "Is Grace okay? Are you okay?"

"Yes. Yes. Everything's fine." Though Mrs. Calvano's voice was weaker than he remembered, she managed to convey her impatience.

"Oh. Good." Levi was at a loss. As far as he knew, there was no playbook for talking to the mother of the woman you loved but couldn't be with because of said mother. "Do you mind if I ask why you're calling then? If this is about me and Grace, I can assure you that there's nothing—"

"That's the problem," Mrs. Calvano cut in.

"I'm sorry. That's the . . ."

"Problem. Yes. Did you know that my Gracey loves you?"

Levi backed into the coffee table behind him, dropping onto it with a thud. "I did know that, yes."

"And she says you love her too?"

Levi blew out a long breath. "Yes, but—"

"No buts."

Levi drew himself up. Mrs. Calvano might be Grace's mother, and she might be dying. But that wasn't going to stop him from saying this. "*But—*" he emphasized. "I understand why you don't approve. And I understand why Grace doesn't want to go against your wishes. So you don't have to worry that I'm going to do anything about my feelings."

"That's a shame." Mrs. Calvano's voice had gone quiet. "Because I was wrong."

"You were . . ."

"Wrong." The word snapped through the phone. "You sure could work on your listening."

"Yes, ma'am." Levi scrubbed a hand over his unshaven cheek. "Sorry. You're catching me by surprise here."

"I'm catching myself by surprise too. I thought it was my job to protect Gracey from men like you. But that was just me letting my own past mistakes get in the way."

He heard her draw in a labored breath. "You don't want to hear about all of that. All you need to know is that Gracey is going to need you. She's a strong girl, and feisty."

Levi chuckled, picturing all the times she'd proven that. "That she is."

"But she's soft too. Sensitive. Always trying to make sure everyone else is taken care of before herself. I need to know you're going to put her first, before yourself. Can you promise me that?"

Levi closed his eyes, an image of Grace filling his whole being. "Mrs. Calvano, the only one above Grace in my life is Jesus." He'd never thought of it in those terms, but it was true, he realized now. His rekindled love for his Savior burned with a fierceness that had taken him completely by surprise. Not even his love for Grace could hold a candle to it. But he knew that was the way Grace wanted it too.

"That's all I wanted to hear." Mrs. Calvano's voice trailed off, and Levi was at a loss as to what to say next.

He was searching for a way to end the conversation when she spoke again. "And you plan to marry her?"

A bright, unbridled hope flared through him. Until a few minutes ago, he hadn't even allowed himself to hope for a moment alone with her. And now her mama was talking marriage.

"Yes, ma'am. If she'll have me."

"Good. Then I think my work here is done. You take good care of my baby girl, Levi Donovan."

"I will." Levi swallowed against a sudden swell of gratitude for Grace's mother, who even as she faced her own death was taking care of everyone else. "And Mrs. Calvano?"

"Yes?" She was sounding weaker.

"I think I know where Grace gets her habit of putting others before herself. You've raised a wonderful daughter."

"Thank you, Levi. Son."

Levi pressed his fingers to the insides of his eyes as he hung up. That might be the first and last time he'd ever hear that word from the woman he hoped would be his future mother-in-law.

Chapter 51

"You're sure you'll be all right, Daddy?" The airport buzzed around them, but Grace set down her luggage. In the two weeks since Mama's death, Grace had been busy helping with funeral arrangements and receiving guests who came to offer condolences and keeping Daddy and her brothers fed and cared for. But now the boys had returned to their lives—and Daddy insisted it was time for her to do the same. But she couldn't bear to think of him going through his days alone.

"You know I'd be happy to stay with you." She tried again. "Make your favorite hot chicken every day."

Daddy laughed. "I don't think that would be too good for my heart. Or for yours." He gave her a shrewd look, and Grace ducked her head.

"Your Mama told me about how she tried to keep you from seeing Levi." Daddy poked a finger under her chin to lift her head. "She also told me to make sure you didn't let that stop you from being with him. You can't stay here with me to hide from that."

"I'm not hiding," Grace mumbled, even though some small part of her knew that wasn't true. Because going back to Hope Springs meant facing Levi—and the possibility that he'd already moved on and found someone else.

"Gracey." Daddy pulled her into a hug. "You've spent so much of your life taking care of others. Now it's time for you to go and live your someday."

"I'm scared." The whisper slipped out before she could stop it. Daddy had enough worries of his own. She didn't need to burden him with hers too.

He squeezed her tighter, then let go and passed her the luggage. "I know. But you know what I always say."

"Do not be afraid; do not be discouraged, for the Lord your God will be with you wherever you go." Grace quoted Daddy's favorite verse from Joshua.

"That's my girl." Daddy patted her cheek. "Now go. With my blessing. And Mama's."

She nodded and steeled her shoulders, pointing herself toward the gate.

"Wait. Grace." Daddy passed her a piece of paper. "Mama wanted you to have this. She said she doesn't know who adopted your sister. But the adoption agency was in Nashville."

"She told you?"

Daddy nodded as Grace peeled the piece of paper open. It had the address of an adoption agency. And a name: Lydia.

"She didn't know if they kept the baby's name or not," Daddy said. "But she thought it might be a starting point."

"A starting point?"

"To look for her."

Grace watched him. He'd aged over the past month and a half, but he still stood straight and tall. She'd always thought of him as an unmovable force. "Do you want me to look?"

Daddy gazed out over the bustling crowd. "I still can't believe she kept that secret for almost forty years. But I'm glad she told me in the end. And this daughter is a part of her. So yes, I'd like to get to know her." Daddy cleared his throat and nudged her away. "Now get going before you miss your plane. I'll talk to you soon."

Grace obeyed, tucking the slip of paper into her pocket. She had no idea how easy or difficult it would be to find someone who had been adopted nearly forty years ago. But for Mama's sake, she was going to try.

She was so caught up in her thoughts that the flight passed in a blink. As she stepped off the plane, she took a deep breath. She was glad she'd been able to be there for her family.

But it was good to be home.

She made her way toward the coffee shop Jade had offered to pick her up from.

But she stopped short thirty feet from it.

That was not Jade.

Unless Jade had gotten a major makeover.

The moment he spotted her, Levi was on the move, dodging bodies, weaving against the current of people to get to her.

Never once did he take his eyes off her, and his face wore a mix of concern and joy and love—at least she thought it might be love.

Grace's pulse hummed as she waited for him to reach her, and her lips rose into an involuntary smile. But most of all, her heart sang.

And then his arms were around her in a bear hug of football player sized proportions.

She could barely breathe, but she didn't care. His arms around her offered her comfort and reassurance she hadn't even realized she needed.

"What are you doing here?" Her voice was muted by his shirt, but he must have heard her because she felt a chuckle rumble through his chest.

"I may have bribed Jade to let me come pick you up."

"Bribed her with what?"

"A night babysitting Hope and Matthias."

It was her turn to laugh. "You know, you probably could have gotten a lot more out of her for that."

"This was all I wanted."

He loosened his hold on her, leaning back so he could look into her eyes. "I'm so sorry about your mom. I've been praying for your family."

"Thank you." She swallowed hard. A lot of people had told her they were praying for her family over the past weeks, but none had meant quite as much as this. Levi took her bag as they headed for the exit.

She considered slipping her hand into his but decided against it.

Just because he'd come to pick her up, just because he'd hugged her, didn't mean he wanted to start over where they'd left off. She'd walked out on him over a month ago. And she wouldn't blame him if he couldn't get over that.

"I have a surprise for you." Levi nudged her shoulder as they stepped into the parking garage.

"Oh yeah? What's that?"

"You'll see." They walked in silence, Levi grinning the entire time. Finally, when her curiosity was about to get the best of her, he paused at a silver sedan. "Ta-da."

She stared. Why was he showing her some stranger's car?

Levi rolled his eyes and pulled out a key fob. He pressed a button, and the car's trunk popped open.

"This is your car?"

"Yep."

"You didn't get rid of the bike, did you?"

He stowed her bag in the trunk, then turned to her. "Why?"

She shrugged. "It's just so . . . you."

"And you like the bike."

"I mean, I—"

"You like it," Levi crowed. "I knew it. And to answer your question, no, I didn't get rid of the bike. Just thought it was time to get something a little more practical too."

"Okay . . ." She slid into the passenger seat as he opened the door for her.

She didn't remember ever telling him that "drives a sensible car" was item number five on her checklist for Mr. Right. He now officially checked every box, even if not in the way she'd expected.

Tell him, a voice urged. *Tell him you want to be with him.*

Grace opened her mouth. "Did I tell you I have a sister?" Those were not the words she'd been planning to say. But now that they were out, she knew she needed to talk about it.

Levi looked at her in surprise. "You do?"

She launched into the story of Mama's confession, of how she'd lived all those years with a secret of that magnitude eating at her heart.

"Wow," Levi finally said as they drove into Hope Springs. "That's a lot to take in."

"You're telling me." She chewed her lip. "I haven't said anything to the boys yet. I thought I'd wait and see how the search goes."

Levi turned to glance at her. "And you're sure you want to find her?"

"Yes. I mean, I think so. I don't know." She laughed. "Sorry, my emotions have been a little mixed up lately."

He took his hand off the wheel to give hers a quick squeeze, letting it linger a moment. "You're allowed. You've gone through a lot. But if you want to try to find your sister, I'll help."

A fresh rush of love for this man washed over her.

"Look—" Levi spoke up as he signaled to turn into the driveway of her house. "I have another surprise for you. But I'm not sure you're going to like it. And if you don't, you can tell me. I promise I won't be upset."

"Why wouldn't I like—" But as Levi stopped the car, tears filled her throat and kept her from saying anything else.

At the side of the driveway was a beautiful wooden sign carved with the words, "Heather House Inn."

Grace brought a hand to her mouth, pressing her lips tight in a vain attempt to hold back the sobs.

"I know I had no right to name your place. But it came to me the other day, and I just thought, with the heather on the hills behind the inn, and your mom's—"

"My mom's name." She managed to control her tears enough to say it. "It's perfect. I don't know why I didn't think of that. It's what this place was meant to be all along. Thank you."

Levi nodded and continued down the driveway to the house. "You ready for the tour?"

"I have one more surprise for you." Levi had loved every minute of taking Grace through the completed bed-and-breakfast. Watching the sparkle come back to her eyes, the flush to her cheeks, the joy to her voice—it made every ounce of sweat and effort worth it. "Close your eyes."

"I'm not sure if I can handle any more surprises today." But she dutifully closed her eyes and let him take her hand in his.

Perfect.

She'd used that word a hundred times as he'd shown her around the place. But *this* was what was perfect.

The two of them.

Together.

He only prayed she felt the same way. If not now, then maybe someday.

He steered her carefully through the kitchen to her living space at the back of the house. Opening the new French doors that led into her sitting room, he took her elbow and gently pulled her into the room.

Nerves tried to wriggle into his gut. What if she didn't like it? But he pushed them aside. It was too late to undo it now. And if she hated it, he'd put it all back the way it had been before.

"Open your eyes."

Without a second of hesitation, her eyes sprang open.

"Oh my goodness. Levi." Her hands went to her mouth, and she took a step back. She shook her head. "I don't . . ."

There was no holding the nerves back now. She didn't like it. "I'm sorry. This is your space. I shouldn't have—"

But she threw herself into his arms, nearly knocking him off his feet with her petite form.

"Are you kidding?" She was laughing and crying all at once. "I love it. It's just so . . . me."

She stepped out of his arms, and he forced himself not to grab her back up as she took a slow tour of the room, exclaiming over how he'd chosen the perfect colors and the perfect furniture. She paused especially long at a wooden sign he'd purchased from the little store Sophie and her family ran at Hidden Blossom Farms.

She ran a finger over the words: *Faith, Hope, Love.* "Daddy's message at Mama's funeral was based on 1 Corinthians 13:13. Same as their wedding day," she said. "It's perfect."

Then her eyes fell on the flamingo Levi had won at the Messtival, drawing out a laugh. "And so is this." She picked it up and hugged it, then tucked it back onto the shelf.

When she'd finished her tour of the room, she returned to his side. "I don't know why you did all of this for me, Levi. But thank you."

"You don't know why I did it?" Levi caught her hands in his, letting his eyes roam her face. "It's because I love you, Grace. I love you so much that it feels like you're a part of me sometimes." He lifted a hand to her cheek. "The best part."

"Levi, I . . ."

"Did you know your mama called me?"

Grace's head popped up. "She did?"

He nodded, leading her to the white love seat he'd picked out for this room. "A couple days before she died. She apologized. Said she'd been wrong to keep us apart. Was pretty adamant that we be together, actually."

Grace shook her head. "And here I thought I was going to miss Mama meddling in my love life. She told me the same thing, but I didn't know if . . ."

He caught her hands in his, pulled them to his heart. "Here's the thing, Grace. I love you. And I'd love for you to consider being in a relationship with me someday. But not because your mom told you to. Not to please me either. I want this to be completely your decision. Okay?"

Grace shook her head, and he forced himself not to fall to his knees right here and beg her to give him a chance. He'd told her it had to be her decision, and he'd meant it. "I understand."

"No." Grace brought his hands to her heart now. "I don't think you do. The part that isn't okay is that I'm done waiting until someday. I want to be with you now."

"But—"

Grace touched a finger to his lips. "Trust me, Levi. I'm not doing this to make Mama happy or to make you happy. I'm doing it because you make *me* happy. And I don't want to waste another moment waiting for someday. I love you *now*."

Chapter 52

"You look more nervous than I do." Luke slapped Levi on the back as Dad adjusted the bow tie threatening to cut off Levi's air supply. Why Luke had insisted that his groomsmen wear the torture devices was beyond him, but being that it was his brother's wedding day, Levi was trying to go along with it.

"I think I might be." Levi tugged at the bow tie. "At least your girl already said yes. You're sure you're okay with me asking Grace today? It's your big day. I can wait."

"I doubt that you can." Luke grinned at him. "Besides, I shouldn't be the only one who gets to be this happy today. How much longer? I can't wait to get out there." Luke's excitement was almost tangible as he moved a little closer to the door of the church conference room where they'd been getting ready.

Across the hall, May and her bridesmaids were doing the same. Levi couldn't count how many times he'd been tempted to pop over there and talk to Grace. But he'd held himself back.

It may not be his wedding day, but he still wanted to be surprised the first time his eyes fell on Grace today. He wanted to experience that heady rush of joy that washed over him every time he saw her. To imagine what it would be like when it *was* their wedding day. Because over the four months they'd been officially dating—since that day she'd said she didn't want to wait until someday to be with him—he'd grown more and more certain. Grace Calvano was the woman he wanted to spend the rest of his life with. The woman he wanted to wake up next to in the morning and lie down next to at night and spend every waking moment of every day with in between.

"There you are." Dad finally finished adjusting the bow tie and clapped a hand on Levi's shoulder. His eyes met Levi's. "I'm proud of you, son." Dad cleared his throat. "Of the man you are. I'm glad you found your way back."

Levi rolled his shoulder out from under Dad's clasp. Now was not the time to get all mushy. Even if Dad's eyes had grown misty and his own felt a bit prickly. "Thanks, Dad."

A knock drew everyone's attention to the door, and Dan poked his head in, giving Luke a thumbs-up. "It's time."

As the men filed out of the room, Levi grabbed Luke's arm. "Hey. Before we go out there, I want to say thank you."

"For what?" Luke moved his cane forward a step, and Levi could tell he was in a hurry to get to his bride.

"For, you know, being there for me. Even though I wasn't always there for you."

"You're here now." Luke threw a quick arm around Levi's back. "And that means a lot to me. Now if you don't mind, I've got a bride to meet."

"What are you waiting for then?" Levi opened the door and waited for Luke to pass through, then followed him down the hallway to a door at the front of the church. Levi patted his jacket pocket. He'd been careful to put Luke's rings in there. He didn't want to get them mixed up with the one in his pants pocket.

The one for later.

As he took his place next to Luke at the front of the church to wait for the bridesmaids to file in, Levi let his gaze drift over all the people gathered in the seats. The church was full, and Levi's heart was fuller. All these people were here to wish his brother and May well in their new life together. They were all here as witnesses to the vow that Luke and May would make before God to love and honor and cherish one another until the end of their days.

Neither of them knew when that would be. But both of them were willing to step out in faith, trusting that God would guide their lives.

A year ago, Levi had almost entirely written off that kind of faith. And now?

Now God had restored that faith to him—strengthened it, actually. As a kid and into his teens, he'd mostly believed because it was what his parents had told him to do. But his faith had never been tested, never really become his own.

Now, after years without God, he could genuinely say that his faith was real, and that it mattered more than anything else in his life.

As the processional began, Levi watched two of May's friends start down the aisle, met halfway by Luke's two other groomsmen. And then Grace was gliding toward him, her face a picture of pure radiance, her smile seeming to glow from the inside out as her eyes met his.

He had no idea if the music was still playing, no idea if people were watching them, no idea even if he was still upright. The only thing he knew was that he was approaching the woman who had woven herself inextricably into the very fiber of his being.

"Hey you," he whispered as he tucked her hand into the crook of his elbow.

"Hey yourself." She let him lead her to the altar, where he reluctantly let her take her place with the bridesmaids as he took his with the groomsmen.

But all through the ceremony—as Dan offered his message, as Luke and May exchanged vows, as he handed the rings over to them—his eyes kept coming back to Grace. And every time, hers were on him too.

By the time the service was over, he was ready to drop to one knee right here in front of the entire congregation.

But he knew Grace wouldn't like that. She would want something more private. Quiet. Just the two of them.

Still, he couldn't wait much longer or the words would burst from him.

He managed to wait until they had walked back up the aisle and congratulated Luke and May with hugs all around.

But as guests began to filter out to greet the beaming bride and groom, he tugged Grace's hand. "Will you come with me for a moment?"

She looked from him to the guests. "Now? Don't we need to get to the reception to make sure everything is ready?"

"We will. I just want a minute alone with you first. Luke knows about it." Levi tugged her hand, pulling her to the new stairway that had been put in alongside the church after the old, worn one had been damaged in the tornado.

"Levi, we really should—" She tried to slide her hand out of his, but he kept pulling.

"I know. I promise, we'll go right back up. It's just I—" He stopped in the sand at the bottom of the steps. He'd been planning to lead her down the beach, to the water's edge, but he was done waiting. He was going to do this right here, right now.

He dropped to one knee, ignoring the sand spilling into his shoe.

"Levi." Grace's hands clutched at his shoulders.

He'd spent months trying to come up with the right thing to say when this moment came. But now that it was here, there was only one thing that mattered. "Grace Calvano. You told me once that you wanted to get married and have a family someday. With the right man. I know I'm not the man you expected, not the man you—"

She dropped into the sand in front of him, on her knees. "Levi Donovan. You are exactly the man I want."

His heart was already soaring, but he had to do this properly. He took the ring out of his pocket. "In that case, I want to make today our someday. Will you marry me?"

"I will." She launched herself into his arms, her lips meeting his as they tipped over. Their kiss was filled with laughter and sand and so much love Levi was pretty sure his heart had burst into ribbons of confetti.

When they finally pulled apart, Levi brushed a patch of sand off her arm. "We should probably get back up there."

"In a minute." Grace brought her lips to his again. "I've been waiting a long time for this someday, and I'm going to savor it."

Epilogue

G race ran her hands down the smooth white satin of her dress.
How many times had she put on a bridesmaid dress, wondering when it would be her turn to wear white? And now here she was.

Was this how Mama had felt, looking at herself in this dress all those years ago when she'd married Daddy?

Like she was the most blessed woman in the world to be marrying a man who loved her so completely?

She picked up the picture of Mama that sat on her dresser. "I miss you, Mama," she whispered. "I wish you were here to share this day with me."

She swiped a quick finger under her eye before she could ruin the makeup Jade had so carefully applied only moments ago. The ceremony would start in a few minutes, and Grace was ready.

So ready.

There was a tap on the door, and Grace called, "Come in."

Daddy popped his head in the door but froze the moment his eyes fell on her. He blinked. Then blinked again and cleared his throat.

"Daddy." She went to him, and he wrapped her in the same hug he'd been giving her since she was a little girl.

"You look just like your Mama on our wedding day." Daddy's voice was choked up but also filled with joy. "She would be so proud of you."

"Thank you, Daddy. That means a lot." She hesitated, then made herself ask the question that had been weighing on her. "And you?"

"What about me?"

"It's been nine months since Mama . . ."

Daddy patted her hand. "I'm happy, Grace. Mama's in heaven with our Savior—and someday I'll get to be there too. But today I'm so happy I get to be here for this."

"You ready?" Jade ducked into the room. "Oh my goodness, look at you." She circled Grace. "You look like that dress was always made for you."

Daddy held out an arm, and Grace looped her hand around it as he led her into the kitchen, where her bridesmaids were lined up, waiting their turn to step through the French doors that led out to the backyard of the Heather House Inn, which had been transformed into the perfect outdoor wedding venue. The Heather House Inn had been open for six months now, and the rooms were almost always full. But Grace had blocked off this week for her family, and she was so grateful for the time she'd gotten to spend with her father and her brothers over the past few days. Her only regret was that she hadn't been able to locate her half-sister yet. But she wasn't giving up.

The processional music began outside, and a flutter of something went through Grace's middle. Not nerves. More like pure, unbounded joy.

She burst into laughter.

Daddy cut a glance at her, the same way he had from the pulpit when she was little and would start acting up in church.

But she couldn't help it. God had been so *good* to her. There was nothing else she could do.

Fortunately, she managed to get her giggles under control seconds before she stepped through the French doors and onto the patio.

Because the moment she saw Levi, tears shimmering in his eyes, she was in tears too.

It was too much. This love she felt surrounding her. She didn't know what to do with it all. What she'd ever done to deserve it.

Nothing.

That was the beautiful thing. She'd done nothing to deserve this love. But God had given it to her anyway.

As she reached the front of the aisle, she turned to kiss her daddy on the cheek, then took Levi's hand.

That first day when he'd knocked on the door of her house, she'd had no way of knowing that he'd come knocking on the door of her heart too.

No way of knowing that God had knocked it out of the park, answering her prayer to send Mr. Right to her doorstep.

But now she could see that God had a plan for her all along. What was it Jade had said? God saw her plans and laughed, then showed her that his plans were even better.

She really should listen to her friend more often.

Levi led her to the spot where Dan stood, waiting to marry them.

As he began the service, Grace committed to remembering every word, remembering every detail, of this day. The way Levi's calloused yet gentle hands felt in hers, the way the breeze played with the loose hairs around her face and blew her veil across her shoulders, the way the scent of the heather drifted up from the hill to remind her of Mama, the way the crash of the waves on the beach below formed the perfect backdrop to Dan's message about faith, hope, and love.

"But the greatest of these is love," she and Levi whispered along as Dan read.

All too soon, the ceremony was over, and they were greeting their friends and family, enjoying the meal Leah had catered, and dancing under the stars long into the evening.

Finally, when the grounds had grown quiet, with the last of the guests on their way home and Grace's family tucked into their rooms inside, Grace got the moment alone with her new husband that she'd been waiting for all day.

"Hey you." Levi drew her into his arms, teasing her lips with a slow, lingering kiss.

"Hey yourself." She wrapped her arms around his neck, letting his breath play across her lips.

"So how was your day?" Levi pulled her down onto a chair with him, settling her onto his lap, and snugging her in tight.

"I'd say it pretty much met the definition of perfect." She traced the outline of his lips with her finger. "This someday was well worth waiting for."

"My wife," he whispered. "Our someday is just beginning."

Thanks for reading NOT UNTIL SOMEDAY! I hope you loved Grace and Levi's story! Catch up with them and all your Hope Springs friends in NOT UNTIL NOW, the next uplifting, emotional book in the Hope Springs series!

Also be sure to sign up for my newsletter to get Ethan and Ariana's story, NOT UNTIL CHRISTMAS, as my free gift to you. Visit www.valeriembodden.com/gift to join.

And if you're wondering about all those brothers (and mystery sister) of Grace's, don't miss the River Falls series.

A preview of Not Until Now

"Now what, Lord?" Kayla whispered the words into the silence of her car, an unfamiliar restlessness gathering in her soul as she eased the hand accelerator toward the steering wheel to pick up speed on the highway.

She'd always believed God opened and closed doors in a person's life for a reason—but she was struggling to understand the reason he'd literally close the doors of the camp for disabled children that she'd worked at for the past decade. The place that had gotten her through the hardest time in her life. That had given her a purpose again. That had helped her find him again.

Even so, she trusted he would open another door eventually. "It'd be nice if you'd let me know what kind of door to look for," she muttered, although she knew that wasn't how God tended to work. More likely, she'd walk through the door without realizing it, not seeing it until she had the benefit of hindsight.

In the meantime, she'd focus on enjoying this visit with her brother and sister-in-law in Hope Springs. The small tourist town on the shores of Lake Michigan always eased her spirit. And with Vi's baby due in a little over a month, she could be there to help out. Her heart filled with joy once again that after years of worrying it would never happen, Vi and Nate's dream of starting a family was at last coming true. And that she was going to be an aunt. She had every intention of spoiling her niece or nephew rotten.

Her own biological clock gave a tiny twinge, but she ignored it. In order to have a baby, she'd have to marry, and in order to marry, she'd have to date—and in order to date, she'd have to give up some of her independence. An independence she'd worked too hard to regain after her spinal cord injury to give it up for any man.

She settled back into her seat, letting herself pour out her hopes and fears and joys and disappointments to the Lord as the miles passed. By the time she neared Hope Springs, the sun was setting, but her soul felt like new life had been breathed into it. Whatever happened next was in God's hands.

She turned onto the road that would take her the last ten miles into the town, lowering the car's visor as the angle of the setting sun directed its beams directly into her eyes. The car in front of her was driving slower than the speed limit, but she didn't mind. She opened her window a crack, inhaling deeply even as she shivered in the frigid November wind that whistled into the car. The scent of pine and cold tickled her nose, and she smiled. She'd enjoy Thanksgiving and Christmas with Nate and Vi, then figure out her next step from there.

"See, Lord, I can be pa—" She gasped as the car in front of her swerved once, then veered off the road and into the ditch, where it traveled a good fifty yards before coming to a stop.

Shoving the hand control forward to slow her own car, Kayla jerked the wheel toward the shoulder. Jamming the car into park, she grabbed her phone and punched in 911. As soon as it started to ring, she hit speaker and tossed the phone into the center console, then opened her door. Reaching toward the passenger seat, she gripped her wheelchair frame and flipped it over herself and out the open door. With her other hand, she shoved a wheel onto the frame. Then, balancing the chair against the door, she yanked the other wheel across the seat and rammed it on before she shoved her seat cushion into place.

"911. What's your emergency?" The voice came from the phone she'd stashed in the console.

"There's been an accident on Highway 10." Thank goodness she'd driven this way enough that the roads had become familiar to her. "A car went in the ditch."

Kayla barely heard the woman's reply that a squad car was on the way as she braced her hands on the seat to scoot her bottom as close to the edge of the car as possible. Bracing her left hand on her wheelchair and gripping the steering wheel with her right, she shifted her body into the chair. Quickly, she lifted one leg at a time onto the chair's footrest, then backed away from her car. She scanned the scene but could see no indication of what had caused the accident. The road was deserted, and though it was cold, there was no ice.

She eyed the shallow ditch, then with a quick decisiveness leaned back and gave a tug on her wheels to pull her chair into a wheelie. With her hands firm on the hand rims, she guided the chair in a controlled roll down the small hill and through the dried grass toward the car.

When she reached the car, she let her front wheels drop. Through the driver's window, she could see a woman's form slumped over the steering wheel, and her breath caught. "Please, Lord, no."

"Please help." The faint sound of a child's voice yanked Kayla's attention to the back seat. A little girl with tear streaked cheeks gazed at her with wide eyes.

Kayla turned her wheelchair so she could open the girl's door. "Help is coming. Are you okay?"

"Mommy!" The girl bolted out of the car and tugged open the driver's door, clutching her mom's arm and shaking it.

Kayla reached gently for the girl. "Help is coming," she repeated. "They'll help your mommy." *Please, Lord, let that be true.* "Can you tell me what happened?"

The girl blinked at her, and Kayla wasn't sure she'd understood the question. But just as she was about to ask again, the girl said, "We were coming home from riding lessons, and I asked Mommy if we could get ice cream, and she said no, and I said, 'pretty please with a cherry on top,' and she said, 'Ruby Jane.' And then she took both hands off the steering wheel and grabbed her head and didn't say anything else. And then we went off the road. I didn't mean to make her mad." The girl's eyes filled with tears again.

Kayla reached for her hand and held it tight. "I'm sure she wasn't mad. Your name is Ruby Jane?"

"Just Ruby. Mommy only calls me Ruby Jane when I'm sassy."

"Okay, Ruby. My name is Kayla."

In the distance, the sound of sirens cut through the sharp air. "Here comes the ambulance. Let's get out of their way." She and Ruby moved away from the car as an ambulance pulled onto the shoulder and paramedics scrambled out.

"Kayla?" One of the paramedics did a double take. Nate and Vi's friend Jared. "Are you all right?"

She nodded. "I was following their car when it went off the road."

"Did you see what caused it?"

Kayla shook her head. "Nothing that I noticed. But Ruby said her mom grabbed her head before driving off the road."

Jared nodded, giving her a grim look. His eyes went past her to Ruby. "And you're Ruby? I think I've seen you at church."

The girl nodded.

"Are you hurt?"

The girl nodded again, and Kayla's stomach dropped. How could she not have thought to check the girl for injuries?

"Where does it hurt?" Jared moved closer and squatted in front of Ruby.

She held up her hand, revealing a band-aid on her finger. A relieved laugh escaped Kayla.

"Anywhere else?"

Ruby shook her head.

"Good." Jared straightened. "Can you tell me your mom's name?"

"Bethany Moore." Ruby's voice was timid but proud.

"All right, good job, sweetie. Why don't you go with Kayla and wait over there? We're going to help your mom." He jogged toward the car, where another paramedic had already begun working on Bethany.

"Come on." Kayla led Ruby toward her own car. It was too cold for the little girl to stand out here without a jacket.

"What are they doing to her?" The girl's eyes went straight back to the car in the ditch the moment Kayla had gotten her settled into the back seat.

Kayla glanced over her shoulder, to where the paramedics were lifting Bethany onto a stretcher. "That's my friend Jared, and he's really good at helping people who are hurt, so you don't have to be scared. He's going to help your mom." She sent up a quick prayer for God to guide Jared's hands.

"Where are they taking her?"

Kayla bit her lip. "They're going to bring her to the hospital to get her more help."

"What about me?" The girl sounded so lost that Kayla wanted to sweep her into her arms. But she didn't want to scare her more. The truth was, she had no idea what would happen to the girl now.

"Can you stay with her?" Jared called as they reached the shoulder with the stretcher. "Ethan's on his way in another rig. He's going to want to check the girl. And the police are going to need your statement." They slid the stretcher into the ambulance.

"Of course." The words were barely out of her mouth before Jared climbed into the ambulance, pulling the door closed behind him seconds before the ambulance roared off, its sirens shrieking and lights flashing in the gathering dusk.

"Mommy." Ruby's voice cracked, and this time Kayla leaned over to pull her into a hug.

"It will be okay. We'll go see her in a few minutes." She didn't know where the *we* had come from. But she *did* know she wasn't leaving this little girl until she knew Ruby wouldn't be alone.

A police car and a second ambulance rolled to a stop, and Nate and Violet's friend Ethan jumped out of the ambulance and jogged toward them, a police officer close behind.

"Hi, Kayla." He squatted next to her wheelchair and looked at the girl in Kayla's arms. "Who's your friend?"

"This is Ruby." Kayla shifted so Ethan could get a better view of the girl.

"Hi, Ruby. How old are you? Wait—" He held up a finger. "Don't tell me. Twenty."

"I'm seven." The girl giggled, and Kayla could have hugged Ethan. She supposed knowing how to comfort kids came with the territory, since he was a dad.

"Seven?" Ethan feigned shock. "You're way too brave to be seven. Does anything hurt?"

The girl shook her head, and Ethan pulled out a pen light and shined it into her eyes, then unwound the stethoscope from around his neck. After listening to her heart and checking her pulse, he felt her arms, legs, and head. "Well, it looks like you're as healthy as a horse."

The girl giggled again.

Instead of getting up, Ethan settled onto the gravel, as if he were going to stay for a chat. The police officer, who had been examining the crashed car, came up behind him. "Can you tell me what happened?"

"Mommy was driving me home from riding lessons, and I was asking for ice cream." Guilt flooded into the girl's face again, and Kayla rubbed her back. "And she said my name, and then she grabbed her head like this—" Ruby lifted her hands to her temples and squeezed her head. "And then she drove off the road."

"Did she say anything else after that?" Ethan asked.

Ruby shook her head. "I kept calling for her, but she wouldn't answer me. I prayed that God would send someone to help us. And he did."

Kayla let out a shaky breath. *Is that why you brought me here right now, Lord?*

"He sure did." Ethan glanced at Kayla with a quick smile, but his eyes were somber. She wanted to ask what he was thinking but didn't want to scare the girl. Ethan hopped up from the ground and held out a hand to Ruby. "Want to take a ride in my ambulance?"

Ruby looked to Kayla. "Can you come with me?"

"Of course." She had no idea if that was allowed or not, but one way or another, she was sticking with this girl.

"Actually, I need you to stay and give your statement," the officer chimed in.

"I don't want to go without Kayla." Tears splattered onto the little girl's cheeks.

Kayla turned to Ethan. "Can you wait a few minutes?"

Ethan nodded. "For my friend, Ruby? Of course."

"Let's go over here." The officer gestured toward his car, and Kayla followed, making sure to give Ruby a reassuring thumbs up over her shoulder.

After she'd recounted how the car had gone off the road, the officer lowered his voice, asking, "And was the driving erratic before the incident? Crossing the center line, changing speed abruptly . . ."

Kayla bit her lip. "The car was going a little slowly, but nothing erratic that I noticed."

The officer gave a knowing nod. "Probably drunk," he muttered.

Kayla's heart sank. She had only too much experience of the cost of drunk driving. But she didn't want to believe that any mother would drive drunk with her child in the back seat.

An overwhelming desire to protect the girl overcame her. "What will happen to Ruby?"

The officer shrugged. "We'll notify family. I found the mother's phone, but she doesn't have any emergency contacts listed. Hopefully, the little girl knows her dad's name. Otherwise, it could take a bit to track someone down."

They made their way back to Ethan and Ruby, who had Ethan's stethoscope tucked into her ears and was holding it to her own heart. She pulled it off and looked up as Kayla and the officer reached them. "Can we go see Mommy now?"

"Yes. But I need to call your dad to have him meet you at the hospital," the officer said. "Do you know his name?"

Ruby shook her head. "I don't have a daddy."

The officer nodded, as if he'd suspected as much. "What about your grandma and grandpa?"

"My grandma and grandpa are in heaven."

Kayla's heart melted a little more for the poor girl. "How about an aunt or uncle or—"

The girl brightened. "I have an uncle!"

"Yeah?" Kayla reached to squeeze her hand. "That's good. What's his name?"

"Uncle Cam." Pride filled the girl's voice. Cam must be some uncle.

"Do you know where he lives? Close to here?"

"Far away, Mommy said. That's why he doesn't come to visit."

The radio on the officer's shoulder crackled to life and a voice spewed out some codes Kayla didn't understand. The officer closed his eyes for a second, shaking his head. "I need to get to that. Take her to the hospital and have them contact child services to start processing her. We'll try to track down the uncle, but we don't have much to go on . . ."

"Wait." Kayla pointed to the phone in his hand. "Ruby, does your mom have your uncle's phone number?"

Ruby shrugged. "I think so."

"It's locked." The officer said, before speaking into his radio, saying that he was en route to the next emergency. He passed the phone to Ethan. "Have them give it to CPS. Maybe they can get someone to unlock it and track down the uncle." With that, he dashed for his car, taking off in a spray of gravel a second later.

"All right. Ready for that super cool ambulance ride?" Ethan turned to Ruby, who gave Kayla an uncertain look.

"Will you come with me?"

"I can't leave my car here, but I'll be right behind you, okay?"

As Ruby nodded, Kayla's eyes fell on the phone in Ethan's hand. "Ruby, do you know your birthday?"

Ruby gave a proud nod. "Yep. April 10."

Kayla quickly tapped 0410 on the phone's keypad, letting out a sound of triumph as the phone unlocked. She held it up to show Ethan, then quickly scrolled through the contacts until she came to the name Cam.

She glanced at Ethan. "I'll make the call, then meet you at the hospital." She had a feeling this wasn't the kind of conversation a little girl should overhear.

"You're sure you want to make the call? We have people who can—"

Kayla shook her head. She didn't know why she felt it was important that she be the one to call, but she did. It was like the moment she'd opened Ruby's car door, she'd forged a connection with her. She felt responsible for whatever happened to her next.

Ethan studied her for a moment, then nodded and led Ruby to the ambulance.

Kayla waited until it pulled onto the road, then drew in a breath and tapped the number.

Hopefully in the next three seconds she'd receive some divine insight into how to tell a complete stranger that his sister had been in an accident.

More Hope Springs Books

While the books in the Hope Springs series are linked, each is a complete romance featuring a different couple.

Not Until Christmas (Ethan & Ariana)

Not Until Forever (Sophie & Spencer)

Not Until This Moment (Jared & Peyton)

Not Until You (Nate & Violet)

Not Until Us (Dan & Jade)

Not Until Christmas Morning (Leah & Austin)

Not Until This Day (Tyler & Isabel)

Not Until Someday (Grace & Levi)

Not Until Now (Cam & Kayla)

Not Until Then (Bethany & James)

Not Until The End (Emma & Owen)

And Don't Miss the River Falls Series

Featuring the Calvano family in the small town of River Falls, nestled in the Smoky Mountains of Tennessee.

Pieces of Forever (Joseph & Ava)

Songs of Home (Lydia & Liam)

Memories of the Heart (Simeon & Abigail)

Whispers of Truth (Benjamin & Summer)

Want to know when my next book releases?

You can follow me on Amazon to be the first to know when my next book releases! Just visit amazon.com/author/valeriembodden and click the follow button.

Acknowledgements

As I sit to write these acknowledgments, all I can think is that Grace said it best on her wedding day:

> It was too much. This love she felt surrounding her. She didn't know what to do with it all. What she'd ever done to deserve it.
> *Nothing.*
> That was the beautiful thing. She'd done nothing to deserve this love. But God had given it to her anyway.

That's exactly how I feel. God has filled my life with so much love. And I thank him today and every day for giving me this wonderful privilege of sharing that love through my books.

As always, my next thank you goes to my husband, because without his support and encouragement, these books never would have made their way into the world. We've walked quite a winding road together, and as our path continues to weave its way through this world toward eternity, there is no one I would rather have next to me. I love that we've brought our four wonderful children right alongside us. And I'm so grateful to them for their unwavering support—it's like having my own personal cheerleading squad every day.

And speaking of cheerleaders, thank you to my parents, my in-laws, and my extended family. Though we've been apart due to circumstances for a long time now, still you find ways to support and encourage us.

And I am grateful to have even more cheerleaders (how blessed can one writer get!): my amazing advance reader team. A super-huge-giant thank you to them for their constant support, encouragement, and feedback. Thank you especially to Vickie, Lincoln Clark, Rhondia, Katie, Michelle M., Gary Richards, Jeanne Olynick, Jaime Fipp, Chris Green, Vickie Escalante, Cheri Piershale, Nana Sue, Ilona, Terri Camp, Melanie A. Tate, Barbara Miller, K. Hartman, Marlize Meyer, Kellie P., Joy Lacey, Aurélie, Kris Vanica, Seyi, Becky Collins, Diana A., Carolyn Shelley, Norma Jean, Jenny M., Malinda Broughton, Sara, Debra Payne, B. Willoughby, Sharon, Deb Galloway, Chinye, Lynn Sell, Trista Heuer, Sandy G., Jan Gilmour, Bonny D. Rambarran, Vicki, Mary, Shelia Garrison, Sharon, Tandy O., Patty Bohuslav, Jenny Kilgallen, Alison K., Teresa Martin, Mary T., Christine Workman, Sandy H., Sarah R., Ann M. Diener, Shavona Thompson, Kori Thomas, Kelly Wickham, Roseann, Joan Arning, Shari Lamona, and Diane Hartmire.

And thank you to you, lovely reader, for spending time in Hope Springs with me. My prayer with every book I write is that I may glorify God and share his love with everyone who reads it. I pray that this book has been a blessing to you.

About the Author

Valerie M. Bodden has three great loves: Jesus, her family, and books. And chocolate (okay, four great loves). She is living out her happily ever after with her high-school-sweetheart-turned-husband and their four children. Her life wouldn't make a terribly exciting book, as it has a happy beginning and middle, and someday when she goes to her heavenly home, it will have a happy end.

She was born and raised in Wisconsin but recently moved with her family to Texas, where they're all getting used to the heat (she doesn't miss the snow even a little bit, though the rest of the family does) and saying y'all instead of you guys.

Valerie writes emotion-filled Christian fiction that weaves real-life problems, real-life people, and real-life faith. Her characters may (okay, will) experience some heartache along the way, but she will always give them a happy ending.

Feel free to stop by www.valeriembodden.com to say hi. She loves visitors! And while you're there, you can sign up for your free story.

Made in United States
Troutdale, OR
12/01/2023

15165608R00195